ICED BLUE

Books by Sherri Leigh James

ICED BLUE
BLOOD RED

LADY AND THE DON
SAGA OF A LADY

GIRL WITH A PAST

ICED BLUE

SHERRI LEIGH JAMES

A Cissy Huntington Mystery

BLACK HAWK PRESS

2019 Black Hawk Press Trade Paperback Edition
2019 Black Hawk Press eBook Edition
Black Hawk Press
P.O. Box 57737
Sherman Oaks, CA 91413

BLACK HAWK PRESS and the colophon are trademarks of Black Hawk Press, Inc.

Cover design by David Oh
Cover Copyright © 2019 Black Hawk Press, Inc.
All rights reserved.

Library of Congress Control Number: 2019938321
Trade Paperback Edition ISBN: 9780999858271
eBook Edition ISBN: 9780999858264

To all the women in my life—daughters, sister,
sisters-in-law, sorority sisters and girlfriends.
Thanks for all the fun and laughs!
You inspire these characters.

*"A building has integrity just like a man.
And just as seldom."*
~ Julia Morgan, Architect (1872-1957) ~

First woman architect licensed in California (1902)
who designed more than 700 buildings
including Hearst Castle.

Prologue

The woman struggled to sit upright on the slippery blonde leather seat of the limousine as her driver navigated the streets of West Hollywood gliding past the Robertson Boulevard boutiques and The Ivy restaurant.

Pull yourself together, you silly old broad, she scolded herself. What is the matter with you?

"Madame, are you alright?"

How many times had she asked Thomas to call her by her first name? She lacked the energy to remind him again. She nodded.

Apparently, he missed her motion.

He asked again, "Are you okay?"

He turned the corner onto Melrose.

Did she look as bad as she felt?

"I'm fine," but her voice was no louder than a whisper. What had happened to her strength? Was this a stroke? Was it her heart? She pleaded with God, "Don't let me die until I set things right."

"Madame, do you want me to help you in? I could park instead of using the drop off."

"No." Worry had sharpened her voice. "Thank you, Thomas." Softer. Better. "I'll be fine." She sank into the leather for a quick rest while Thomas walked around the car to her door.

He opened the door and offered his sturdy brown hand. Covering her frail, trembling hand with his, he drew her from the car and on to her feet. "You are very pale. I don't think I should leave you here."

She waved him off, smoothed her auburn hair, concentrated on putting one foot in front of the other, and walked to the entrance. She had to fix the stupid, selfish things she'd done. She had to speak to her.

Chapter 1

"Who is that woman in the front row?" I leaned over to whisper in the ear of my fellow panelist, Alexa Hamilton. We sat in pale blue Eames chairs pulled up to a white Saarinen tulip table on the stage of the Silver Screen Theater in LA's Pacific Design Center.

"The one in the ice blue jacket? The one who's staring at you?" Alexa gave an imperceptible nod toward the woman who had fixed her pale blue-eyed gaze on my face.

"Yes," I said. "Does she look familiar to you?" She definitely did to me, but I wasn't certain if it was another instance of my mistaking an actress from the last movie I saw for an acquaintance. Whoever she was, her stare was creeping me out.

Alexa grabbed the chrome frame of her chair and scooted it closer to mine. "I think maybe she's an actress, but I don't remember her name. She sure looks familiar. I wonder why she's so-o intent on you?" she murmured, her face turned away from the audience.

Good question. But the moderator, Linda Desante had begun to speak. My curiosity would have to wait.

"First, this lovely lady on my left is Cissy Huntington, designer to the stars.

I nodded and smiled at Linda.

"I'd like to, somewhat belatedly, welcome her back to LA. As many of you know, she had been retired in San Francisco raising her family until last fall. Now that her youngest is a freshman at UC Berkeley, she has returned to both our city and the business. I don't imagine any of you missed the *Architectural Digest* cover featuring her project last month. And Cissy and her charming daughter, Emma, are currently working on a residence for super star Sally Abbey. Cissy will give you the inside scoop of what it's like to work for the super stars."

I was roped into this panel at the last minute, when fellow interior designer Rose Tarlow came down with a severe case of laryngitis. What a great excuse! Too bad I hadn't thought of it. Although Rose was probably disappointed: she had a new book to promote.

I had no idea that Linda, the moderator, was looking for a replacement panelist when she called the evening before. I set myself up by telling her that I was fine and planning to attend the discussion of LA design.

It wasn't that I minded being on a panel, but I was in no way prepared. I would normally have done some research, and, of course, there was the what-shall-I-wear issue.

Emma, my daughter and design assistant, insisted I had to wear something more hip than my two-year-old black Armani suit, now that I was to be on the stage. So, we spent what felt like hours last night with me trying on outfits and

Emma critiquing. I'd ended up in my usual black slacks and one of Emma's white ruffled shirts.

Ironically, Alexa, daughter of recently deceased designer Mark Hamilton and closer to Emma's age than mine, was dressed in a grey suit that looked suspiciously similar to my Armani.

"Next is Alexa Hamilton. Alexa has just completed the re-do of the décor for Blair House in D.C., and she also has a beautiful new furniture line for Baker. She has some very nice slides of her pieces to show you. The actual pieces are on display upstairs in the Baker showroom. Alexa will address how best to use her furnishings in LA."

Alexa tossed back her chestnut hair and smiled sweetly in response to the applause.

"On Alexa's right is Buff Drake. Buff has some slides he would like to show you of his unique interior designs that make use of intense, bold color palettes. He also has a beautiful book that he will be happy to sign for you after our discussion. And he will recommend how to use his book in designing LA interiors."

Buff was dressed in his usual flamboyant style: a hot pink suit, a pale pink shirt, and a lavender tie. Where in the world had he found those spectator shoes in shades of pink?

Having seen him, certainly no one was surprised to learn that Buff is known for his unusual use of showy furnishings as well as bright colors in designing interiors.

I looked past Buff's new book, covered in purple faux ostrich skin displayed at the front of the white tulip table and noticed that the pale woman was still staring at me. I returned her gaze and smiled. My smile was not returned.

The moderator had begun without our fourth member, but he needed no introduction.

Frank Gehry entered the room shouting as he stormed down the aisle to the stage swinging his cane.

Every head in the auditorium but one turned to watch him. The auburn-haired head of the elderly woman remained forward, and her eyes remained fixed on my face. What was the deal with her?

Frank wore blue jeans, and a gray sweater with a black cashmere sackcloth blazer and black Doc Marten's all of which contrasted with his full head of snowy-white hair. Frank's the guy who does those way-out-there sculptural metal buildings: Bilbao's Guggenheim Museum, Seattle's Rock 'n' Roll museum, and our very own L.A. Disney Concert Hall.

The LA Times had to pick that particular morning to print a story about the park that was to be built around the Disney concert hall. "This is just bullshit," he roared at us all. "The city never even had the decency to reject our submission of over a year ago. Not one damn word. And then, out of the blue, this announcement of their selection of a new landscape architect. They're going to ruin my building! The setting is vital!" He was evidently oblivious to the fact that the moderator was attempting to talk. He stomped down the aisle, walked up to the microphone and continued to rant.

The thing about Frank is he's charming as hell, even when he's pissed off. And he's that rare phenomenon: a genius artist—in this case architect—who is popular in his own time.

I needn't have worried about what I was going to say. Frank's rage pre-empted most of my time, and I yielded much of what was left to Alexa. Between Alexa's delightful presentation of her new furniture line, Buff's proud showcasing of his new book on design, and Frank's blistering anger with the city management of LA, there was really no opportunity for me to say much more than that designing for the stars is a delightful, occasionally demanding, challenge.

The moderator barely got the words out that it was time for questions from the audience when several hands shot up. I was surprised that some of the younger guests yelled out their questions without bothering to raise their hands.

"What is the hardest part of designing for the superstars?" one young lady shouted from the back of the auditorium.

"Cissy, I believe that question is for you," said the moderator.

"The bad news, for those of you aspiring to be designers to the stars, is that you must be on call 24/7," I explained to the audience. "Movie stars tend to keep odd hours. Three a.m. phone calls from clients are standard. One way of avoiding paparazzi or over-eager fans is to go out in the middle of the night. I once dropped off a mega star at a gym at one o'clock in the morning . . . after our meeting. It was the one time of the day he and his personal trainer could use the facilities in peace."

Several people hollered, "Who was that?" at once.

I smiled. "Of course, I won't be telling you who that was. Which leads me to the next bit of news: you won't be entertaining your friends with tidbits of gossip about your clients. In fact, keeping quiet will soon become such a habit that you'll find yourself out of the gossip loop entirely as you have nothing to exchange. Because, you see, you will inevitably be asked to sign a confidentiality agreement, the ubiquitous NDA."

The moderator said, "Thank you," as she pointed to a young woman in the second row with her hand raised.

"Is there anything good about designing for the stars?" asked the young woman whose head-to-toe black ensemble was punctuated with a pale pink statement necklace.

My fellow panelists smiled at me as I took the question. "There are some perks: traveling via private jet at someone else's expense is great. And a few of my clients have become good friends. On the rare occasions that you take your celeb client out shopping, it's fun to watch the reactions, as long as you avoid being caught in the crush."

"Do you have any advice for us wannabe designers to the stars?" asked a black-clad lad.

"Here's a tip: avoid the valet parking stand at The Ivy. I'm sure you've noticed the tourists hanging around there waiting to get a photo of a celeb. I walked by there with John Travolta once and was nearly trampled by the stampeding herd of tourists trying to get a shot of John." I ended on the gratifying laughter that story elicited from the audience. The only one who wasn't at least smiling was the woman in the front row who stared stone-faced at me. She looked too delicate to be dangerous. But what if she had a gun?

I shook off my discomfort.

"Have you slept with any of your clients?" That was shouted anonymously from the back of the hall.

"Have I mentioned those confidentiality agreements?" I winked. Alexa was squirming in her seat. Frank was scowling at me. "That's enough questions for me. Ask Frank about his new project."

But apparently no one wanted to chance Frank ranting again. Even the Gehry groupies in the left section of the auditorium were quiet.

A sweet young man in the center section asked Buff if any of his clients ever resisted Buff's bright color palette.

"Why would they call me?" he answered. "Actually, I sometimes have clients who want such intense color and shocking combos, they're too over the top for me . . . if you can imagine such a thing."

There were a few more questions before the moderator announced, "That's all folks," and we were free to mingle with the audience briefly. I shook a few hands. Buff and Alexa both had agendas. Buff had a book to sell and Alexa a furniture line to promote.

My only agenda was to get out of there as fast as possible. I glanced around the auditorium. Despite the thinning crowd, I didn't locate the woman from the front row.

I had a lunch date in Beverly Hills with two of my movie star friends/clients. I had made the date when I knew

I would already be at the PDC and could easily hop over to the restaurant right after the panel. Of course, at the point when I made that plan, I had no idea I was to be part of the panel and therefore possibly trapped.

I pushed through the crowd of BevHills matrons, design and architecture students, and Frank Gehry groupies that had rushed toward the stage, and flew up the aisle past the ceiling height maple doors. I dashed through the grey flannel anteroom and down the stairs past the round security/info desk. Hoping to exit the parking tollbooths before the bulk of the crowd, I hurried to my car on the second floor of the garage structure.

The line for the valet had been long when I arrived, so I'd self-parked. Having learned a while back where the parking lot filled up last, I usually park there unless I have clients with me. I dashed up the stairs rather than wait for the elevator.

My gray Prius was parked behind the bank of elevators. As I turned the corner of the building, I saw an ice blue jacket on the hood of my car. What the hell?

I got closer. It wasn't just a jacket. It was the upper part of a person. Whoa, I recognized that auburn hair. Christ, it was the woman from the front row. What the hell? Draped over my car. Had she fainted?

Now I could find out who she was.

Her Jimmy Choo-clad feet grazed the ground while most of her body rested on the hood of my car.

"Hello." I tapped her on the shoulder. No response.

"Hey!" I shook her. Still no response.

10

I bent down to look at her face. Her once pale blue eyes were now black and had that nobody's-home-look of the dead.

Oh, damn! Shit, shit, shit!

I searched for a pulse with one hand while I dialed 9-1-1 on my cell. I felt her wrists and her neck. She was limp. I couldn't find any sign of life.

911 put me on hold—why the hell do they do that? I really hate that!

I have got to learn CPR. This was the second body I'd found.

Chapter 2

"Please stay on the line. Your call will be answered in the order received." I removed the phone from my ear and looked at the time on my cell. I had been on hold for two minutes.

What if she wasn't dead?

I was pretty sure she was, but what if?

Maybe she had overdosed on something. Was she comatose?

People must breathe when they are in coma. I pulled a compact mirror out of my purse and held it in front of her mouth and nose. She definitely was not breathing.

I reminded myself not to panic, to think through what to do.

Damn, I wish I hadn't parked in this isolated section.

I couldn't hear anyone on the other side of the elevators.

I hurried over to the peek around the corner. No one over there.

Didn't anyone else self-park? Had all those students taken a bus? Where was everyone?

No sign of the blue Kelly bag I had seen on her lap in

the theater. I dug in each of the pockets in her jacket. No ID. No medical alert bracelet or tag.

"Please stay on the line." Oh, for Chrissake, I'd been on hold for five minutes.

I remembered the security guard at the round info desk back in the lobby. I made a dash for help.

I sprinted down to the lobby and grabbed the security guard by his beefy arm. "Come quick!" I panted. "There's a woman in the parking structure. I don't know what's the matter with her. I think she's dead. But she might be passed out." I gasped for air.

"Ma'am, I can't leave here." The security guard held firm to his swivel chair and munched on a donut dribbling white powdered sugar down the front of his dark uniform.

"Listen!" I squinted at the nametag on his barrel chest. "Butch, do you know CPR?"

"Of course."

"Then you have to come with me! You have to hurry up! She might not be dead!" I yanked on his arm.

"Call an ambulance! Call the police," I yelled at the info officer at the desk. Maybe the woman on my car could be revived.

When I yelled, Butch stood up. I pulled him toward the parking structure.

We pushed past one or two people in line for the valet who tried to tell me hello and wanted to chat.

Deborah Holland stood right in our path to stop me. "Cissy, I have to tell you what happened at the last ASID meeting."

"Deb, not now." I brushed her aside and shouted back at her, "I've got to get this man to my car. I'll explain later." Where the hell were all these people when I needed help a few minutes ago?

"Hurry up!" I rushed the guard up the stairs to my car.

Only thirty something, Butch was already overweight and slow. One flight of stairs and the dirty blond hair that stuck out from his cap dripped sweat.

It couldn't have taken more than five, maybe ten minutes to return to my car. The timer on my phone said I had been on hold for thirteen minutes and 34 seconds. I showed the timer to Butch. "Can you believe this? Look at how long 911 has had me on hold."

Butch took the phone out of my hand just as we approached my car.

What? I could see the overhead light reflected on the hood. The entire hood—no longer occupied!

There was no body!

Chapter 3

I checked the area around the car. She hadn't fallen off; she wasn't on the concrete floor of the parking structure.

What the hell? Was I on the wrong floor? Had I somehow gone up more flights of stairs than I thought?

No, no. I was sure it was my car she was on. I remember seeing my scarf on the passenger seat. The scarf was still there.

The security guard glared at me. "Where is she?"

"Don't look at me like that." I tried to remain calm. "Look, she was here on the hood. Maybe she wasn't dead, but I couldn't find any pulse on her wrist or her neck. She definitely did not get up and walk away!"

I got on my knees to see under the car. I looked underneath the neighboring cars. I scanned the tops of the cars in the back section of the garage.

"You're sure this is the right car?" he asked.

"Yes, it is my car and it was parked right here. Call in reinforcements. We've got to search the garage. If she wasn't dead, then she's awfully damn sick, and we need to get her help."

He put his radio to his mouth. "Willie, what's your 20? Can you come up to the second floor?"

I remembered Willie: African American, with a big grin. He'd been around the PDC almost as long as I had been going there. Since he knew me, I had hope he'd be more help.

"Come up to the second floor of the garage. Over."

"Copy that. 10-16." Willie was enroute.

Then Butch spoke into into my phone. "No. No. This is security officer Butch Talbot at the Pacific Design Center. Doesn't seem like we need you. False alarm." He clicked my phone off.

"What? What did you do?" My God, the nerve. He'd hung up my phone. "Call your supervisor. Get him here now! Tell him that Cissy Huntington needs him," I ordered in my most authoritative voice.

"Lady, my boss isn't gonna like me calling him just cause you think you saw a body on your car. You haven't been hittin' the sauce kinda early today, have ya?"

I ignored his insolent question. How rude. He won't be working here long with that kind of attitude.

I could hear sirens in the distance. Naively I thought maybe now I would get some real help. I looked under cars farther down the aisle. Butch watched me.

Willie finally showed up. "Oh, it's you, Mrs. Huntington. Wassup?"

"Oh, Willie. Something terrible has happened. Please. You've got to help me. A woman was lying on my car. Now I can't find her. She might be sick, . . . or dead."

Willie gave me one of those looks but he said, "Sure, sure." Willie and Butch, who resembled a black and white Laurel and Hardy, sauntered over to the main section of the garage in front of the elevators and began a slipshod search, flitting their flashlights around the cars.

I systematically searched in and under every car in my section of the parking structure.

Minutes later a patrol car, followed by an ambulance, roared up the aisle in front of the elevators. Willie and Butch ambled over to speak with the officers and the paramedics as they exited their vehicles.

I was farther away. By the time I arrived on that side of the elevators, Butch had already done his damage. I don't know what he said to them, but they shook their heads and got back into their respective transport.

"Wait, wait!" I waved my arms and yelled as they drove away.

"Lady, er, Mrs. Huntington," Butch said. "We've looked all over this floor for almost an hour."

"Nowhere near an hour," I protested.

"There is no body, on your car, under your car, or anybody else's car." Butch looked at me as though pitying a lunatic. He and Willy walked away.

I had been ignoring my cell, and anyone who tried to engage me in conversation for the last hour that we had spent searching the garage. Abandoned by the security guards, I finally answered the persistent ring.

"Oh Sally, I'm so-o sorry. You won't believe what happened." Nor it seemed would anybody else.

"Are you going to get here before we pass out? We're doing cosmos," Sally said.

"I guess I can meet you soon. Have another cosmo, and order one for me too. Glad that Nikki is there to keep you company."

I had to get some help. Aah, good. Detective Manuel Rodriquez's number was still in my phone. I'd put him on speed dial favorites when Nikki was in danger last month. I scrolled to his listing and hit send.

"Hey Manny, it's Cissy." It reassured me to hear his voice. "So look, here's the thing. I found another dead body."

"Slow down. Did you say dead body?"

"Yes. On my car, but she—that is, her body—has disappeared. I don't know what to do. I'm supposed to meet Sally and Nikki for lunch, but it seems like I shouldn't move this car."

"Where are you?"

"In the parking structure at the PDC, second floor, behind the elevators. The security guys here think I'm nuts."

"I remember that thought." He laughed.

It had only been a matter of weeks since my daughter Emma, and my movie star friends had helped me snare a murderer for the detective.

"And you called me, why? I'm a Beverly Hills cop. You're in West Hollywood."

"Please! I helped you with that last case. Admit it. You owe me one."

Manny exhaled a deep breath. "Okay, I'm not too far away. I'll come check it out."

I called Sally back. "You're going to have to drink that cosmo for me. I'm stuck here until Detective Rodriquez arrives."

"You mean Manny? As in Homicide Detective Rodriquez?"

"That's the one."

"What the hell are you up to now?"

"Just a little matter of a dead body I found on my car . . . and then it vanished."

"Fuck, you are a magnet for dead bodies!"

That's my friend Sally. She's a gorgeous, mega movie star with a lexicon of colorful language. She's particularly fond of the F-word.

I could hear her explain to Nikki what I had just said. Their friendship proved the truth of "opposites attract". Sally's big expressive eyes and personality reminded me of an over-friendly golden retriever. Nikki's blue eyes, and gentle demeanor, a playful gold point Siamese kitten.

"Nikki's worried about you. She thinks we should come over there."

"Please tell her thank you, but other than being terribly disappointed to miss lunch with you two, I'm fine." At least I would be when my hands stopped shaking. "And Detective Rodriquez said he was nearby. As soon as he's been here, I can go down to that little snack bar and grab some food."

"Never mind that. Nikki has already ordered you a pear,

gorgonzola, and arugula salad to go. Apparently, we are bringing lunch to you." Sally lowered her voice to a whisper. "I should've known when I told her Manny would be there. She thinks he's hot. But I should have first dibs. She's already got her own hottie." Aloud Sally spoke to Nikki, "Hey bitch, remember your fucking husband."

I could hear Nikki protesting in the background. Nikki must have won the fight for the phone because her breathless, Marilyn Monroe voice was the next one I heard. "Cissy darling, we'll be right over. Sally's nearly done stuffing herself. Call you when we get close. Love ya. Ciao."

I remembered the water bottle in my bag. I had just chugged the last of it when Detective Rodriquez pulled his Ford Escape Hybrid up behind my car.

"So, what happened?"

"There was this woman in the audience, she was staring at me, she creeped me out she was gawking so intent—"

"Hold it, hold it—slow down . . . deep breath. Now start again."

I took a breath and then I explained as calmly as I could. Everything from the staring to the missing body.

"What did she look like?"

"She had on a Chanel jacket, the wool one in ice blue with a matching t-shirt, silver Jimmy Choo shoes, grey pinstripe slacks—I think those were Michael Kors—"

With a sigh of impatience, Detective Rodriquez interrupted me. "What did her body look like?"

"Dead."

The detective pursed his lips together and looked at me with those gorgeous, dark chocolate eyes. Now we were back on familiar ground. He often just looks at me when we're having a conversation.

"Okay," I took a deep breath. "She had auburn hair, dyed of course, but probably not too far off her original natural color, judging from her skin tone—which was pale even before she was dead—"

He broke in again. "Give me her height and weight."

"I never saw her standing up, but I would guess she was pretty close to my size. Five six, maybe size four, probably 125 pounds, light blue eyes. Older."

"Where was the wound?"

"A wound? Hmm, . . . I didn't see one."

"No visible sign of a wound?" He shook his dark head.

I continued, "She had on some good-sized diamond studs and a diamond tennis bracelet. She looked familiar, but I couldn't place her."

He looked me in the eye. "What do you suppose happened to her body?"

"No idea."

He continued to look at me. I could see doubt in his eyes.

"Hey, I've got no reason not to tell you everything I know." I knew he was thinking of a few weeks ago when I had stumbled upon another dead body and I kind of didn't tell him every little thing right away. But that was different.

"Why was she on your car? Did you run into her?"

Now it was my turn not to answer and just look at him

in disgust.

He turned away and walked over to the hood of the car. "Which side was she on?"

"This one." I stepped forward and pointed to the right side of the hood.

"Stay back." He raised his hand, palm toward me.

"I am, I am. She was just in front of the windshield, chest down, face turned toward the front bumper. Her hands were palms down, next to her shoulders. Her head was more than halfway across the hood and her feet were barely touching the ground—uh, the concrete."

He shined a flashlight across the hood, leaned over and looked sideways across it.

"What makes you think she was dead?"

"I couldn't find a pulse."

"You do know how to find a pulse?"

"Of course." I was pretty sure I did anyway.

"Any other reason?"

"Her eyes had that vacant look . . . that dead look. Her pupils were fully dilated."

"Are you sure she wasn't just passed out?"

"With her eyes open?"

"That doesn't mean anything. Dilated pupils could have been too many diet pills."

"I'm sure she was dead. Her eyes were all pupils. I couldn't get a pulse on her wrist or her neck. When I felt her neck, she was absolutely still. Shit. You still don't trust me."

"You haven't exactly been stellar in the trust building

department."

"I've never lied to you. I just left stuff out."

In my defense, I still maintain that the stuff I left out didn't have anything to do with the murder of Dr. Martin.

He looked me in the eye. Silently, as usual.

"I know there was a dead woman here," I said. "Believe me, with those diamonds and that hair, she was a long way from being a nobody. When she turns up missing, or the dead body surfaces, you're going to want to know she was the body I saw. Can't you get some DNA off the car, or me, and identify her that way?"

"Despite what you may have seen on TV, we don't have some universal DNA database that will do that for us."

"What about fingerprints?"

"A big maybe."

"Don't you think the hood of the car would have her fingerprints?"

"Hers and the guy at the car wash and the parking attendant and—"

"I get it, I get it.

"Then there's the question of whether or not her prints are even on file."

"I'm telling you, you're going to wish you had some physical evidence."

"Okay, I'll do what I can. I've got a kit in the trunk. Don't touch anything." Detective Rodriquez was back on duty.

He walked over to his car and opened the back. He lifted up a flap of carpet.

My phone rang. "Hi!" I explained where we were to Sally and Nikki.

Detective Rodriquez opened up a metal box and pulled out a bag. "You sure you don't know who she was?"

"She looked familiar, but I haven't thought of who she was, or how I know her. I absolutely promise, I'll tell you the second it comes to me. She might be an actress."

I noticed a line of auburn on my sleeve. "Hey! Look here's one of her hairs on my sleeve! That proves she exists, doesn't it?"

"It doesn't prove she's dead."

Sally's Porsche pulled up. Nikki hung a delicious smelling bag out the window, handing me my lunch. Must have been a lot of garlic on the focaccia bread that came with the salad.

"U-uh, I can't take it right now. I'm not allowed to touch anything. But . . . thanks." At least he was humoring me.

The girls parked a few stalls down.

"I should have known the gang would be close behind," Detective Rodriquez muttered without lifting his head from his task.

Sally and Nikki were bearing down on us fast with Sally about to engulf me in one of her huge hugs.

Detective Rodriquez knew the drill. "Halt!" he shouted.

Sally slid to a stop about five feet away from me. Nikki crept up behind her. Sally is jumbo sized; tall and voluptuous with rich bittersweet brown hair and jade eyes; Nikki is petite, delicate, champagne blonde and blue eyed.

"God help me, if I don't collect some evidence Cissy

will never let me hear the end of it. If there was a body . . . she," he pointed at me, "could be covered in the only evidence we may have. If we can get some thing off her, or the car, it might be useful when—and if—a body turns up. So, you need to stay back. Got it?" Detective Rodriquez never had been the slightest bit intimidated by Sally and Nikki's mega movie star status.

"Ga-w-d, I'm starving," I said.

"Can I feed her?" Sally offered.

He turned to Sally without cracking a smile. "What part of what I just said did you fail to understand? Back off."

"Hey, start with me, not the damn car." Hunger was making me cranky.

Detective Rodriquez wiped down my hands and bagged the wipes. He used his gloved fingers to carefully remove the auburn hair from my sleeve. Then he ran a cute little hand vacuum over the arms of my jacket.

When he was done with me, Detective Rodriquez—I can't get used to saying Manny—nodded to Sally and Nikki that it was okay to hand me the salad and latte. They laid out a napkin for a placemat and set a place with plastic utensils for me on the hood of his Escape. From there I had a good view of his quick examination of my car hood, including the collection of fingerprints. While I ate, Sally and Nikki bombarded me with questions.

"Okay, that's it." Detective Rodriquez was ready to move his car.

"Will you let me know when you find out something?" I asked as we scrambled to remove my lunch from his hood.

25

"Like what? There's quite a backlog on lab work. I don't know how usable these prints are. We don't even have a body, so this isn't going to be anybody's priority."

"Don't you want to interview any of the people that were at the panel discussion? Maybe one of them knows who she was." I couldn't understand his lack of interest. Did everyone think I was hallucinating?

"Send me a list of who was there. I'll call you." He slammed the car door.

"I get it. 'Don't call me, I'll call you'," I said.

"It's the ol' brushoff, fuckoff." Sally works the F-word into every sentence.

"And I thought he liked us," Nikki sighed.

Chapter 4

"Oh, darling. He's going to be sorry. He should've listened to you," Nikki said.

"He'll feel like a fucking idiot," Sally added.

The three of us watched the Escape disappear from view behind the elevator bank.

"What do we do now?" They both looked at me for instructions.

God. It's good to have girl friends.

"I'm going to go back into the theater and see if anyone is still there. Wanta come with?"

"Of course, darling."

"Abso-fucking-lutely."

There were still a few people sitting on the edge of the stage and on the chairs. Buff was signing books. Alexa had a circle of design students at her feet. Linda, the moderator, was chilling in the first row.

I sat down next to Linda. I had but a few minutes before Sally and Nikki's presence would distract the hell out of the remaining audience. "Linda, there was a woman in the front row, towards the middle. Auburn hair, Chanel ice blue jacket. Do you know who she was?"

"I noticed her. She stared at you the entire time. She looked familiar, but I couldn't place her. Why?"

"Uhm, well, . . ." I wasn't prepared for that question. What do I say? 'Cause I think she's dead, but every man I've told that to thinks I'm nuts?

"Yeah, if she had been staring at me like that, I'd be wondering what her story was too," Linda said.

"Will you call me if you remember who she is?"

"Of course."

By now the students were crowded around Sally and Nikki. I sat down in the chair next to Alexa who was gathering her brochures together. "Did you ever figure out why that woman, the one staring at me, looked familiar?" I asked her.

"Maybe we've just seen her around the design show-rooms." Alexa's knitted brow demonstrated her concentration. "You know, if you really want to know, that photographer who was here might have gotten a shot of her."

"Right! Brilliant. Do you know who he was?"

"Buff was flirting with him. Maybe he got his number." Alexa glanced at Buff to see if he was listening and then winked at me.

"I beg your pardon, I was not flirting with him." Major attitude from Buff. "But I do know him. He works for the company that does the design center newsletters. Check with the administration office."

"Buff, do you by any chance know the redhead who was

in blue in the front row?"

"Didn't notice her. Must not know her."

"Thanks, both of you," I said. Alexa, if you think of who she is . . ."

"No worries. I'll call you."

Frank was gone. I made a mental note to call him.

I walked over to where Sally and Nikki were holding court. The crowd surrounding them had doubled in size while I wasn't watching. I placed my hand on Sally's arm. "May I interrupt?" I asked.

"Hey guys, quiet. Cissy wants to say something," Sally ordered. The room immediately went dead quiet.

"There was a woman with auburn hair and an ice blue jacket sitting in the front row. Do any of you know her?"

Silence.

"Or, know who she is?"

The crowd of fans all looked at me, but no one answered. A couple of them shook their heads.

"Sally, Nikki, I'm going to go over to the PDC office. I'll be back."

The office was only a few steps away from the theater, and the photographer was there leaning against the counter and chatting with the receptionist. What luck!

"Hi! So glad I ran into you."

"Hey, Cissy." The photographer was in his late twenties with a very short buzz cut, a silver ring in his pierced eyebrow, and six rings climbing the outer edge of each ear.

"Listen I need a photo of one of the people in the audience of this morning's panel. Would you, . . . did you get any shots of them?"

"I took a few shots into audience."

"She was in the front row."

"Sure, I got the front row. I'll email you whatever I got, and you can crop out whoever you want."

"Great." I gave him my card with the email address. "Thanks a lot. Send the bill with it."

"Not necessary. Just recommend me to your clients."

"No problem. Can you do it today?"

"For sure."

That meant that I could take the photo around to the showrooms the next day and find someone who recognized her. I hurried back to the theater and explained my plan to the girls.

"Fuck, I love this detecting shit," said Sally as she signed the sleeve of a young fan.

Chapter 5

That evening I organized a posse to take the photo around to all the showrooms in the PDC the next day. We had two detective teams: one consisting of Sally and Nikki, the other of Emma and me.

While I waited for my fellow sleuths to assemble in the office the next morning, I printed off the list of questions each team was to ask of anyone who recognized the photo.

"Good morning, Susan. You're going to have to hold down the fort here today," I said as she closed the front door. When I got back to the office the day before, I had spent nearly an hour explaining about the dead woman to both Emma and Susan.

"It's okay, Cissy. I have to get the sales tax report done." Susan hung her hat and jacket on the Eastlake coat tree in the entry hall. She checked her reflection in the mirror above the console where she smoothed her soft brown hair, slicked lip-gloss onto her cupid bow mouth, and pinched her cute plump cheeks.

"Thanks. I promise we'll arrange another outing that includes you."

Susan had come to work with us two months ago. She ran the office and acted as receptionist. Emma and Susan had set up the dark mahogany paneled library as the office and the adjoining sunroom as my workplace. Susan sat at the large desk at the front of the library just inside the double doors that open to the entry hall and stairwell.

Behind Susan, Emma used an antique writing table to hold her laptop and phone. Between their workspaces, the window bay facing the street had a built-in seat with a thick cushion and down pillows. It was my favorite resting spot.

Beyond their room, my sunroom office contained a massive library table with drawers in both aprons and an inlay top covered with messy piles of fabric, wallpaper, and carpet samples.

I had just handed the list of detecting questions to Susan to make copies when the front door flew open and Sally barged in with Nikki in tow. Sally was outfitted in her version of Sherlock Holmes garb: tweed jacket over skin tight riding pants and knee-high boots, all topped off with a fedora. Nikki had on a soft pink cashmere Nina Ricci twin set and grey flannels.

Emma, my beautiful blue-eyed blonde daughter dressed in her usual jeans with a stylishly cropped jacket, walked down the stairs, and the three of them entered the office wing of our house together.

"Mom, I haven't walked Lulu yet today." Emma patted the head of Lulu, our chocolate brown labradoodle, who looked at me with her big, black, sad eyes and whimpered.

"I'll take Lulu," Susan volunteered. "I want to walk over

to Yvonne's to check out how the nursery is comin' along. Mr. Paint did those wide pink stripes on the cream-colored walls. Cissy, you were so right. They look great. I'll go over there now so that I'm back in the office before you get to the PDC. Just in case you need anythin' from me."

"Thanks." Emma hugged Susan.

A round of good-byes, and then a reminder from Susan, "Don't forget the baby shower on Saturday." Our nearby neighbor, Yvonne, was pregnant.

"And keep your eyes open for weddin' gifts for Poppy. You'll have to come up with somethin' pretty inventive for those people who have everythin'." Emma's best friend was getting married in San Francisco soon.

"I bought the sweetest teeny little pink outfit," Nikki said as we loaded into my car. We discussed baby clothes most of the drive to the PDC. "I bought the softest, most darling his and her cashmere robes," Nikki said changing to the subject of wedding gifts.

I half listened to the women discuss wedding gifts the rest of the drive to the PDC while I wondered why the dead person looked familiar.

As we waited in line for the parking garage of the enormous royal blue, grass green, and blood red buildings, I pulled the list of questions from my bag. "Here's what we need to know if you find anyone who recognizes the photo. Sally and Nikki, you take the green building. Emma and I'll do the blue. We'll meet at the Red Seven for lunch at one."

"Let's take the elevator to the sixth floor," I said to Emma. "Then we can work our way down."

We started at Brunschwig and Fils. "You take the front desk. I'll do the sample counter."

"Shit, I should have brought returns with us." Emma referred to the piles of rejected fabric samples that required sorting in order to be returned to the showrooms.

"Sorry, didn't give you much chance to organize the returns, did I? We'll do it another day." I smiled at my daughter.

"Mom, what are you doing?"

"What do you mean?"

"Why are we spending this much of our time identifying this woman? We have lots of paying work we should be doing."

I knew Emma was once again wondering when her mother was going to grow up and stop playing Nancy Drew.

"If only you'd seen how she stared at me."

Emma rolled her eyes at me. "Well, I didn't. So maybe I'm being objective about this."

"Emma, I feel somehow responsible for this woman. I'm apparently the only one who knows she's dead." I shook my head. "Well, other than whoever it was who moved her. Which just might be the same person who killed her. I think she was trying to tell me something. She has some connection to me. For all we know it has something to do with your father's disappearance."

Her eyes filled with tears. "Okay, Mama. We'll do this . . . . Especially if there is the slightest chance it'll help find Daddy." She gave me a quick hug before she moved on to the front desk behind a counter.

"Hey, do you recognize this woman?" Emma asked the receptionist. I headed for the back of the showroom.

I paused for just a second to admire the black and cream furnishings with red accents décor of the window vignette. At the sample counter, I asked the same question, but the young man said he definitely didn't know the woman.

We covered the entire sixth floor with the same result. On the fifth floor, we finally found someone to whom the woman in the photo looked familiar. I walked between the racks covered in layers of fabric samples until I found Jeanne, the showroom manager at Pindler.

She said, "Maybe an actress, definitely not a designer. I don't think I've seen her in the showroom. Seems like it was some other context, but it's not coming to me. Damn."

"Don't fret. Call me if you think of who she is. Here's my cell number in case it comes to you in the next couple hours." I thanked Jeanne and Karen.

"Mom, I'm really hungry, and it's close to one," Emma said.

We headed for the restaurant on the first floor of the blue building. The café named for Wolfgang Puck, the owner, had once been on the second floor, which made it accessible only to PDC patrons. Now that Wolfgang had relocated to the ground floor, the Red Seven was far busier. The food there was a real treat.

Although we were early, Sally and Nikki had already arrived and were seated at the best table in the room. Emma and I slid into the comfortable upholstered benches at the table.

Sally and Nikki were sipping iced teas.

"This detecting is hard work." Sally pointed at the Manolo Blahnik stilettos on Nikki's feet. "And Nikki wore the wrong fucking shoes, so we had to take a break a little early."

"No cosmos, or lemon drops?" I remarked.

"Nah, this is a working lunch," Sally said. "No one has the faintest idea who she is, but we've only covered a couple floors.

"One person thought she looked familiar," Emma said. "Shit, this isn't so easy. After lunch we should split up, Mom. You do the fourth and second floors. I'll do the third and first."

"We'll do the same," Sally said.

We all ordered salads with dressing on the side and asked that the bread platter be removed from the table.

Nikki and Emma excused themselves to go to the ladies room.

"You got any ideas how we are going to find out who your dead woman is—or was—if this doesn't work?" Sally asked.

"How does one post a photo on the Internet?" I wondered aloud.

"Maybe I could put it on my website. I get a lot of hits. You and Nikki could put it on yours, too. Emma can post on Facebook." Sally grinned. "On another subject, I saw an oval ottoman covered in cream-colored croc with pewter nail heads that would look fucking great in my dressing room. It's in Schumacher's window."

"Sounds good. Show it to me after lunch."

Nikki and Emma giggled their way back to the table. "Sally darling, you aren't going to believe who's in the bathroom."

Sally shrugged. "Who?"

"Your ex's new wife," Emma said.

"Bunny? They let her in the ladies?" Sally waited in vain for a laugh. "Fuck. I wish she was his wife, but she's his live-in bitch. He'll never marry her."

"Why not?" Emma asked.

"He likes that fucking alimony too much." Sally took a gulp of her iced tea. "Shit, maybe we should've had martinis."

"You pay him alimony? Hey wait. I thought he was a trust fund baby." Emma asked. "Isn't he some relative of the Spreckels?"

"A very distant relative. He's a compulsive liar. I fell for his story. Took me a long fucking time to catch on." Sally slapped her forehead. "He's one of those guys who never has any cash or cards on him when it comes time to pay the fucking bill."

"Kinda typical of really rich people, isn't it?" Emma asked. Emma's upbringing had exposed her to a lot of wealthy people, including her own father and his family.

"And of fuckheads who are actually broke." A nearly visible black cloud had obliterated Sally's usual sunny disposition. "I suppose she's here spending my money on that fucking McMansion Ted bought."

"Do you think Bunny knows where the money comes from?" I asked.

"I doubt it. He's pretty fucking good at fooling people. I didn't realize that his so-called trust fund was miniscule until we'd been married for months."

"I still don't get the alimony thing." Emma knit her brows into a scowl of confusion. "Didn't your prenup handle that?"

"Oh honey, when it comes time for you to make 'those kind of decisions,' come to your aunt Nikki for advice . . . not Sally." Nikki bestowed her gentle smile on Emma and patted her hand. "And try not to do that with your face. Unless you plan to invest heavily in Botox."

Sally glared at Nikki. "Scheming bitch. You think you're so fucking much smarter than me."

"Darling, I don't think with my C-U-N-T." Nikki flashed a fake smile at Sally.

"No, you think with your fucking calculator."

"Ladies, you know you love each other. Kiss and make up," I said.

"Not a chance in hell." Sally looked across the room. "Oops, here comes the bimbo."

Sally took a deep breath, exhaled, and whispered, "I actually, like a fucking idiot, refused to do a prenup cause I thought he had more money than I did. Part of his attraction was that he couldn't possibly have been after my money. I didn't get how he was conning me until after I faced the fact he was sleeping with every bimbo starlet in town."

Perhaps the maitre'd knew the relationship between

Sally and Bunny the Bimbo. He seated her and her decorator as far from our table as possible on the opposite side of the room in dark, windowless Siberia.

So that was Bunny. The attraction was hard to miss. The tight-fitting leopard print jacket and pants showed off her assets and blended well with her blonde and tan coloring. But her brassy, in-your-face sexiness didn't come close to Sally's breathtaking, voluptuous beauty.

"You know, I really don't have a problem with her anymore. She's too stupid to give a shit about." Sally sighed. "I just really fucking hate having to give him money every month on top of what he already got from me."

"The condo in Aspen, the house in Cabo, the Malibu estate, the vintage 190SL, the Jasper John painting . . . ," Nikki said as she ticked off the list on her fingers. She'd heard this tirade before.

"And what did I get? Not even a good fuck."

"You got the dogs."

Nikki referred to Sally's pair of miniature pinchers. But not even the holy mini-terrors, as Sally was fond of calling them, could distract Sally from her subject.

"He was a lousy lover. Best thing I can say is at least he was fast." Sally had her head in her hands now. "I'd like to say he sucked at it, but that would be wishful thinking. His idea of oral sex was talking about himself."

I recognized sour grapes. Sally had been famously, jumping on sofas, madly in love with Ted. He'd seriously hurt her.

"Does Bunny have any money?" I asked. A plan was starting to form in my twisted mind.

"Who knows? Why?" Sally looked up at me and grinned. "What do you have in mind? Something really fucking nasty I hope."

Chapter 6

"I think we should get Bunny to insist that Ted marry her. And we find a way to get him thinking that she is about to come into some serious money so that he goes along with it," I said.

"Fuck. I like it. How?"

"Let's start by making her jealous. Did you two . . . ." I looked at Emma and Nikki. "Did you let on that you recognized her?"

"No. I didn't have a clue who she was. Nikki told me after we left the bathroom," Emma said.

"And I didn't even hint that I knew who she was when I saw her," Nikki said.

"Good." I looked at Sally. "As we walk out of here, you just happen to mention within her earshot that Ted called you and was dropping hints that he wants to get back together." I smiled at Sally. "We'll figure the rest out later. On the drive home you can tell me everything you know about who he hangs with and where. He's big on racquetball, isn't he?"

"Yeah."

"Where does he play?" Emma asked.

"LA Athletic Club."

"Jeff, my fiancée plays there. Maybe they know each other?" Emma offered.

"They could certainly get acquainted," I said. "Sally, you come with me for the rest of the day. We have to check out that ottoman anyway. We'll finish the Blue building." I smiled at my daughter. "Emma, Nikki, call me if you happen to spot Bunny in any of the showrooms." I was ready for some fun.

We finished our salads, split the bill, and headed back to work via Siberia. All four of us looked straight ahead as we passed Bunny's table as if we had no idea she was sitting there. Sally announced, "I told Ted he really had to stop fucking calling me unless he was serious about getting back together. He's breaking my heart. Can you believe, he called me again two hours later?"

"Don't look back," I hissed as we exited the restaurant. Sally and I took the escalator up to the fifth floor.

Sally and I started at Schumacher's.

"So nice to see you ladies again. Cissy, what can we help you with?"

"Hello Dennis. Two things. One we need a tear sheet, price and lead time for the croc ottoman in the window." Dennis had been at Schumacher's back almost twenty-five years ago, when I first started coming to the PDC.

"I'll get the tear sheet and put the price on it. If you like that leather, you can have that one.

"Good. Just might do that," I said. "Next, please look at

this photo. Do you recognize this woman?"

Dennis studied the photo. "Now why does she look familiar?"

Behind his back, Sally silently bounced from foot to foot until she had my attention and then motioned out into the barrel ceiling atrium. There was Bunny and her decorator entering Baker, Knapp and Tubbs. I nodded and gave her a thumbs up signal.

"Cissy, I'm sorry, I just can't think of who she is. Why do you want to know?"

I ignored his question. "Would you please show it to the rest of the staff? We'll look at fabrics for a while. Do you know if you have a pewter or gray on ivory toile?"

Dennis led us to a fabric sample rack. "Here's the toiles. I think Mary is the most familiar with them. She can help you while I show the photo around."

As soon as Dennis walked away from us, Sally said, "Cissy, what the fuck are you doing? Don't we want to follow them into Baker?"

"Relax, Baker is a huge showroom. They'll be in there for ages. Let's look at the toiles and give Dennis a chance to ask about the dead woman."

We didn't find a gray on ivory toile. And Dennis reported that no one in the showroom recognized the woman in the photo.

Sally rushed me over to Baker. Baker is the one showroom in the PDC that makes designers and their clients register to get inside the door. "Mrs. Huntington, your salesperson will be with you in a moment," said the receptionist without taking his eyes off of Sally's gorgeous face. In light of his obvious sexual orientation that did not include the female, it was interesting to note his fascination with her beauty. It *is* startling to see such flawless skin close up.

"No problem. We'll just look around. Have him catch up with us," I said to the receptionist.

"Do you see the bimbo?" asked Sally.

"Shush," I whispered and pointed to my left. I had spotted Bunny in the adjoining alcove. Aloud I said, "Sally, you really ought to give Ted another chance. After all, there's all that Spreckels's money to consider."

Sally caught on immediately. "I don't need his money, even if it is more than I'll ever make. I've got all I need." She paused. "But still Spreckels's money is fucking big-time. And the payoff is coming up soon too."

"Maybe that's one of your attractions for him. You don't need his money. But you used to have such a good time together," I said a little louder than necessary.

"Before he got involved with that slut."

"But he says he's through with her."

To our satisfaction, seconds later Bunny tore out of the showroom holding her hand to her mouth. Her decorator hurried after her.

"Whoa, fucking score!" Sally high-fived me.

"Did we over do it? I feel a little bad."

"You feel bad!" Sally scowled at me. "Remember, she's the one who broke up my marriage. Even so, I guess I can't blame her. That prick was fucking every willing thing in

44

skirts even before her." Sally shook her head and ran her fingers through her thick brown hair. "What's the plan now?"

"Now we get Ted to believe that Bunny is an heiress. Let's see, maybe with a recently deceased mega-rich uncle. Then we just have to find a couple of guys to discuss her impending wealth in the locker room at the LA Athletic Club when Ted's around. He is a member, right?"

"Fuck yes."

"My son Skip's home for Spring Break. He and Jeff will have to play a game or two of racquetball." Skip attends the University of California at Berkeley. Jeff is my daughter Emma's fiancée.

"Too cool," Sally grinned and hugged me. "It would be so nice to be rid of that expense. Just think of all the money we could have for furnishing my house. I give him sixty-fifty grand a month."

"That's nearly a room a month. But we need to get back to detecting."

Sally took the photo from my hand and marched over to the receptionist. He was still staring at her in awe. "Have you seen this woman? Do you have any idea who she is?' Sally demanded.

His mouth hung open and he shook his head without uttering a word.

Our salesperson showed up at that moment, and Sally repeated her questions. Unfortunately, the saleswoman was also speechless with awe and repeated the receptionist's headshake.

"Fuck, this isn't so easy."

Sally and I moved on to the next showroom.

"I guess you're not so jazzed about this detecting stuff anymore?"

"It's not quite as exciting as I hoped. No shoot-outs . . . , or car chases. And nobody seems to recognize her. My fucking feet hurt more every time someone says no."

We had just stepped onto the escalator down to the fourth floor when my cell rang. I looked at the screen. It was a 212 number. Who was calling me from New York? Or from a New York cell phone? "Hello."

"Hi Cissy! It's Alexa." Oh, Alexa Hamilton. Probably from her cell. She was on the road pushing her furniture line.

"Hi, how are you?"

"I'm good, and I figured out why that woman looked familiar."

Chapter 7

"I'm pretty sure she was a client of my father's. If she's the one I'm thinking of, I met her when I was a little girl. I can't remember her name, but I can find the info in Dad's records once I'm in New York. I'm headed back now."

"That's great. Do you remember anything else about her?"

"Not really. I was maybe eight. We had come to LA on a family trip and ran into her with some other women in the Bullock's Wilshire Tea Room. They used to have fashion shows there into the early '80s. It was a special treat to get to go there since I was too young to go to fashion shows in New York."

"What do you remember about her?"

I prided myself on sounding more patient than Rodriquez did when I wandered off the subject.

"It was her eyes. I remember her eyes. I'd never seen such light blue eyes before. My mother and father talked about her later, but I don't remember exactly what they said. Something about her having left the husband that she had when Dad designed their interiors. It'll take a bit to find her but I think I can."

Sally was looking at me questioningly. I had silently led her off the escalator and into the first showroom while I listened to Alexa. When Sally exited the showroom shaking her head, I followed her into the next one. I stood at the entrance and continued my conversation with Alexa.

"Thank you, Alexa. I really appreciate you taking an interest."

"I'm curious too. She was fascinating to me as a child. Very chic. Along the lines of Slim Keith or Babe Paley."

"Well. Thanks again. I'm anxious to hear back from you."

"It may take a while, but I'll let you know. Gotta go. Plane's about to take off."

I explained the conversation to Sally. "You know Alexa is Mark Hamilton's daughter."

"He's a designer, right?"

"Big time. Alexa took over his company when he died."

"Cool that she might have a line on the woman. Does that mean we can stop doing this?"

"So, you're finished with the glamorous life of the detective? Back to boring celebrity life?"

"Well fuck, nobody seems to recognize her."

"Let's zoom through this floor. I'll do every other showroom, and then we'll hit the big ones on the next floor. We have to do Aga John. Jerry and Michael know everybody."

We leap frogged our way down the hall, each of us doing every other shop. I had no luck and Sally continued to shake her head as she exited each one. Discouraged, we headed for the next floor.

When we entered Aga John, brothers and owners Michael and Jerry greeted us with hugs and offers of diet cokes. The previous month, Sally and I had spent quite some time in their place looking at hundreds of new and antique hand-knotted rugs from all over the world. Sally threw herself down on one of the tall stacks of rugs with a huge sigh.

"Do either of you recognize this woman?" I asked Michael and Jerry. They shook their handsome dark gray heads initially, but then Jerry took the photo from me.

"You know, I think maybe she has been in here. It was awhile back. How old is this photo?" Jerry said.

"It was taken yesterday."

"Re-ally. Then she's had some work done, because my recollection of her is of an older woman than she looks here." Jerry pointed to the photograph. "I'll have to think about who brought her in. She's definitely not a designer."

Sally spoke up from where she was lounging on the pile of rugs. "Think about it as long as you like."

"Ms. Abbey, would you like a latte?" asked one of the sales assistants.

"Oh fuck, yes! Nonfat decaf with two packets of sweetener."

"And you Ms. Huntington?"

"No thanks." I called Emma and Nikki, "How are you guys doing?"

"Not so good. We've had no luck. She's not a designer,

Mom."

"That seems to be the consensus of opinion. We're at Aga John's. Care to join us?"

"We'll be right there."

After the girls arrived, and while Nikki lectured Sally about her lack of decorum, I gave Jerry one last chance to tell me which designer had brought the woman into his showroom.

"I'm sorry dear. I'll call you when it comes to me."

Sally climbed off her stack of rugs and the four of us headed to the parking structure. We waited for the valet to fetch our car as I filled the girls in on everything Alexa had told me.

Later in the car, Sally and I described what had happened with Bunny in the Baker showroom. Emma called Jeff and her brother Skip. She gave them their instructions for their racquetball game.

"Cissy, since we're on the subject of husbands, you know I've don't think I've met yours. Nikki and her husband used to say nice things about him, but they've been mum on the subject ever since you moved here. Would you please tell me what the story is with your Jamie?" Sally asked.

Chapter 8

I sighed, realizing I couldn't avoid the subject any longer. The playfulness had left the car. Sally's previously innocuous strong perfume cloyed my lurching stomach. My head began to pound. This subject wasn't fun to Emma and me.

Emma glanced at me, her eyes filled with sorrow before she spoke. "My dad disappeared last summer before we moved down here and met you."

"Wow. Fuck! Don't you have any idea where he is?" Sally asked.

"Our assets were frozen and he split," I said. "I had no idea he was even having financial difficulties. We were in shock for several months."

My heart sank remembering the pain of those first weeks.

"Finally, I refused to think about it and moved on. My father had this house in Los Feliz so we came here. I had worked for a BevHills design firm before I married, and I went back to doing interiors."

"Fuck, I had no idea. You guys are okay now though . . .

right?"

"Financially, yes," I hesitated. "Nothing like before. We've had to learn a new lifestyle." I sighed. "We get by thanks to clients like you. I've stopped freaking every time Skip's tuition is due," I paused. "The numbness is starting to wear off. I realized recently that he might have left because he loved us, not the opposite. That he felt so bad that . . ."

It was too damn hard to talk about Jamie.

"But Mom and I are going to find him now. Jeff wants to get married soon, and I need my dad to walk me down that aisle."

An unusual silence fell over the car.

I dropped Sally and Nikki at Sally's house a few blocks from ours.

Sally reached in the driver's window to give me a consoling hug. "Cissy, if I can help you in any way with finding your husband—with finding Jamie—you let me know."

"Same goes for me," Nikki said as she gently pressed her cheek to mine. "Love ya, darlings"

As we drove away, Emma said, "You can tell right away how sweet Nikki is, but Sally is even more compassionate."

"Tough exteriors are often meant to protect soft hearts," I said.

"Mom, what possible connection do you think that woman could have had to dad?"

"I don't know. She couldn't have showed up at that panel knowing I was to be there, because I wasn't listed on the program. I only knew I was going to be on the stage a few hours beforehand."

I slowed the car to miss the dog walker grasping a half dozen leashes restraining tiny yappers including Sally's.

"Maybe she came thinking you would be in the audience. Maybe she was going to sit next to you and tell you something."

"Unfortunately, I don't think we'll ever know because I'm certain she's dead."

I pulled into our drive and turned off the car. I reached over and put my arms around my beautiful daughter.

"Emma, I love you very much. I would give anything not to see you hurting like this." I held her away from me, smoothed her blonde hair back from her face, and looked into her eyes.

"I got the name of a private detective from Don Hager—you know—the criminal attorney. I called him right after the last time we discussed this. I was waiting for some news from the investigator before I mentioned it to you, but I'll call him as soon as we go inside and see if he's found out anything at all."

Emma nodded and returned my hug. "I love you too, Mama."

We went in through the kitchen Dutch door. Addie Mae Daniels sat at the scrubbed pine table, holding her purse on her lap, sipping tea and supervising the two girls who were cleaning the kitchen. Maria mopped the terracotta tile floor. Naomi wiped down the hand painted blue and white tiles on the back splash. This was the last room cleaned each day.

The house my father had generously made available to my children and me was a two story, u-shaped Spanish Colonial Revival style built around an interior courtyard bounded by the living room on the front side, the kitchen on the back, and a lap pool with a fountain on the outside of the courtyard. Through the kitchen window I saw a cheery blaze crackling in the double-sided fireplace that served both the living room and the courtyard.

"It's about time you got home. I been waiting to leave."

Addie Mae had taken care of me when I was a child. When my parents were first married, they lived in the guesthouse on my grandfather's estate. Addie Mae cleaned up after the three of us and kept an eye on me. She had never stopped. She still bossed me around like I was her charge. I asked her once if she was ever going to treat me like an adult, to which she answered, "You be my baby girl 'til the day I die."

As I wrapped my arms around her now-frail body, I worried that day may not be far off. It used to be impossible to get my arms around her full figure. "I love you very much, Addie Mae."

She shook me off, but welcomed Emma into a mutual hug. Addie was the one tie my children had left to the life they once knew. Her presence always made me feel as though no real harm could come to them, but it couldn't ease the heartache they felt whenever they thought of their father.

Damn, I had to find him.

When Skip came into the kitchen, I was struck once again by how much he looked like his handsome blonde father. He ignored all the feminine affection and emotion, greeting us with a grunt, and heading straight for the refrigerator. He opened the door, studied the contents, then finally reached for a soda.

"So, what's up? What's this Jeff said about picking me up to play racquetball? We're supposed to hang out in the locker room until some guy shows up? What's with that?" Skip took a slug of the soda.

"I'll fill you in. Is Jeff on his way over now?" Emma asked.

She put her arm through her brother's and led him out to the atrium. Through the kitchen window, I watched them pull the cushioned armchairs closer to the outdoor fireplace. Emma's obvious delight at having Skip home for spring break warmed my mother's heart. And increased my determination to find their father.

"That sleazy private detective man called. Did I tell you I don't like him much?" Addie Mae said as she reorganized the contents of her tote on the table.

"When did he call?"

"Just a bit ago," she answered.

"You can tell people like that to call my cell," I reminded her. I gave her a quick hug and wished her a goodnight before heading into my sunroom office to return the call.

He must have some news. I hoped it was good.

Chapter 9

In my office, I sat down at the huge library table strewn with fabric, carpet and tile samples. Moving aside a design board covered with Buff Drake's colorful paisleys, I picked up the message that Susan had taken with the PI's phone number on it.

My hands shook as I punched the buttons and held the receiver. I stood and paced as I listened to the ringing at the other end of the line.

A man's voice answered with a curt, "Yeah?"

"Hello, Mr. Pelancono?"

"Yeah."

"This is Cissy Huntington."

"Yeah."

"You called."

"Yeah"

"Do you have some news?"

"Yep."

"Did you learn something about my husband?" My hand clutched the phone so tightly it hurt.

"Yeah."

Oh, for Gods sake. "Well?"

"He's alive. Or he was a week ago."

"Thank God!" I took a deep breath. "How . . . how do you know that?"

"We won't be discussing my methods over the phone."

"Where is he?"

"I can't tell you where he is right at the moment."

"Where was he a week ago?"

"In Tucson, Arizona. But he left there and we don't have a handle on his current whereabouts."

"Tucson. That's not so far."

I'd been afraid he was in the South Pacific, having sailed off to some forgotten island, or another equally remote location. Tucson. That's not so bad.

"What was he doing in Tucson?"

"It seems he was looking at a mine."

"Oh."

"There's something else."

"Oh?"

"He's got a woman with him."

"O-h!"

"They're traveling in her jet."

"O-h."

"We haven't got our hands on the flight plan yet, but we will."

"Oh."

"We'll keep you informed." And he hung up.

"O-o-oh" I collapsed into my desk chair. I was so

57

shocked I had failed to ask who the woman was. So damn naive. I had never considered the possibility that Jamie had left us for another woman. Another woman? I couldn't get my head around the idea. How could he?

My hand clutching the receiver shook so violently it took both hands and several tries to get the phone back on the cradle.

Damn fool! I was convinced that he was so embarrassed that his famous business talent had failed him that he had run away rather than face his friends, business associates, . . . or even his family. I had some ill-conceived, romantic idea that he went off to recoup his fortune and would reappear on our doorstep someday, announcing that all was well. What a damn fool I'd been!

Later. I had to think about this later. For now, what do I tell my children?

Rather than head directly out to the atrium patio, I stopped in the kitchen for a glass of wine. I found an open Sauvignon Blanc in the fridge and poured the wine into a large goblet. I refrained from my usual habit of adding San Pellegrino.

Maybe one of my annoying habits had finally gotten to my husband. Or maybe it was because I wasn't young anymore.

Jamie was still a very attractive man. Shit, it's so unfair how men get better looking as they age. He probably found someone young and rich—with a private jet. I took a couple swallows and plastered a smile on my face. Then I walked out to the join my children.

"Good news." I sat on the hearth in front of the blazing fire. "I just spoke with the private investigator I asked to find your father."

They both looked at me expectantly.

"He's alive."

Emma breathed a sigh of relief.

"You guys actually thought he might be dead?" Skip frowned at each of us in turn.

"Well, we haven't heard from him since August. It's been more than six months. It was a definite possibility." Emma rolled her big blue eyes at her brother. "Where is he?"

"Mr. Pelancono says he was in Tucson a week ago. But they don't know where he is now."

"Yeah, I guess with all the security these days it's not so easy to find out who is on what flight," Skip mused.

"He's traveling by private jet."

"What? Whose?" Emma stood up.

I shook my head.

"He sold his plane, right Mom?" Skip asked.

"The bank sold his jet," Emma reminded her brother. "Wow, what do you think Mom?"

"I don't know what to think." I went back to the kitchen to refill my glass. I leaned against the blue and white tile counter and took a deep breath.

Emma followed me. "What's wrong? What aren't you telling us?"

I shook my head. "Nothing."

I had to pull myself together. I took a drink.

"I just don't understand why he wouldn't have told me any of the problems he was having. How could he leave us without a word? And how could he be so close by and not make any effort to see us? I know he loves you both very much. No matter how upset he could be with me, why wouldn't he be in touch with you and your brother?"

Emma studied my face. "Mama, I've never wanted to bring this up before. You've had enough to deal with. I kind of assumed . . . . Well, did you guys have a fight or something?"

"No, not at all. But in retrospect, I obviously wasn't there for him when he needed me." I looked her in the eye. "Strange we haven't talked about this isn't?" I brushed her hair away from her face. "He kissed me good-bye that morning. Messed up Skip's hair. Yelled upstairs to you. And he never set foot in that house again."

I took a gulp of wine. "When he didn't come home that night, I thought he'd gotten caught up in a meeting that went really late. Often when he was dealing with developers overseas the teleconferences would go into weird hours. Sometimes, rather than come home in the middle of the night and then have to be back in the City early the next morning, he would sleep on the sofa in his office."

Or so he told me.

"I left a couple messages on his voicemail. I figured he'd come in during the night, and I'd lecture him the next day about staying in touch. Turned out he'd left his cell at the office when he went to lunch. His secretary said he never came back."

Emma poured herself a glass of wine.

I continued, "The next morning, a sheriff showed up and confiscated two of the cars. When I called your father's attorney, he was shocked to hear that I didn't know about the bankruptcy. That's when we moved in with Grandpa in Atherton. Your father definitely knows how to get a hold of your grandfather, and I kept the same cell, even when we moved down here so that Jamie could call me whenever. I thought he'd call as soon as he calmed down. I never dreamed he would be out of touch this long."

"He's had business deals that went wrong before, hasn't he?" Emma asked.

"Yes. That fly-in community he built with Jeff Trevor barely came out even. And those Chelsea Harbor Townhouses . . . , remember how beautiful the view of the Thames is from there? Anyway, it took a long time to sell all of those units. But in the end the London real estate market caught up with the value. I know he had some bad moments juggling loans because he had so much money tied up in the London project. But, it seems, this time he had a much worse problem."

"It's amazing we've never really talked about this. I'm sorry. I assumed you'd had a fight." Emma placed her arm across my shoulders. "I wouldn't have thought Dad ran away in shame. Do you think he hooked up with someone?"

I ignored my daughter's question. I wasn't ready for that yet.

"Or Mom, there is another possibility. Do you think he

could be protecting us from something worse than the bankruptcy? Frozen assets could mean legal problems, right?"

"I'm beginning to think—anything's possible.

Chapter 10

"Hey dude! Good to see ya." Jeff had arrived. He and Skip clasped hands. "Ready for racquetball?"

With the two young men standing next to each other in the atrium, I could see that although they both were tall, Skip was a couple inches taller than Jeff. They were both slender, with the natural tan of outdoor athletes, but Jeff's hair was black-brown in contrast to Skip's blonde.

"I can't believe we got roped into this. Are we actually going to play?" Skip asked. "Or just lie in wait in the locker room?"

"Let's play. Have to be convincingly sweaty, right? We can check out where he is and then figure it out."

"Do you know what he looks like?" Skip picked up an L. L. Bean tote bag from the terracotta tile floor in front of the fireplace.

"Yeah, and you do too," Jeff said. "You'll remember him once you see him. Good-lookin' dude. Pulls girls. About your height, light brown hair, year-round dark tan, blue eyes, ripped. Looks like a movie star, but he's mostly

TV. Works out everyday. I've often seen him at the club about this time."

Emma went to the atrium and greeted Jeff with a kiss and a hug. "Hello, gum drop."

Jeff grabbed Emma and pulled her close for a deeper kiss.

I hung back for a moment and then I hugged Jeff too.

"So, do you guys know what to do?" I asked.

"Yep, casually discuss within hearing range of Ted Greer that Bunny's rich uncle is in really bad health."

"You think the rich uncle bit is a little too obvious?" Skip asked. Skip was less than enthused about this project. Once again, the women in his family had him doing something silly. Probably made him miss his father even more.

"Improvise," I said. "Whatever you decide you want to say, just make sure he gets the idea that her wealth is imminent."

Skip carried his bag upstairs to get his racquet and clothes.

Emma and Jeff went for a clinch and deep, soulful kisses as soon as I cleared the door to the kitchen. When he came up for air, Jeff murmured sweet nothings in Emma's ear. "Ah, my little bonbon."

I made for the wine bottle. I decided not to think about what Pelancono had told me. I would concentrate on finding out who the dead woman was. I went into the office and located the photo on my computer.

I heard Skip's footsteps run down the terracotta steps.

When the front door slammed I called out to Emma, "Sweetheart, would you please help me post this photo on the Internet?"

"Right there, Mom."

I sat at Emma's writing table, watched the young men get in the car and drive away. Emma came into the library with a piece of cheese in one hand and her wine glass in the other.

I moved out of her way and sat in the window seat next to her desk.

"I transferred the photo to your computer. Do you have any idea where and how to post it?"

"Sure." Emma sat down, hit some keys, and deftly maneuvered through cyberspace. "Are you going to tell me what the PI said?"

"I told you."

"You didn't tell me what upset you so much."

"No, I didn't." I punched one of the down pillows and stuck it behind my back.

"So?"

Oh, hell. What was the point of trying to keep something from my daughter? Now that she was an adult, I couldn't protect her from the bad stuff in life

"Your father is traveling with a woman."

"Mom, I'm sure that doesn't mean anything."

"And why are you *sure*?"

I turned and stared out the window hiding my tears from my daughter.

"Daddy loves you, Mom." Emma wasn't looking at me

anyway. She gazed at the screen and poked keys on the computer.

"And that's why he left me?"

"Okay, it doesn't make total sense, but how many times have you explained that people's behavior doesn't always make sense? God knows what he's thinking. Besides you're the one who said that he left because he couldn't face us after bankrupting his company." Emma scowled and turned to face me. "How did he do that, anyway?"

"I told you I don't know." I wiped my eyes. "I guess it was that fly-in community in Florida. Didn't sell as well as he hoped. Seems there aren't that many jumbo jet owners around."

"Is that the place that had that extra heavy-duty runway that was built for flying horses around?" Emma asked while her fingers flew over her keyboard.

"Yeah. Bo Derek used it to ship her horses. Before your dad bought it and expanded the runways."

"But one project wouldn't ruin Dad. Was there more to it?"

"I don't know, sweetheart. Something was draining off capital."

"But Dad wouldn't touch capital, Mom. How many lectures did he give us about *NEVER, EVER, UNDER ANY CIRCUMSTANCES, SPEND CAPITAL*?" Emma spun in her chair and looked at me.

"Well," I grimaced, "it seems he did. Look at everything the banks took. The Tahoe house, the house in the City, the flat in London, the office building, the jet, five cars, the boat—"

"Okay, Okay, Mom! I get your point. But think about it. There's something really freaking wrong here that you're avoiding." Emma's eyes were glued to mine. "What if there was something he didn't want us to know, and somebody found out about it?"

"What? You think he was being blackmailed?"

"Maybe extortion?" She turned her attention back to the computer, but continued to speak. "Maybe someone was threatening him—or us. Maybe he left to protect us from a real threat. Not something so stupid as not being able to tell us he was broke."

"You could be right," I pushed my side swept bangs off my forehead and turned back to the window, "but at the moment it looks more like he ran off with another woman."

Emma sighed. "I don't think so." She pushed away from the computer. "Okay, I've posted the dead woman's photo several places: on Sally's website, on Facebook, on our website, and a bunch more. I left the design firm email address as a contact point."

"Great. Thanks. Got any other ideas how else we can find out who she was?"

"Wait to see what Alexa finds out?" Emma suggested. "I don't get why you give a shit about this dead woman."

"I've got a feeling about her. She's connected to us."

"We don't know her."

"Maybe your father does."

"And maybe you're just looking for a distraction. Or something you can *do*?" Emma said. "You still want to head up to the Lake?"

"Hmm, I'd like a change of scenery." I thought about it for a second. "This is the last weekend Skip will be home for awhile."

Emma smiled. "And hitting the slopes would be a good distraction. Jeff and Skip would like to board one last time before the hill closes, and Skip won't be home again until Easter when they might be closed. What do we need to pack?" She sat down beside me in the window seat, put her arm around me, and rested her head on my shoulder.

"There's a basket of clean ski clothes in the laundry room. Stuff we brought home last time. I think everything else is up there."

"How about food?"

"Addie Mae left enchiladas in the oven. I'll make a salad." I started toward the kitchen with Emma on my heels.

"I'll set the table, and then throw some books and my laptop in the Highlander with the laundry. We can leave right after dinner. The Friday get-away traffic will be over by then."

Emma and I completed our chores, loaded all we would need for a few days in the car and sat down in the atrium with the last two glasses of wine to wait for the guys.

Emma held a handful of creamy white envelopes she had taken off the refrigerator door. "Mom, did we remember to RSVP to Poppy's wedding?"

I stared at my daughter blankly. I'd forgotten Emma's best friend's wedding. Shit. When was the damn thing?

"The RSVP card is still in the envelope." Emma raised an eyebrow at me. "The wedding is in two weeks. We should have sent it in by now." Emma studied the cards and then handed them to me.

The engraved invitation read "Mr. and Mrs. Cameron Wells request the honor of your presence at the wedding of their daughter Penelope Olivia Priestly Wells . . ."

Poppy's wedding. Cameron and Joan were always correct. The stiffest people of my generation that I'd ever known. I wouldn't have failed to respond to an invite from them.

I remembered. "We got two copies of this invite. That's yours. I sent in the return card saying that four of us, you and Jeff, Skip and I would attend."

"Don't forget that I'm going up to the City a week earlier for the shower and the spinster bachelorette party. Poppy really wanted me to come even sooner for other parties, but I didn't want to desert you for two weeks."

"You could fly up for the parties."

"Yeah, I was trying to work it out with Poppy. Which days were what, but she hasn't been answering her cell."

"Did you try her house?"

"That-ever-so-correct butler of her mother's—what's-his-name? Philip?—refuses to give out any numbers. He says 'Miss, I am happy to take a message for Miss Poppy.' and he just keeps repeating the same damn thing."

"Email her."

"I did."

Jeff called as they were leaving the club. Emma put her

cell on speaker. I could hear Skip whooping in the background.

"We did it. Went smooth as silk. We'll tell you all about it in ten minutes. Oh, and we're bringing a surprise."

Chapter 11

The early March evening turned cool enough that even directly in front of the outdoor fireplace was too chilly to sit comfortably. Emma and I adjourned to the kitchen where Emma had set the scrubbed pine table for our informal dinner.

"Mom, should we at least take a carton of milk and some eggs from here? Would save us having to stop for groceries tonight." Emma grabbed a small cooler, filled it with breakfast essentials, and returned it to the laundry room.

Minutes later, the laundry door entrance to the house slammed open and Skip burst into the kitchen. He turned his head to speak to someone behind him. "Was that your cousin Cameron we saw you talking to?"

Skip cursed as he tripped over the breakfast cooler. "Shit, goddamn, who put that there?" Skip stumbled into the kitchen.

"I'm sorry," Emma said. "I packed it to take to the mountain."

My children looked at each other and laughed.

"Look who we found at the club."

Right behind Skip were his childhood babysitters and distant Cowles cousins, Tommy and Robby. Not my favorites.

Robby and Tommy were trust fund babies. No-need-to-do-anything-useful-in-order-to-survive bums who filled their days with surfing, skiing, and boarding, and their nights clubbing and partying. Their bodies were tan and lean, but they had killed more than a few brain cells with intellectual atrophy as well as drugs.

"Hello, cream puff!" Jeff gathered Emma into his arms.

"What are you two doing in LA?" Emma wiggled out of Jeff's embrace and turned to her cousins.

Robby stepped forward to give her a quick hug. "Hey, cuz."

Emma laughed as Robby's dark blonde buzz cut grazed her cheek.

"Uh, just comin' back from a surfin' safari in Baja. Got cleaned up at the club. Thought we'd . . . uh, like, hit a couple of nightspots." Tommy tossed his streaked blonde hair out of his eyes to check out Emma. "Uh. You've grown up good, cuz."

Emma squirmed out of Tommy's lingering hug just in time to avoid Jeff jumping to her rescue. She pushed Tommy's shoulder to arm's length and then slapped his hand away.

"Jeez, Tommy, when was the last time you got a haircut?" Emma looked pointedly at the top of Tommy's head and a good size bald patch fringed with long, stringy hair.

"Join us for dinner?" I asked as politeness dictated.

Robby frowned at the table set for four. "Hey. Nah, just wanted to like say hello. We gotta meet a guy. Like, maybe we'll come back later."

"We going up to the mountain after dinner," Emma said quickly.

We exchanged quick hugs and Tommy and Robby said good-bye. I thanked God for my wonderful children.

Emma said, "Mom, why the hell did you invite them for dinner?" She shuddered and shook her hands at her sides. "Tommy is so disgusting—they're both creeps. I've never understood why you let them hang around."

Before I could answer, Skip came to my defense—sorta.

"Hey, they're cool. I liked it when Mom let me hang with them up at the Lake." Skip grinned at his sister. "They taught me to smoke."

Emma pointed at Skip but looked at me. "My point exactly. What were you? Eight?"

Jeff put his arms around Emma and nestled his head over her shoulder. "Cookie, I know you don't like those guys. I'll protect you from them."

Emma smiled and patted Jeff's cheek. "I packed the car with the laundry we brought down last trip." She turned to face Jeff. "What happened with Ted?"

Skip surveyed the neatly set dinner table. "I'm starving. Can we tell you over dinner?"

In response, I took the enchiladas out of the oven and placed the dish on a trivet in the middle of the table. We sat down and dug in.

Ignoring the refrain-from-talking-with-one's-mouthful "rule of manners" Skip filled us in, "So, we checked the courts when we got there and found Ted. He was mid-game. Sweaty enough that we knew he had been at it awhile."

He jammed a large bite of salad into his mouth.

Jeff picked up the story, "So we got the court next to his and kinda screwed around, pretending to play, but mostly listening for him to quit."

"When he did, we gave him a couple minutes to hit the shower—"

"That was a gamble. What if he had left without showering?" Emma said.

"Not a chance." Skip gave his sister that look that only brothers can get a way with. That disdainful but affect-tionate look. The one that says, "Oh God, you're dumb, but I do love you anyway."

Ignoring the siblings, Jeff continued the story, "We went into the locker room and strategically placed ourselves in the next aisle over from where he'd dropped his clothes. When we heard him and his friend come back from the showers, we had a loud conversation."

Skip said, "So, I said plenty loud, 'I was thinking about getting to know that Barbara Brown, the one they call Bunny. She's hot!' "

"And then I said," Jeff added, " 'Not just hot, she's soon to be plenty rich.' "

Skip picked up the next line. "Then I said, 'I'm down with that. But how is she going to get rich?' "

Jeff grinned as he delivered the punch lines to their play acting. "I made sure to say plenty loud 'Just happened to hear some of the partners at my law firm. Her uncle, the one whose wife died a few years ago, the one with no children. Seriously ill. Even though they're not all that close, he's leaving it all to Bunny.' "

"To which I said, 'No way,' " Skip interjected.

Jeff continued to explain what he had said, " 'But he seems to think she's a moron. Stipulates that she has to be married before she gets the money, and that the husband is to be the executor of the estate.' "

I high fived them both. "Nice touch," I said.

"Then Skip said, 'She may not be the smartest thing, but I'm down with how sexy. Not a bad deal.' "

"Another nice touch," I said. "Are you sure he heard you?"

"Oh, de-fin-ite-ly. He checked us out when he left the room."

We clinked our goblets. "Well done!"

Skip set down his glass and studied the light fixture over the tabletop.

"What's the matter?" I asked my son.

"The guy he was with, Ted's friend—I didn't really get a look at him, but his voice was familiar. I caught a glimpse of him when he rushed out. I thought it was Poppy's father, ya know Cameron, but when he didn't say hello . . ." Skip shrugged his shoulders.

Cameron? In LA? Was he doing business with Ted? They seemed a strange combo, although from things I'd heard, they both engaged in some questionable business occasionally.

We efficiently finished dinner in silence, knowing we'd have better than an hour to chat as we drove to my father's place at Big Bear Lake. We cleared the table, grabbed a few more things including our chocolate brown Labradoodle, Lulu, and piled into the car.

"Let's hit the road." Skip pulled the car out of the driveway.

Chapter 12

Despite the fresh mountain air, the skies bright with stars, and the reflection of the moon on the lake and the snow, I couldn't hold my immense sorrow at bay. Once in my cozy bed, a cloud of overwhelming gloom descended on me. I was afraid the dull ache would turn to a broken heart if I allowed myself to think about Jamie's absence.

He was such a shit, but I missed him so much. As soon as I admitted that to myself, I burst into tears and I cried until there were no tears left. I sniffled and tossed and turned for what seemed like hours.

Eventually, I gave up on sleep, turned on the light, and tried to distract myself with a book. My favorite: Agatha Christie's Miss Marple. When that didn't work I headed for the kitchen and nuked a mug of milk to which I had added sweetener and cinnamon. Finally, at about five thirty, my eyes felt heavy, and I drifted off.

"Mom, are you getting up?" Emma inquired from my bedroom doorway.

It seemed like minutes later, but it must have been eight o'clock.

"I had a miserable night. I'll walk down to the shuttle and meet you for lunch. Maybe by then I'll have rested enough to take on the hill. The way I feel at the moment, I'd probably have trouble avoiding trees."

I heard the bustle of activity as they tossed down some breakfast and packed up their gear. Skip fed Lulu on the back porch and yelled to Emma that he was going to leave the dog in the yard.

The door slammed shut and a peaceful quiet fell over the mountain home. It was comfy, cozy in my warm bed. I snuggled deeper into the down duvet and fell back asleep to dream of Jamie and a lazy afternoon siesta we'd spent in a comfy bed behind shuttered windows in Tuscany. I felt warm and safe nestled in his arms after an afternoon of gentle, sensual lovemaking. The light streaming through the cracks in the shutters lit stripes on the leg he'd thrown over me. I wanted to stay in that world forever, but even in the dream I couldn't shake the sadness that threatened to overwhelm the bliss. And the barking—what was the barking?

I awoke with alarm to Lulu barking frantically. A squirrel couldn't have elicited that much noise. Maybe it was a bear . . . or worse yet, a snake. A rattlesnake! A mountain lion?

Shit, Skip had left Lulu outside.

I threw on my robe, slipped my feet into my sheepskin clogs, and exited the log house onto the back porch. The barking came from the side deck, off the living room, where the cedar porch faced the lake and the ski resorts on the far side of the water. It was a nice location for enjoying the view, soaking in the spa, and sipping après ski wine.

"Lulu, hush. Lulu, quiet!"

Lulu stopped pacing and sat next to the spa.

Lying across the cover of the spa was the same body that had been spread across the hood of my car just a couple days before: the same auburn hair, the same ice blue jacket and the same jewelry. The Jimmy Choo sandals were missing. And her lovely pale skin was a pale shade of blue. Ice blue. She looked frozen. Iced blue.

I'd probably never feel the same about that deck . . . definitely not about the spa.

Chapter 13

Not this again!

Again, I was alone.

This time I didn't even have a car.

If I were to leave the area, would this damn body disappear again?

Could whoever had dropped this body here still be around?

Did Lulu scare them off?

From where I stood, I could see through the French doors to the portable phone on the counter between the living room and the kitchen. Could I possibly make it to the phone without letting the body out of my sight? Just grab the portable and bring it back?

I gave some thought to where the nearest camera might be. Where was my cell? Damn! Upstairs in the bedroom.

The hell with the camera. I'd go for the landline portable.

I backed up to the French door that led to the living room. I twisted the handle with my hands behind my back. Damn, locked. And bolted.

We'd only unlocked the main entrance. I'd opened the back door when I came out to investigate what Lulu was barking about. The "kids" had gone out through the mud-room. None of those doors were within sight of the spa.

Could I see through the windows of the living room to the spa?

Recalling times that I had come through the main entrance knowing that there were people in the spa—could I see them from the front door? It was the best bet.

"Lulu, stay," I ordered. She wouldn't let a stranger onto the deck.

Well, at least not without barking. Who was I kidding? She'd at worst lick a stranger to death.

I backed around the exterior corner of the living room and onto the front walk, raced through the front door, down the short hall and into the kitchen where I grabbed the phone and burst through the living room, through the French door, and back onto the deck.

The body was still there.

Lulu tilted her head at me with one ear raised.

Both of my hands shook as I stabbed at the buttons on the phone. 9–1–1. Please, please don't put me on hold.

Hopefully the Big Bear police weren't as overloaded as the LA cops. The phone rang a third time. A fourth. A fifth.

Oh Christ, were they not even going to answer?

"If you wish to reach the Big Bear police department or Big Bear Station, please dial 909-866-0100. For the San Bernardino Sheriff's Headquarters call 909 387 3545. If this is an emergency, please stay on the line."

Oh no-o-o.

"What is the nature of your emergency?"

"There's a dead body on my spa."

"In your spa."

"*On* my spa."

"Did it drown?"

"How should I know?"

"Did he or she drown in the spa?" The operator now spoke slowly, enunciating deliberately. "Has anyone administered CPR?"

"She didn't drown in my spa. She's been dead for days."

"What? How do you know that?"

"Please just send someone over here quickly. It's freezing out here." My robe was useless in the cold wind on the deck. And then there was the possibility—that I was doing my best not to think about—that the murderers were still close by.

"Ma'am, if you are certain the body is dead, there's no need to stay with it."

"Oh, yes there is."

"Is she a relative?"

"No. I have no idea who she is."

"Are you sure she's dead?"

"Oh yeah, I'm sure."

Nobody could look like that and be alive. I poked the body. Cold and hard as ice. Frozen solid.

Chapter 14

"How soon can they get here?"

"Ma'am, if she is already dead—"

"Just tell 'em to hurry. I could be in danger." I hung up, ran into the living room, pulled a throw off of the hunter green sofa, wrapped myself in it, and sat down on the floor next to the window where I had a clear view of the spa. And the body.

I endured a few minutes of violent shivering before I decided to chance making myself a cup of tea. I slid into the kitchen, grabbed a mug, looked out the French doors, saw the body, grabbed a tea bag, looked out the French doors, filled the mug with water, looked out the French doors, stuck the mug into the microwave, and went back to my post by the French doors. When the microwave bell rang, I retrieved my mug of tea, tossed sugar and splashed milk into it, and returned to my watch while my trembling hands sloshed tea.

I hadn't taken my eyes off of the body for more than three seconds at a time.

She was still there.

Lulu barked outside the door demanding entrance.

"Okay, come in. Sit."

Lulu and I huddled together with both of us keeping close watch on the body. If the bad guys were still around somewhere, maybe the size of the dog would give them second thoughts about harming me. I reached up and locked the French door.

From the center of town where I remembered the police station was, to our cabin was normally a ten-minute drive. The first vehicle arrived fifteen minutes after I hung up the phone.

I made my way to the front door sideways so I could keep an eye on the body as I walked.

"Officers, please come in. The body is right this way." I ignored their drawn guns and ushered the two uniformed men through the living room and out to the deck.

"She's dead all right." The older of the two deputies made the pronouncement.

A wave of relief washed over me. This body was no longer my problem. "If you gentlemen will please excuse me, I'd like to take a hot shower and get some warmer clothes on."

"Oh, no! Whoa. Have a seat right in there. Where we can see you."

The sheriff's deputy motioned to the living room while the other man used his radio to call for crime scene investigators and the medical examiner. It sounded like the forensics personnel were coming up all the way from San Bernardino.

I sat down on the sofa. Lulu curled up at my feet. I finished my tea. I wanted to call Detective Rodriquez and tell him I'd found the body again. The dead body! But I didn't know his number.

"Officer, I need to make a phone call, and the number is in my cell which is upstairs in my bedroom. May I please get my cell?"

"Calling your lawyer?"

"No, a detective with the Beverly Hills police."

"Bruce, walk up to her bedroom with her. Make sure she doesn't touch anything but the phone."

Bruce escorted me down the long, pine-paneled hall to my room, where I grabbed my phone.

Out the front windows I saw the other deputy move his white Explorer so that it blocked the drive onto our property from the main road.

"Can we stop in the kitchen on the way back to the living room?" I asked.

"What for?"

"I'd like another cup of tea." Maybe the warmth of another cup would calm my shaking hands. "Would you like one?"

"No thanks."

But we stopped off. Full mug of tea in one hand and cell in the other, I settled into the sofa in the living room.

"Detective Rodriquez. So glad I caught you. Listen, I found that body again. Or I should say, it found me."

"What?"

"This is Cissy Huntington."

"I know who it is." Deep sigh. "What's this about a body?"

"The body that disappeared off my car showed up on top of my spa."

"In Los Feliz? Did you call the LAPD?"

"No. I called the Big Bear Police Station, which is apparently part of the San Bernardino Sheriff's Department."

"What the hell?"

"I'm at my father's house at Big Bear Lake. I was kinda hoping you would consider coming up here because these sheriff deputies seem to think I'm a suspect, or something. They won't even let me get dressed."

"Are you naked?"

"No. I'm in my nightgown."

"Who is with you?"

"Two deputies. The forensic support team is coming up from San Bernardino from someplace called Sid. Or maybe the investigator is named Sid?"

"That's capitals S. I. D. It stands for Scientific Investigations Division. When the investigators show up, have the lead give me a call."

"I heard the deputies ask for CSI . . . and something like CAL-ID latent and ten print unit. What's that?"

"Those are fingerprint units. The latent unit will be looking for prints left at the scene. The ten print will be using fingerprint cards, probably to identify the body."

"Oh. I'm going to be here for awhile, aren't I?" At least I was comfortable at this crime scene. "Are you coming up here?"

"Just have him call me."

He hung up.

I looked at the time on my phone. Eleven fifteen. I called the kids to let them know I wouldn't be meeting them for lunch. I got Emma's voicemail. Cell service on the hill was spotty. I tried another number. I was relieved to get Skip.

"I'm not going to make it for lunch, sweetheart."

"Are you alright, Mom?"

"I'm fine."

I was surprised to realize I *was* fine. The morning's events had distracted me from and put my own problems in perspective. Shit, at least I wasn't dead.

"But I'm a bit tied up here. Something's come up. What time will you quit for the day?"

"We'll just take a couple more runs after lunch. It's crowded and cold. Major clouding over too. We'll quit for sure when it starts to snow. Should get in some runs today, because we probably won't want to ride or ski in a blizzard tomorrow."

"Okay."

"We could just come home now."

"No, don't do that. Have a good lunch."

My stomach was growling. "Sheriff, I'd like to go back to the kitchen and get some food," I called out to the two men on the deck standing half in the open doorway presumably so that they could keep an eye on me. Interesting how the authorities assume that the person reporting a crime may well have had something to do with it.

If only they would close the door it would be a lot warmer in here. They both had on khaki green parkas over their light khaki uniform shirts, dark khaki powder pants and heavy boots. Their caps had fur-lined earmuffs attached. The cold wasn't a problem for them.

"Ma'am, we need you to stay right where you are until the SID personnel arrive. We really can't allow you to touch anything before that."

"But it could be hours before they arrive. Especially if the weather gets any worse."

From where I sat, I could see the sky darken. In spite of the daylight hour, the room was gloomy.

I looked at the cold fireplace longingly. "A fire sure would be nice."

The deputy looked at me as though I was crazy, but politely said, "Sorry Ma'am. If the weather holds and the traffic isn't too heavy, they should be here in less than an hour."

I punched a tapestry throw pillow and placed it against the arm of the sofa, pulled an additional cashmere throw over me, and curled up with my head on the pillow. My heart had stopped pounding. Maybe I could catch a nap.

But napping in the midst of a crime scene wasn't all that easy.

I looked around the familiar room furnished with memorable items or hand-me-downs from the houses of my childhood. Above the rustic, rock fireplace hung a pair of wood skis that had belonged to my great grandfather. I took a deep breath. The smoky sweet smell of burnt oak had penetrated the thick wool curtains. The two sofas, the armchairs and all eight beds were purchased new for this cabin, comfort being an important concern in a vacation home. Everything else had been handed down to this house.

Comforted by the well-known surroundings, I must have dozed off because the next thing I knew, heavily-booted personnel tromped through the living room and out to the deck. Blue booties covered their shoes.

I had a panoramic view of the property. From where I perched on the sofa in the living room, I could see the lawn rolling down to the lake on one side, and out the windows facing the drive on the opposite wall. I had the perfect vantage point to keep track of the investigation.

A heated discussion was taking place between the new arrivals and the two deputies. The CSI team wasn't pleased that I had touched numerous objects while we awaited their appearance.

That all seemed rather nonsensical to me. After all, I could have scrubbed my hands, changed my clothes, hell, even taken a shower before I'd called the authorities.

One of the investigators carried his bag over to where I lay on the sofa.

"Ma'am please give me your hands."

Young and deferential, he spoke softly.

"Homicide Detective Rodriquez with the Beverly Hills Police would like the person in charge here to call him," I said. "I'll give the phone number to that person, if you would be so kind as to send him to me."

"She is busy at the moment, but I know she'll speak to you."

I held out my hands and he placed a plastic bag over each one.

I was getting to know this routine all too well.

Deftly using a pair of tweezers, he picked up a hair from my sleeve and placed it in a small folded paper. The paper was then placed in a bag. He labeled the bag with the date, my name, and location of removal. After he picked over my clothes and the throw, he used a hand-held vacuum that he ran over my robe and my clogs.

I wondered if they all used that same brand of cute little vacuum.

Next, he removed the bags and sprayed something on my hands and wiped them down.

"What's that?" I asked.

"Thank you," was all I got for an answer.

Then he rolled each of my fingers in ink and made copies.

From where I sat I could see a row of white Explorers with county sheriff seals on their sides lined up at the edge of the main road, blocking entrance to the property. Our drive was made of decomposed granite. The edges and the parking area had patches of partially melted snow that had iced over in the night and had yet to melt on the cold morning. The dark clouds threatened a new layer of snow.

Investigators strung familiar yellow crime scene tape across the drive and wrapped trees fifty feet away on both sides of the gate. The investigators who were stringing the tape gestured at the drivers of the Explorers to get farther away from the drive. Barricades were placed onto the asphalt ten feet from where the crushed granite drive began. I guessed that the investigators wanted to examine the tire treads on the harder surface and in the mud that oozed between the asphalt road and the crushed rock drive. I assumed that the rock failed to offer an ideal base for tire tracks.

Meanwhile on the deck, a man I took to be a medical examiner, or a forensic investigator, checked out the body while a photographer took shots. Through the open door I heard, "This isn't the primary."

Meaning that the body had been moved from where she had been killed. Duh! They could've asked.

"Yeah, check out the double lividity. This body was moved in the first four to six hours after death."

I knew that!

The yellow tape now stretched all the way to the water delineating a hundred feet of shoreline. The tape marked a trapezoid—one hundred and twenty feet at the entrance end, one hundred feet at the water, and two hundred feet deep. The boundaries of the crime scene exceeded Dad's property by several feet in each direction.

One team of investigators shined lights at an angle along the shore. One man made casts of whatever it was they found. I wondered if they had found signs of a boat coming ashore. We never used powerboats and, therefore, had no need of a dock. Thus, any boats would have had to land at the water's edge.

A second team examined the drive with angled lights and made casts of tire tracks.

A third used their wide beamed flashlights and laser lights to study the tracks at the asphalt road, at the muddy shoulder, and at the junction. A photographer looked down and held her camera at a ninety-degree angle, shooting tracks on the asphalt.

I figured they must be looking for where the suspects who dumped the body on the spa entered and exited the property.

On the deck, the photographer, together with his note taker and the forensics investigator working on the body, were documenting and collecting trace evidence. The criminalist used tweezers to pick up items so small I couldn't see what they were and placed the items in bags. A second man wrote labels on the bags. Paper bags had already been placed on the hands of the corpse. A young woman used a measuring tape and then made notations on a sketch pad. Wish I knew what they were finding. Maybe I could get Manny to tell me?

An hour after the boots stomped through the living room, a second set of investigators arrived at the property. Frequently someone would study the threatening sky as if they were judging how much time they had left before a layer of snow covered the evidence.

The second team encircled the spa, studied the deck, and then the ground, as they moved in a spiral pattern away from the body. Occasionally an investigator would bag something.

What they were looking for? What they had found?

The railing at the steps leading up to the deck was dusted for fingerprints. The fingerprint examiner then waved his finger print wand at the railing and built-in seat that ran the length of the deck.

I called out to the closest deputy. "May I please speak with the lead investigator?"

"Ma'am, she'll be with you soon. We're working against what is forecasted to be a heavy snowfall. Any evidence that is outside will likely be lost unless we deal with it now."

"Then will you at least take a message to her. She needs to call Detective Rodriquez with the Beverly Hills Police." I scrolled my cell phone contact list down to the detective's number. I scribbled his name and number on a notepad. "Here, give her this, please."

I watched the deputy exit the front door and walk alongside the drive to where a cluster of sheriffs and investigators were gathered in a small clearing. He spoke with an investigator who even from the back and in the sheriff's uniform parka was clearly a woman. She waved him away, but I was pleased to see that he persisted until she took the paper. She stuffed it in a jacket pocket.

She obviously wasn't going to call anyone until after the evidence gathering was complete. I hit the send button on my phone and waited to hear Rodriquez's voice.

"Hi, it's Cissy."

"Did you tell him to call me?"

"No, well yeah. It's a she. And I had a deputy give her your number, but the investigators seem intent on gathering evidence outside before they deal with me. I think she'll wait until they're done with that, or until the storm hits, before she calls you."

"That's fine. She's right," Manny said, "I can wait."

"I guess that means you aren't coming up here?" I sighed.

"Actually, I'm on my way. But now that you tell me there's a storm expected, I'm wondering if I ought to forget it. I only have today off."

"Oh, thank God. What a relief it is to know you are on your way. We have plenty of room here . . . if you should get stuck."

I pictured the small guesthouse off the garage and made a mental note to turn on the heat in there as soon as I was released from my sofa prison.

"Aren't you driving your Escape? That will handle the snow."

"Not a big storm. Oh, what the hell! I'm almost there. Probably a half-hour away."

"Thank you so much for coming. I can't tell you what a relief it is to know you are on your way."

"Yeah."

"See you soon."

"Yeah. Don't be in the house alone." He hung up.

Being alone didn't seem likely.

The investigators were making casts of tire tracks in the drive. The fingerprint guy was using what looked like white glue to do the same on the deck railing.

At the edge of the now choppy lake, waves slapped the investigators and their equipment as they continued to mold plaster. The sky was now deep, dark charcoal gray. Winds whipped through the swaying pine trees and manzanita bushes sending sprays of needles and leaves against the deputies.

I snuggled deeper into my sofa and afghan nest.

Was I safe?

Chapter 15

"Mom, are you asleep? In the middle of all this?"

Emma's voice woke me.

"She's asleep?"

That was Skip.

"And you were panicking! Look. She's fine." Jeff's voice.

I opened my eyes to see the three of them standing over me. "I'm not asleep. How did you get in here? They won't even let me off the sofa."

"Yeah, well, we aren't supposed to leave the living room. But they couldn't very well make us stay outside in a blizzard." Emma pulled off her cap and shook it over the stone hearth.

I looked out the picture window. All I could see was swirling white.

"The lead investigator wanted us to stick around. And Emma was desperate to get in here and make sure you were okay." Skip unzipped his parka.

"Oh—and you weren't worried, too." Emma punched her brother's arm.

"So, Detective Rodriquez is on his way up," I announced.

"He's here. Manny's here," Emma informed me.

"Yeah. How do think we got in here?" Jeff leaned into the enormous river rock fireplace to shake the snow off his jacket.

"He's out there with that hot investigator," Skip said

"Oh, she's hot? Maybe he'll be glad he came up."

I would feel a lot safer if Detective Rodriquez stayed at least overnight.

Jeff dipped his head toward the window. "He's probably going to be stuck."

At least the doors were all closed now, but unfortunately my views of the investigation were gone thanks to the heavy snowfall.

"What are they doing out there?" I asked.

Skip sat on the arm of the sofa. "Hurrying like hell to pick up all of their equipment and castings and the body and get the stuff into the trucks before they lose it all in the snow."

"Manny's talking to the babe, the investigator." Emma sat on the coffee table and leaned over to pat my shoulder.

I could hear stomping boots at the entry door. Two uniformed investigators shook snow off their jackets in the hall. "Ma'am. We need to check out some things inside now."

I nodded, and soon the hordes descended on us: photographers, laser lamp handlers, and finger printers.

Oh God. Fingerprint dust everywhere. I hate that shit.

"We're going to have to do some serious cleaning up," Emma observed.

"I don't think anyone came in the house." I tried to get the attention of the two men working in the living room.

One man used a wand to scatter charcoal gray powder on surfaces that fingers would touch. Another waved a light around the room.

"How do you know the bad guys weren't in here before we arrived?" Skip asked.

"I think the killer, or killers, followed us here," I said. "Lulu started barking just after ten this morning. That's got to be when the body showed up. There had to be at least two of them to carry a frozen body."

What was the purpose of putting this body first on my car and then on my—well, my father's—spa? Was somebody trying to tell me something?

Like maybe scare me? Maybe the message was, do you want to end up like this?

But why scare me? I had no money to give them. Did I know something that threatened someone?

Oh, shit. I sat bolt upright. Was somebody going to ask something of me. Something they had to scare me into doing.

"Where's Manny? I need him, now." I looked down at my nightgown. 'Merde, I want to get dressed." I stood up. "Look, I'm getting dressed. Have someone check out my bedroom and bath—whatever you need to do—but I'm getting dressed." I announced to the room.

Not one of the investigators responded.

"Emma, can you guys get back out of here? If this is a major storm we'll need more food than what we brought up last night. You should go down to the market."

"The pantry is full, Mom. So's the freezer."

"See if you can pick up some fresh stuff, milk, eggs, bread, lettuce. We may be here for days. I'm not interested in surviving on the food in the freezer and the pantry. God knows how long some of that's been there."

"Mom?" Emma said.

"I'm in no mood for arguing. Go to the market. Jeff, take the Land Rover that's in the garage. Just take it nice and slow. That car will get there and back."

"Skip. Come with me."

I shuffled my slippers toward my bedroom, expecting one of the deputies to stop me, but no one paid me any attention.

As we walked down the hall, I quizzed my son. "Sweetheart, do you know anything at all about this woman? Did you see her when you let the dog out this morning?"

"No. And Mom, there wasn't anything on the spa when we were eating breakfast."

"Okay, please go tell whoever is in charge that I'm in here."

"I saw who's in charge. She's a little old, but she's hot." Skip grinned.

"How old?"

"At least thirty."

I had to laugh. "Yeah, she's ancient."

"Manny thinks she's hot."

"Hmm." I considered that development for a few seconds. "Anyway, sweetheart, get permission to bring in a pile of firewood and turn on the heat in the guest house. I told Manny he could stay there tonight if he gets stuck here. Also, make sure we've got a supply of candles. If you see anything we're missing, call your sister."

He nodded and hurried down the hall.

I stripped off my night clothes and hopped into the shower so fast the water hadn't had a chance to warm up. But it was worth it to get dressed properly.

Once I had on my cashmere turtleneck and sweats, I felt much better. I decided not to think about why the body kept being dumped near me until I'd organized the household in preparation for the storm. I would think about that later. Later . . . when I could discuss it with Manny. I slipped back into my sheepskin-lined slippers and headed down the hall to the livingroom.

Detective Rodriquez stood looking out the window towards the Lake. I doubted he could see much.

"Detective, I'm glad to see you. Thank you so much for coming all this way. I really appreciate it."

"Cissy, I have to be honest. I didn't come up here just out of concern for you. I've got a missing woman who just could be your dead woman."

"Really? Who?"

"I'm not going to discuss possibilities."

Jeez, such a hard nose. "Got it. Can I get you a drink?"

A very attractive brunette entered through the French

door off the deck. She took off a cap and shook snow off her long black ponytail.

"Cissy, this is Deputy Sheriff Rosalind Vasquez." Manny turned to the brunette, "Rosalind, Cissy Huntington."

"Ms. Vasquez, or should I say Deputy?" I said as I extended my hand.

"Please call me Rosalind." She firmly grasped my hand.

"And call me Cissy."

"I hope we didn't interfere with your investigation, but I really couldn't stay in those nightclothes, and I'm concerned about getting in some supplies before the storm strands us here."

"I do understand, but . . . well, let's talk." Rosalind looked around the room.

I motioned to the chairs flanking the fireplace. Rosalind and Manny each took one and I returned to my sofa.

As soon as she sat down, Rosalind continued. "You're pretty certain this body was left here between 9 and 10:30 a.m.?"

"Well, my children didn't see it, or anyone here before they left for the ski hill. And the dog went berserk at 10:30 and woke me up. I think it was a stranger or strangers coming on to the deck that set off Lulu."

"Lulu's the dog," Manny explained.

"Do you think anyone came inside?" Rosalind asked.

"I doubt it. Lulu maybe would have gotten a piece of 'em. And only two doors were unlocked. The doors off the deck were locked."

"Sorry to make such a mess checking for fingerprints."

Unfortunately, from previous experience, I knew we were in for a terrible mess—plenty of black or gray powder all over the house. But I wasn't asked for permission.

I had no more than nodded when a whole cadre of CSI entered the house and began shooting photos and laser lights in every room.

Skip came back into the main house from turning on the heat in the guesthouse. I heard him stomping snow off in the mudroom while he soothed Lulu with a soft voice.

He called out to me in the living room. "Mom, I think someone has been staying in the guest house."

"What?" I asked.

"A bed in one of the bedrooms, one of the lower bunks, is messed up and there are things—papers and wrappers in the bathroom. I personally was assigned to clean up the guesthouse the last time we were here, so I know we didn't leave it like that. Plus, I found some wild underwear behind the toilet."

Rosalind was right on it. She hurried to the mudroom. "Please show me."

Skip took one look at the deputy without her outdoor gear on and was more than willing to brave the storm. They both replaced their caps and covered their heads with their hoods as they exited the house via the mudroom.

"She's quite attractive." I looked at Manny. "Have you found out if she's single yet?"

Detective Rodriquez did his usual—no answer. Didn't even look at me. He looked at the white swirls in the window for thirty seconds and then said, "Cissy what do you think? What's the story?"

"I don't know. I know I've seen her before, but where— it's just not coming to me."

Detective Rodriquez raised one eyebrow and studied my face,

"Really, I don't."

"Have you figured out who she is yet?" Manny looked at me as if to read my mind.

"There's a good chance she was one of Mark Hamilton's clients back in the eighties. Mark's daughter, Alexa is planning to check their files on Monday. She remembers meeting the dead woman back then. And when Alexa told me that it twigged something, but I haven't quite got a hold of it yet."

"So, she's rich?"

"I told you she was. I could tell from her clothes and jewelry. Especially the jewelry. Is she the person you're looking for?"

"Maybe."

My turn to raise my eyebrow at him.

"Fingerprints should tell us. But I got this tingly feeling on the back of my neck when this big time TV producer's personal assistant called to say that the producer's wife was missing. Has been missing for days—but they just discovered that she wasn't traveling, or at another one of their houses."

"Whose wife?"

He shook his head.

"Aaron Spelling?"

He looked ever so slightly alarmed. I was close.

"Oh, but he died, didn't he? And of course, I've met Candy," I realized. "Harvey Greenwalt?"

He looked relieved, I was way off.

"Let's see, I know Jerry Bruckheimer's wife, so not her."

Even more relieved. Had to be someone older and in Spelling's class. All of a sudden, I realized who she was. Finally. I did know the dead woman. And she had to be Manny's missing woman. At least I was pretty sure.

"You're going to tell me when I get it, right?" I negotiated.

"I can't tell you anything. The press hasn't gotten the data yet. They're trying to hold off until Monday before making any announcements and my chief swore me to secrecy."

"Did you tell Rosalind?"

"I'm not telling anyone."

I gave the name a shot. "Well, I know who she is . . . it finally came to me. She's Marty Chaffin's wife. Marty Chaffin, producer of *Survival at Sea, Deal Me In*, and all those other dreadful reality shows."

A quick look at the alarm that flashed across his face, and I knew I had it right.

"What was her first name? Babe, no . . . aah yeah, Honey. Honey Chaffin. Used to be Honey Randolph. Was Honey Sumner. I bet she was Honey Sumner when Alexa's father did that house in Southampton. Yes!" I grinned.

Detective Rodriquez looked at his feet. I was correct.

"You didn't get that from me," he growled.

The fingerprint examiner had entered the room and waited to speak. "Sir, we've finished up in here. We're going to check out the guest house, but we have some concern about getting down the mountain and back to the lab before this storm strands us here."

"Very good. Seems to be some evidence in the guesthouse."

"So I hear. Two of us will stay to deal with that, but everyone else is taking off."

The storm failed to muffle the sound of a dozen SUVs leaving.

The question of identity resolved, I turned my attention to surviving the weekend with a houseful of unexpected guests. Focus on one thing at a time.

"Manny, you should get your vehicle off the shoulder of the road and into the drive," I warned him. "Otherwise you'll be buried for days. When the snow removers come by, they blow the snow into huge piles at the side of the road. But we're going to have to discuss this. You do realize that I'm possibly in danger, that this body dumping is most likely a threat?"

Manny nodded but took off for the road, and I headed for the woodpile. Skip joined me and I loaded his arms. "Let's fill the wood basket in the living room, and then make a pile in the mudroom . . . just in case we can't get out here. Or don't want to come out tonight." The logs were neatly stacked under the covered walkway that led to the guesthouse, but the way the snow was swirling around, any protection afforded by the roof was negligible.

"I'll tarp it too, Mom."

"Good plan. Did you have a chance to check the candle supply?"

"Yeah, we've got plenty, and there's kerosene in both lanterns. The flashlights all work and there are extra batteries. I brought in extra dog food from the storage shed. Next I'll start the fires in the living room and the kitchen."

"Thank you, sweetheart." I patted my son's arm.

I hung my jacket on one of the hooks in the mudroom and fixed myself a bowl of granola and yogurt in the kitchen. I was enjoying the first bite when I saw Manny shake out his jacket and hang it in the mudroom.

"Are you hungry? I could make some sandwiches."

"Not yet. I grabbed a burger on the way up here," Manny admitted.

"I'm going to make a pot of veggie stew as soon as I have my breakfast."

"Can I help?"

"You want to chop some vegetables?"

"Sure."

I pulled out a cutting board and dug potatoes, carrots, onions, and turnips out of the cold storage. While Manny washed and chopped, I found cans of beans, corn, tomatoes, and broth. I poured olive oil into the bottom of the soup pot and tossed in the chopped onions. The rich aroma of sautéing onions filled the air.

"Emma and Jeff are picking up fresh veggies, hopefully

zucchini, green peppers, celery, leeks. This will keep us going for a few days."

"Do you really think we'll be stuck here that long?" Manny asked.

"I don't like fighting blinding blizzard conditions all the way down that mountain. Driving off the edge of the winding road and down one of the steep cliffs isn't appealing. Speaking of which, I regret having sent Emma and Jeff out in this blizzard."

"The road's not bad between here and the village. It's kept plowed. The sheriffs still have to get around," Manny said.

Rosalind shook off in the mudroom and joined us in the kitchen.

"Actually, we stay at the Big Bear station rather than brave that drive down the hill in bad weather. It may be a bit crowded there tonight."

"You're welcome here," I offered. "We've got a couple of extra bedrooms."

"That's kind of you, but really not necessary. We may still make it back down the hill."

I looked at the whiteout in the window and doubted that anyone would be going far that night.

Just as I was beginning to worry about having sent Emma and Jeff out into the weather, they burst through the mudroom door, laughing and loaded with grocery bags.

"We got hot buttered rum fixings. Jeff's going to start those." Emma looked into the soup pot. "Smells good."

Manny took the fresh vegetables from Emma and began

washing and chopping. I stirred in the fresh basil and added a few spices.

"I'd like to ask each of you a few questions. After you're done there, is fine." Rosalind said.

"Skip's in the living room if you want to start with him."

Emma looked up from where she was filling the fridge with fresh veggies and dairy. "I'll be in as soon as I get this stuff put away."

I peeked around the corner to see the living room. Skip had the fire blazing in the living room. He had vacuumed up most of the black powder from every horizontal hard surface in the room: the twig end tables, the Arts and Crafts coffee table, and the rough-hewn stone mantle. I saw him switch off the vacuum when Rosalind entered the living room. While she spoke with him, he rolled up the cord. I couldn't quite make out the words.

Without questioning who wanted one, Jeff put a steaming mug of fragrant hot buttered rum in each person's hand. He handed the last mug to Rosalind.

"Detective Rodriquez has explained to us that it's merely an urban legend that law enforcement can't drink alcohol while on duty."

Manny raised an eyebrow at me and I suspected the urban legend story was not entirely accurate.

From where they sat on the hearth, Skip, Emma and Jeff spoke animatedly. Each one described what they had done that morning. The bottom line was they were each certain that the body had not been on the spa that morning when they had left for the ski hill.

Once our soup simmered on the stove, Manny and I picked up our drinks and entered the living room. We sat in the lounge chairs flanking the fireplace and sipped the comforting, hot liquid. I took a deep breath enjoying the smell of the burning oak mixed with the spices in the hot rum.

"We left here about eight thirty," Emma said.

"We had planned to leave at eight thirty. It was actually eight forty-three," Jeff said.

"Did you see anyone hanging around the property?" Rosalind asked.

"No," said Jeff, Skip, and Emma in unison.

"What about vehicles? Any vehicles nearby?"

"No," again in unison.

"Do any of you know this woman?"

"Just from the photo Mom has been showing everyone for the last few days," Emma answered.

"Mrs. Huntington." Rosalind turned to me.

"Please call me Cissy."

"Alright Cissy, what do you know about this woman?"

"Actually, I know a lot. I remembered who she is . . . was. In some circles, she's a legend."

Chapter 16

"Her name is Honey Chaffin. I don't know what her proper first name was. Maybe Honor. But I think the nickname Honey was based on the color of her hair. Before she began to cover the gray with that auburn, it was the color of golden honey."

"What do you mean by legend?" Deputy Sheriff Rosalind Vasquez studied my face.

"She grew up in Carmel near where I did. We were both students at Santa Catalina, a girl's boarding school in Monterey. I went there decades later as a day student. Honey Nickels was still a big deal. Still someone talked about with admiration."

"Why?" Rosalind asked.

"When she was in high school, she was beautiful and wild. An only child. Denied nothing by her father. She would drive down to Palm Springs in her T-Bird convertible on weekends or over Spring Break and stay with an aunt who was either deaf and blind or very permissive. Because once she arrived there, she wasn't a schoolgirl anymore. She glammed up."

"What do you mean?"

"She was rumored to have been involved with Errol Flynn, Clark Gable and Howard Hughes, among others."

"Wow. Clark Gable?" Emma's eyes widened.

"So, the rumors went." I continued, "One part of her story is definitely fact. When she was barely eighteen, she eloped with director Hayward Sumner. Are any of you old enough to remember who he was?"

"Mom, of course we know about him. He's considered to be one of the all-time great directors."

Skip shook his head in disappointment with how out of it his mother was and drank more of his hot buttered rum.

"Fine. Here's the inside story. Hayward was an escapee from old East Coast money. I think as long as they stayed in LA and hung out with the Hollywood crowd, the difference in their ages wasn't an issue. Really the only issue they had was that Honey was so incredibly beautiful the studios were constantly pushing for Hayward to cast her in a film. Hayward was dead set against his wife being a starlet. And Honey wasn't interested in acting. She was already admired for her unique California style in fashion and entertaining. In fact, within a couple years of their marriage, she appeared in high-end magazines posing in designer clothes in glamorous interiors."

"So, what happened? Why did they break up?" Emma asked.

"It must have been when Mark was doing the house in Southhampton for them, that things started to go wrong. Honey was used to a level of adoration . . . . But now they were in the East. She was an unknown Westerner. It was different then. Being from California was not seen as a good thing," I stopped speaking for a moment, remembering from my childhood visits, just how unacceptable Californians were in certain parts of the East Coast.

"Honey began spending most of her time in Europe, especially in France. I imagine the French appreciated her flair and enthusiasm for life. And that's where she got involved with the next husband—who was even wealthier than the first. Or so the story goes."

"Who is she married to now?"

I looked at Rodriquez, then back at Rosalind. "Marty Chaffin."

"Why does that sound familiar?" Rosalind asked.

"He produces reality TV shows. I've never actually known him, or Honey, other than by sight and reputation. But I have reason to believe they live in Beverly Hills."

"Why have you been looking for her?" Rosalind looked puzzled. "Showing people her photo?"

"I wasn't actually looking for her. I was trying to figure out who she was." I explained in detail what happened at the PDC and the lengths we had gone to to find out her identity since. My story was interrupted by the entrance of the two CSI's who had been working in the guesthouse.

"We didn't actually finish up in there, . . . uhm . . . we're thinking that we aren't going to make it even back to the local station the way the snow's piling up . . . unless we leave soon," The investigator explained to Rosalind.

"Okay. When will you finish up?" She looked a bit

uncomfortable to be caught sitting in front of a roaring fire, drinking hot buttered rum and chatting.

"Tomorrow . . . or whenever the storm breaks."

Rosalind looked at me. "I guess you'll have to do without the guest house until then."

I looked at Manny. "We still have two empty bedrooms in the main house. Do you mind staying in here?"

"No. I don't mind, but I'm hoping to get back in time for work tomorrow."

Everyone in the room shook their heads.

"That's not happening," Skip said.

"So Ma'am, do you want to ride down to the station with us?" the younger investigator asked Rosalind.

"I have a vehicle here. And more questions. I'll just have to take it easy . . . and find my way down later."

Again, I offered the remaining bedroom, but she didn't respond.

Instead she said, "Why do you think Mrs. Chaffin was on first your car and then your spa?"

I looked around the room at my children and Manny. "I had an idea that . . . well, I guess, just an idea. I think that someone is trying to scare me."

"Somebody killed this woman just to scare you?" Rosalind was more than a little doubtful.

"No, I suspect they were going to kill her anyway, but then thought they could use the body to frighten me."

"Why?" Rosalind frowned.

"I don't know. It's too creepy to think about." I rubbed my forehead in an effort to slow my heartbeat. "Maybe they want something from me. Maybe they want me to do something. Maybe . . . maybe . . . I don't know. I felt as though she stared at me because she wanted to tell me something."

"Do you have anything else in common with her besides having gone to the same school some thirty years apart?"

"It's conceivable that we would have some of the same relatives. My great grandmother married a Nickels. But then I'm related to a lot of people in California . . . I can't imagine what else."

"How do you know so much about her?"

"I told you—she was a legend at our school, at Catalina. All the girls loved to gossip about her and especially her escapades." I sighed thinking about those innocent days when we thought of someone who had been "around" as sophisticated. "She was the reason we had a debutante dance. She insisted that her father start the tradition. And the practice continued until it became unfashionable in the 1970's. She didn't want to be hampered by her so-called 'humble beginnings', and that sort of thing was important in her day."

"Private girl's school doesn't sound very humble."

"It's all relative. And I did say 'so called'. We were just low key. And compared to the noble society that she moved in later in life, it was ever so humble."

"Do you have friends in common?"

"Certainly not close friends." I thought for a minute. "If we do, I'm not aware of it. We were different generations. Her later husbands were acquaintances of my father's. Her friends were friends of my mother's."

"Why would she have something to tell you?"

I shook my head to indicate my lack of real knowledge on the subject. Then I voiced my guesses. "Possibly something to do with my husband. Possibly something to do with her husband . . . or husbands."

I looked at Detective Rodriquez who I was finally starting to think of as Manny, and directed my next question to him. "Maybe you could ask her husband if he knows mine?"

"Let's verify who she is first," Manny said.

"Oh shit, when are you going to learn to trust me?"

"I'm not going to call her husband and tell him his missing wife is dead until we've checked the fingerprints. She had no I.D. on her."

Rosalind was on her cell with the lab in San Bernadino. "Check to see if you get a match with Mrs. Marty Chaffin, Honey Chaffin."

"Honor Chaffin," Manny supplied.

Rosalind repeated the information into the phone and shut the lid.

"Okay, so we think Mrs. Chaffin went to your school, but the first time you saw her was at the panel discussion in the PDC."

"No, I've seen her over the years. But she must've had some work done recently . . . on her face. Mostly I've seen her in photos but we've attended the same fundraiser a few times. A museum opening here and there. I think she and her then husband were on the guest list when Jamie and I . .

. for our wedding."

"How big was your wedding?" Rosalind's eyes widened as she stared at me. "You don't know who was on the guest list?"

"I was a little distracted at the time."

"So how big?" Rosalind persisted.

"Five or six hundred actually showed up. I couldn't say if she was among them. My parents handled the guest list and the receiving line was a blur."

Jeff decided it was time for refills and started to collect cups.

"No matter what Detective Rodriquez says, I can't have any more of that stuff. Do you have some tea?" Rosalind asked.

"Sure." Emma stood up to assist Jeff with drinks.

"Emma, please stir the soup while you are in the kitchen," I requested.

A gust of wind howled. The lights flickered. Every head in the room turned to look out the windows at swirling bits of white against a deep gray background. Even though it was only mid afternoon, the room was dark in the brief moment without lights.

"I think you should both plan to stay right here until this storm passes over. We'll let that soup simmer for a bit more and then have what will probably be a candlelit dinner."

"Thank you. I'll definitely stick around for that, but I really do need to get back to the lab, or at least to the station tonight," Rosalind said.

Manny looked at Rosalind. "Why?" he asked.

"Well, we are in the midst of an investigation here," she answered.

"In case you hadn't noticed, we are in the midst of a major storm here," Manny said. He didn't seem anxious for her to leave.

The lights flickered again and then stayed off. Skip lit the candles he had previously arranged on the rough-hewn mantle, the Stickley side table and the wood slab coffee table. I lit the candles on the dining table and then carried a candle into the kitchen. "Glad we have a gas stove here, aren't you?" I said to Jeff and Emma.

I took the placemats and napkins from the sideboard and set the table while Rosalind and Manny conversed quietly in the living room. I could make out most of what they were saying to each other. Manny was assuring her that we, especially me, were okay. "It's a complete waste of time to consider any of them suspects. And they'll aid your investigation."

Rosalind spoke softly, and I couldn't quite make out what she said. But then I heard Manny say, "I can see you're not buying my advice here."

Emma brought her a cup of tea. I wondered if Rosalind was worried we would poison her. But she sipped the tea without hesitation.

Emma joined me in the dining area and together we put the bread, the butter, and the soup tureen on the planks of the refectory table. Jeff brought in wine glasses and a bottle of Pinot Noir.

The candles and the blazing fire reflected in the window

glass. Occasionally a squall of wind disturbed the crackling fire and the blanketing storm.

I heard one short ring of a cell that Rosalind quickly answered. She spoke only "Yes, yes, Good, and thank you," before hanging up.

Rosalind murmured something to Manny. He then made a quick call, brusquely identified himself presumably to his office, and then mumbled a very brief statement before closing the phone.

I called to Rosalind and Manny to join us at the table and seated them in the plush green velvet cushioned chairs. We each took our seat and busied ourselves with polite comments—please and thank you—as the soup and bread rolls passed from hand to hand. The tearing of the crisp crusted sourdough rolls, the clink of soup spoons against the bowls, and the ring of the wine bottle against the rim of glasses provided the only sounds other than the moans of appreciation for my culinary skills. The howling storm supplied the background dinner music.

Carrying a stack of dishes to the kitchen, Emma excused herself to make a pot of coffee on the stove. Advising our guests to keep their seats, Skip and Jeff also carried dishes to the kitchen. Jeff returned with a bottle of cognac and six snifters. Skip brought out coffee condiments and mugs. Emma returned with a carafe of filtered coffee and everyone settled back into his or her seat.

Over the bowl of my brandy snifter, I looked around the table and enjoyed the cozy scene. I especially liked that I had both of the investigators trapped and indebted to me. I led with a deceptively innocent question.

"Have you heard back from the lab?"

"Yes," Rosalind replied.

I stared into her deep brown eyes. She returned my gaze.

"You had it right. She was Honey Chaffin. Honor Clarissa Nickels Sumner Randolph Visconti Chaffin."

Emma and Skip turned to me as they repeated, "Clarissa?"

Our two investigator guests picked up on the reaction to Clarissa. Rosalind and Manny turned to me as well.

"Cissy is short for Clarissa," I explained. "Clarissa is a family name."

Chapter 17

"Not exactly a common name," Manny said. "Is it?"

"It was my grandmother Nichol's first name . . . and her grandmother's too." I gave it a moment's thought. "Perhaps Honey and I were related."

"Mom, you might be on to something. That name is all over our family tree. You could share some of the family lore?" Emma asked. "I love those stories."

"Oh, shit, yes. Good stories. Swashbuckling pirates, stagecoach bandits, saloon owning gamblers, swordsman Californios—the Wild West," Skip added.

"I'm sure our family history is of no interest to our guests," I said.

"Somehow I doubt that." Manny grinned at me. "I suspect we should be interested."

"What else are we going to do?" Jeff said. "We aren't going anywhere anytime soon." He glanced at his watch. "And it's still early."

I looked at Rosalind. She nodded in encouragement.

"Before I entertain you, did you learn anything else from

the lab?"

Rosalind returned my gaze and shrugged her shoulders. "It's pretty early. I can't imagine we'll know much more for at least a day or two. There's really no urgent reason to push our case to the head of the line."

"Do you at least know how she died?" I pressed Rosalind.

"That's easy to guess," Manny interjected.

"Really?" I asked.

"I would say she was poisoned," Manny bit his lip as though he regretted having spoken.

"Oh."

"Did you smell anything odd that first day, the first time you found her?" Rosalind asked me.

"Like the smell of almonds?" I guessed she was thinking cyanide poisoning.

"Yeah," Rosalind said.

"No, but the exhaust fumes in the garage could have masked any other odor."

"Maybe." Manny shrugged his shoulders. "Was her face flushed? A bright cherry pink?"

"No. She was quite pale with almost a blue gray tinge to her skin."

"Hmm." Rosalind exchanged looks with Manny.

"This is one for the toxicologists," Manny said.

"Yeah," Rosalind agreed.

"You do know that she was quite a bit older than she looked?" I asked. "She was in my grandmother's generation. She had to be in her nineties."

"If she died of natural causes, why the hell was she moved around so much?" Jeff asked the detectives.

Rosalind and Manny both shrugged. Manny attempted to change the subject.

"So, what is the story with your relatives?" he asked.

"Okay, okay. But first, Rosalind, is there anything else that you can tell us?"

"All we have is the ID. Cause and time of death have yet to be determined. But I agree with Manny on poison and you already have the time of death pinpointed. We've gathered lots of evidence today, but no one has put it all together to see what it says. I'll have to get started on that as soon as I can get back down to the lab."

A quick glance out the window showed that trip wasn't going to occur anytime soon. Rosalind continued, "But once we've established your familial relationship with the deceased, I'll be obliged to keep you informed as the investigation proceeds. Please do tell us more about that relationship."

"My great grandmother married into the Nickels family. Nickels and Cowles are the married names of the two daughters of Henry Minner who once owned fourteen and a half million acres at the center of California, including the entire San Joaquin Valley. Of course, when he owned most of the Central Valley, it wasn't the rich agriculture center of today."

"Yeah, but it certainly wasn't the swampland he claimed it was in the ruse that allowed him to lay claim to most of the acreage," Skip explained to our guests.

"Henry Minner bragged that he could ride from the Mexican to the Oregon border without leaving his own land," Emma added. "Mom, explain about the Nickels and Nichols thing."

"Let's move over to the fire. Bring that bottle of cognac please, Jeff."

I carried my brandy to one of the soft leather armchairs, tucked my feet under my legs, and waited for the rest of the group to find their seats and snuggle under throws.

Emma and Jeff cuddled together on a suede sofa. Manny took the dark green leather armchair across the hearth from mine. Rosalind and Skip each took an end of the other suede sofa.

While we settled in, Skip and Emma recited their favorite nursery rhyme:

> *"The miners came in forty-nine*
> *The whores in fifty-one*
> *And when they got together*
> *They produced the native son,"*

A little ditty our family had long taught generations of our children to keep them centered and kill any high falutin' snobbery they could possibly have based on being one of the older families in California.

"I've obviously told these stories based on family lore a few times. Most of the stories come from journals written by the women in my family—including one written by a young girl who traveled to California in 1848. Clarissa

Barrington Wells was the first English speaking woman in my family to arrive in California," I explained. "My great grandmother, Clarissa's great granddaughter Emma Rose, married the son of Amanda Minner Nickels."

"I'm lost already. Who was Amanda?" Jeff was eager to learn about the family he was marrying into.

"Amanda was one of Henry Minner's two daughters and only heirs." I attempted to continue. "Six years of marriage and three children later—"

"Henry Minner owned the valley," Emma interjected. "The San Joaquin Valley and more. But he also had considerable wealth in other assets."

"Yes, that was apparently true." I smiled my thanks to Emma for filling in the facts for me. "Back to Emma Rose. They had been married for six years when Henry 'Hank' Nickels disappeared. Emma Rose Nickels was left with three children under the age of four and little money. Henry—they called him Hank so as not to confuse him with his grandfather— per family lore was actually some kind of a secret agent."

"A secret agent! For real?" Jeff exclaimed. "No shit?"

I nodded. "His work would often send him into dangerous situations and it was assumed that he had been killed. Emma Rose's parents had not been happy with her choice of husbands. It seems in retribution, Amanda had decided not to be pleased by their union either."

"Why was that?" Skip asked. "I've never understood all of that part."

"Families can be weird, especially when two are joining.

For one thing, Emma Rose was young, seventeen. Also, her family was suspicious of Hank. It seemed like there was something about him that he wasn't being straightforward about—"

"Like that he was a secret agent? And for the Germans no less." Emma smiled.

"He was a double agent. But that's another story." I paused to remember where I was in my story. "Amanda thought that Emma Rose and Clarissa's family was being snobbish. Emma Rose's great, great grandfather and her great uncle were titled Englishmen, the Lords Barrington. Amanda's father, Henry Minner was the son of a German butcher and had himself worked as a butcher while acquiring all his land."

I took a sip from my snifter. "Emma Rose's stubborn pride kept her from asking either family for assistance."

"Now there's a dominant family trait." Manny laughed. "The stubborn, I mean."

I ignored his comment. "When Emma Rose's funds ran short she began selling off assets. Amanda got wind of Emma Rose trying to sell a property that had been Hank's and a piece of the Minner estate, and she was furious."

"Mom, I know you favor Emma Rose's side of this story, but truly Aunt Amanda had her own problems." Emma smiled at me. "You kinda gave away who you favored by the name you gave me."

"Yes." I returned her smile. "And it is true that Amanda had her own problems. Amanda's father, Henry Minner died in 1916. It took Amanda eleven years to get anything from the estate. And then due to a Nickels and Cowles family feud, much of Henry Minner's land was tied up in court battles until 1965. For nearly fifty years Amanda was distracted by her own legal battles and resulting financial ups and downs. She failed to notice that Emma and her grandchildren were struggling to merely survive. A couple years went by without Amanda offering any aid. By the time Amanda realized how seriously Emma Rose was in financial trouble, Emma Rose was so embittered she refused any help from Amanda and even went so far as to change the spelling of Nickels N-I-C-K-E-L-S to N-I-C-H-O-L-S."

An exceptionally loud wail of wind interrupted my story. Each person turned to look outside at the swirling snow blowing against the windows. Skip stood to throw a couple more logs on the fire. Emma and I closed the shutters on all of the windows except the small one that faced the drive. Emma helped me to light the old gas torch on the front porch that would allow us to monitor the storm without leaving our comfy seats. Jeff brought a fresh pot of coffee and a new pot of mint tea.

Rosalind and Manny both attempted unsuccessfully to check in with their departments. "I can't get through to the lab, but I'll get the Big Bear Station," Rosalind said.

"Hello, hello. This is Deputy Rosalind Vasquez . . . . Yes, but I can't get through to my office." She raised her eyebrows and grimaced at Manny. "I see. Yes, I'll stay put. No, I'm not in any danger." Rosalind closed the phone and looked around the group gathered in front of the fire.

"Power is out all around the Lake and throughout much of the basin. There are a lot of people requiring rescue, but the snowfall is exceptionally heavy and visibility is zero. They were in contact with my office an hour or so ago and were told that everyone there headed home for the rest of the weekend." Rosalind forced a sad little smile. "I hope you won't mind me taking you up on your offer of a room? It looks like the storm will last well into the night and no one will be moving about until the snow plows clear the way at dawn . . . . If the storm lets up by then."

"You know we're happy to have you. The beds may be a bit cold. We should make sure the doors are open to all the bedrooms so that the heat from the fire takes off some of the chill. Unfortunately, we discovered some years back—and have never done anything about it—that the gas heaters don't work when the power is out because the pilots are electric."

Emma and Skip went to check on the bedroom doors and opened any that were closed. I brought Lulu in from the mudroom and she settled in front of the fire.

When everyone had returned to the living room we sat in our accustomed seats. "Cissy, you have quite an amazing family." Rosalind poured herself a fresh cup of mint tea.

"I suspect all family histories are interesting. My point being that the reason I never thought about Honey being a relative is because I think of my grandparents as being Nichols with a CHO rather than Nickels with a CKE. And my family has never interacted with the CKE Nickels family—or acknowledged any relationship."

"Mom, we did see Tommy and Robby at the Lake. Skip and I went out on their boat and watched them water ski," Emma said.

"I remember I worried the whole time you were with them, not because of the family relationship though. They're from the Cowles branch. Those two have always been in trouble."

I paused to listen to the storm rage outside our cozy setting. "My God it's wild out—"

Suddenly a loud crack split the air. The one window that had remained unshuttered shattered.

"Get down," Manny yelled.

"Hit the floor," Rosalind screamed.

Wind shrieked through the broken window.

I fell on the floor next to the hearth and pulled Lulu toward me.

Emma, Jeff on top of her, was wedged next to the bottom of their sofa.

Skip was on his knees next to the sofa he had been sitting on. Rosalind motioned to Skip to stay down from where she stood on one side of the window with a gun in her hand.

She snuck a look out the bottom corner. Manny was on the opposite side of the window. He too had drawn a gun from somewhere. He carefully turned his head around the window frame and studied the snowy winter scene out the window.

"A branch must have broken off a tree and blown into the window." I started to get off the floor.

"Stay down! That was no branch." Manny pointed to a hole in the wall, just above the candle on the side table. A hole the size of a very large bullet.

A second and third shot hit the wall next to the first hole.

Chapter 18

"Is there a room without windows?" Rosalind shouted over the storm as she swung her extended arms, a large gun in hand, around the edges of the shattered window.

"Close the shutters over that opening." It took me a full minute to coordinate my mouth with my voice.

The shrieks of the wind were instantly muffled as Manny closed the shutter on his side of the window and Rosalind did the same.

"I want to get you out of this room," Manny said.

"The pantry off the mudroom," I blurted as I thought, this must be a dream—a nightmare.

"Okay, on the floor. Stay as low as you possibly can. Wiggle your way out of this room. Stay down until we get to the pantry," Manny instructed as he too hit the floor.

"Watch the glass," I warned. "Bring flashlights if you can reach them."

Skip tossed me one of the flashlights he had placed on the side table earlier. I shone the light on the floor and he did the same.

"Turn off the damn lights," Manny hissed.

Jeff and Emma led the way, with Skip right behind them. I followed Skip; Manny and Rosalind were next. We made our way through the dining area, the kitchen, the mudroom and into the pantry.

In the windowless room, we sat on the floor with our backs against shelves full of canned goods. It was a tight squeeze for the six of us. Lulu whimpered outside the door. I opened the door and let her land on my lap. As she leapt onto me, I finally remembered to breathe.

"What the hell?" Jeff was the first to speak. He shone a flashlight on Emma's face.

"What was that?" Emma's eyes were bright and as big as blue cornflowers.

"Wait. Hold it." Manny held up his hand, palm toward Jeff and Emma. "Rosalind, can you call for back up?"

"The storm. I don't know if . . ."

"Someone is moving around out there."

Rosalind already had her phone out, using the radio option. "Station two, come in." She called several times but all she was getting was static. She switched to phone mode. The phone worked better.

"This is Deputy Rosalind Vasquez. Immediate assistance needed at 1232 Greenbriar Road, off the old highway at the lake's edge halfway to Fawnskin. Shots fired." Rosalind listened.

"I don't hear anything out there," I whispered to Manny.

Manny checked his gun, and then looked each of us in the eye as he spoke. "I need you all to stay on the floor, and don't leave this room, no matter what you hear out there. I'm going out to take a look around. I need to know that I can count on you to stay put in here. I don't want to accidentally shoot one of you."

"What about the sheriffs who are coming?" I asked.

"Yeah, they might shoot you!" Emma's whisper rose to a squeal.

Rosalind shook her head. "They don't think they can get through right away. They'll have to bring a plow. All the Sno-cats are scattered around the Lake on various emergencies. The snowmobiles are also—"

A loud roar sounding like a motorcycle starting interrupted Rosalind's sentence.

"Speaking of snowmobiles." Manny burst out of the pantry.

Rosalind, gun in hand, was close behind him. "I'll go right," she yelled as she slammed the pantry door behind her.

We heard the backdoor slam.

Emma, Jeff, Skip, and I sat in stunned silence. For five minutes we heard only the moans of the wind.

Finally, Emma broke the silence, "It's hard to believe this is really happening. Who the hell is shooting at us?"

"Quiet, I want to hear what's going on out there," I hushed.

"What for? We can't go out, no matter what we hear?" Emma responded with attitude.

"Was that a shot?" Jeff jumped halfway up and then slid back down to the floor.

"That was definitely a snow loaded branch cracking."

I'd heard that sound so many times in other storms I was sure that was what it was. I couldn't stand the thought that it was a shot. Who would be shooting? At whom?

Another five minutes went by. Then another ten.

"I can't take this." Emma started to stand up from where she sat on a case of Pellegrino.

"Well, you'll have to." Jeff pulled Emma back down to the floor. "SIT there and DO NOT move again!"

Emma looked as startled as I was to hear Jeff speak to her in such a tone. Not even a hint of a sweet nickname. I was relieved that he got her to sit back down.

Lulu choose that moment to bark. "No, Lulu. Hush."

I could make out the sound of a male voice, but I couldn't tell who it was. Then a female voice. It had to be Manny and Rosalind.

Right outside the pantry, we heard, "I saw tracks from one snowmobile parallel to the front drive." Clearly Manny's voice.

"Me too," Rosalind responded.

"Did you see any others?"

"No."

"I think whoever it was is gone."

"So do I."

We four erupted from the pantry.

"Hey, I didn't tell you to come out of there," Manny attempted to complain as Emma and I both enveloped him in a huge hug.

"But you said he's gone." Emma smiled and squeezed.

"Skip. Is there anything we can put over that window?" Manny asked.

"Snow boards? Wait. There's a big old toboggan in the shed. Just might cover the hole."

Jeff and Emma went to the garage to get a hammer and nails and to see what was there that could cover the hole. Rosalind went with them. Manny and Skip went to the shed for the toboggan. Lulu guarded me in the pantry where Manny had shoved me back inside. "You are probably who he was shooting at. Stay in there. Rosalind will be right back as soon as she checks out the garage."

An eternity later—factually probably minutes later—I heard Rosalind, Emma and Jeff in the mudroom. I opened the door and stepped into the circle.

"Mrs. Huntington," Rosalind started, but seeing my look, she changed her approach. "Cissy, please stay in there until we've secured the area."

"What about the rest of you?" I glowered at her. "You aren't safe. No one could possibly see well enough in this storm to see who they were aiming at."

"Emma, Cupcake, go back in there with your mother." Jeff ordered as he shoved us back into the pantry and slammed the door.

"Shit, this is exciting!" Emma's eyes shone. She hugged me, hiding the grin she couldn't wipe off her face.

When I was Emma's age, mortality meant little to me also. It was much later in life that I understood what frail things bodies are.

I returned her hug, wrapping my arms around her

slender young body. Brushing her blonde hair back from her face, I held her away from me and looked into her eyes. "Emma, I'm glad you find this to be exciting, but I need you to recognize that there is real danger here. Be aware of what is going on around you. I love you so very much."

"I love you too, Mom." Emma pulled me close again. "And I'd say you are the one who needs to take care. What is this all about?"

I slid to the floor, crossed my arms around my chest, and leaned against the shelves of canned goods. "At first I thought someone was trying to scare me. Finding Honey's body—not just once, but twice—definitely shook me. The last time, this morning, damn. Too gruesome." I tried not to think about how horrible it was. "The only explanation I came up with was someone trying to scare me, but now, well, do you think the person who shot out the window was trying to actually hit someone?"

Emma joined me on the floor. "I don't see how he could've expected to actually hit someone. After all, it was dark inside. Just a few candles and the fire. Even with the torch lit on the front porch. What could he see through the storm?"

"Maybe he was still trying to scare me. If that's the case, he must have wanted to scare me awfully badly—to come out in this storm."

We were quiet while we considered my last statement. I put an arm over Emma's shoulders and we leaned together. My heart still raced. I hoped Emma didn't notice my hands trembling.

135

If someone was trying to scare me, he was doing a damn good job—especially when my children were endangered.

Skip opened the pantry door. "Hole's covered. It's not exactly leak proof, but it's not wide open anymore. We also closed all of the curtains and shutters throughout the house. Manny and Rosalind even closed all of the storm shutters on the outside." Skip's voice shook. "So, you can come out now."

Emma jumped to her feet and pulled me up. We stopped in the kitchen for calming mint tea. I debated lacing mine with a shot or two of the cognac, but decided to keep a clear head for the time being.

We resumed our accustomed places in the living room. Skip had heaped more logs on the fire. It would take awhile for the blaze to take the chill off of the room.

Manny started the conversation. "Cissy, what is this all about?"

I looked into his eyes lit by the fire. "I really don't know."

Manny shook his head and studied his hands in his lap. "We're going to have to figure it out. What's the story with your husband? Could this possibly have something to do with him?"

"I suppose it's possible, but I really don't know what."

"Where is he?"

"Good question." I stared at the fire. "The detective I hired said he was in Tucson last week. But he left there in a private jet. Destination unknown."

"You have no idea what he's up to?" Manny leaned

forward in his chair and studied my face.

"None. I haven't spoken to him or heard from him in seven months." I held my shaking hands up to the warmth of the fire. "I just can't imagine that this has anything to do with him. I know that Jamie absolutely wouldn't harm me, or our children."

"Okay. Let's go back to the family connection. You said Henry Minner once owned the entire San Joaquin Valley. Are you heir to some of that money?" Manny's gaze never left my face.

"No. By the time the estate was finally settled in 1965, my part of the family had long since changed the spelling of their name. The animosity that started with Amanda and Emma Rose caused a rift that never mended. My part of the family took pride in the fact that they had turned their backs on the entire estate—thus establishing the family motto of 'living the good life' being more important than accumulating tons of money."

"Is there some other connection between you and this woman?" Manny leaned a little closer to me.

"Maybe someone has decided to murder all the attendees of Santa Catalina School for Girls? Or maybe just those with the name Clarissa?" I tried to joke. "Truly, I don't know."

Manny didn't crack a smile. "Let's go back to that day at the Pacific Design Center, the day you found Mrs. Chaffin's body the first time. Did you see anyone else— other than you two—who went to Catalina?"

I thought about it for a minute. "No."

"Anyone who had any connection to the school?" Manny asked.

I shook my head. "Not that I know."

"Anyone who had some involvement with your family?"

Again, I gave the question a moment's thought. "No."

I made a mental note to check the photos of the audience I'd gotten.

"Are you in *any* situation that would cause someone to want to kill you?"

I shrugged. "Not that I know of."

"You haven't received any threats?" Manny turned the statement into a question.

I shook my head.

"Have you pissed off any clients lately?"

"No."

"Dumped any nutcase clients?"

"No. Well, not recently anyway. There was . . ." Could I, should I mention this? "There was a project I resigned from doing. But no, I've since become good friends with his . . . family." Not to mention the intimidating NDA I signed with that famous actor.

"Is there anything with any of your clients that could possibly, by any stretch of the imagination, give someone a reason to shoot at you?"

I flashed on the ruse I had engineered with Sally's ex-husband Ted and his girlfriend Bunny, but decided not to mention it. That silly con couldn't possibly be related. "I really don't know of anything."

Manny turned his attention to Jeff, Emma and Skip. "Do

you guys know anything at all that would give us some clue as to what this is all about?"

"I might," Emma said.

Chapter 19

Even in the candlelight, Emma paled visibly. "We got a strange phone call recently. I didn't pay much attention to it at the time. But now I'm thinking—"

"When did you get this call?" Manny asked.

"It was the morning that Mom found Mrs. Chaffin's body on her car."

The sight of my stricken daughter startled me out of the shocked state I had settled into for the last hour. The emotional trauma of finding the body not once but twice, then, to have that event topped by the gunshot-shattered window had frozen me with fear.

My children were upset by my shock. Skip was watching me. Even Jeff had his eyes on me. I had to pull myself together.

"Emma, tell me what happened." I moved over to where she sat on the sofa her head buried in her hands, and gently placed my arm around her shoulders.

"I thought it was a prank. At the time I didn't know you'd hired a detective, and then when you told us that . . . . With all that's happened—I forgot about that call. I'd already decided it was a wrong number."

"Sweetheart, what was it?" I held her more tightly to protect her from the fear that had her shaking."

"A voice, it sounded like a man's said, 'Call off the private dick. We've got what you're looking for. Do as you're asked, or your husband will end up iced."

"Why would someone say that to you?" Rosalind frowned.

"Mom and I sound a lot alike on the phone. He probably thought he was talking to mom."

"Cissy, you know what this means, don't you?" Manny smiled gently. "It's your husband this is about. Tell us everything," he coaxed. He pulled a notebook out of his pocket and held a pencil at the ready. "We need the details."

I explained what Pelancono had told me, including the private jet and the woman traveling companion. "I just can't imagine that Jamie would do anything that would endanger his children."

"Dad wouldn't do anything to put any of us in danger," Skip said.

"Maybe he's involved in something illegal," Manny said.

"No!" Skip jumped out of his seat.

"No way!" Emma shouted.

"Absolutely not," I said but immediately thought about all the assets frozen and seized. "Someone thought he was involved in something illegal, but it would be so unlike him."

"Okay, okay." Manny thought for a moment. "Is it possible that he distanced himself from you because he was being threatened?" Manny walked over to a French door, lifted an edge of a curtain, and peeked out the window.

"I have considered that possibility. But why not explain that to us?" I fought back the tears that threatened. "Why not even a phone call?" I hated the whining note in my voice.

"Perhaps he fears that his movements, his communication—everything he's doing is being monitored." Manny sat back into the armchair opposite me. "And maybe it is. That woman could be his kidnapper." He stared at me.

I couldn't return his gaze. I looked at the floor. A knock at the door startled me before I could think about Manny's suggested explanation for Jamie's strange behavior.

"Damn."

"Chill, it's the two sheriff deputies. I just heard a plow outside. They circled the house," Manny explained.

Rosalind opened the door, hurried the two men in, and closed the door against the storm.

"Well?" she greeted the deputies.

"Ma'am, we didn't see anything," said the older, heavier man.

"No tracks, no nothing," said the tall thin deputy.

"Of course, you didn't see any tracks. The snow must be falling a few inches every hour. Not to mention what the wind is doing. Do you have any idea how long it's been since we called for back up?" Rosalind scowled at the deputy.

"I'm sorry ma'am. We're spread pretty thin what with some of the men couldn't get back up the hill."

"And some can't get into the station. We were caught off guard. The weather forecasts completely underestimated the extent of this storm."

Rosalind exhibited no sign of sympathy. "What kind of vehicle did you bring?"

"The plow. We parked it down at the main road."

She looked at the older deputy. "You go to the top of the house. Up to the cupola. Keep your eyes open for any movement out there. You see anything—anything at all—you radio me immediately."

She poked her finger into the chest of the second deputy. "You are going to sit in that plow and watch for anyone, any pedestrian, any vehicle—including a snowmobile—that comes anywhere near this place. You got it?"

The two men studied the stone floor of the entry hall while she spoke. Without raising their eyes, they nodded and one hurried up the staircase, the other out the door.

Rosalind returned to the gathering in front of the fire. "Cissy, have you ever been threatened before?"

"No. At least not by anyone who isn't in jail now."

"Do you know of anything that might indicate that your husband was threatened?"

"I don't think so. Nothing comes to mind, and I have thought about that possibility."

"Did your husband make any large withdrawals from accounts prior to his disappearance?"

"Yes, maybe. I'm not sure. I'd have to check bank records to give you any details. I couldn't handle looking at most of that stuff last summer. I left it to the accountants. And the lawyers. I'll do that as soon as we can leave here. I think the authorities took all of the cash."

I was still convinced that this matter, Honey's death and the gunshot that shattered the window, had nothing to do with Jamie. But if the police investigated Jamie and his disappearance, maybe they would come up with something more than Pelancono had. Extortion, or blackmail, might offer a possible explanation.

Whoever had shot out the window probably did not know that two law enforcement detectives were inside. But shooting at cops was bound to get you serious attention.

Manny and Rosalind continued to quiz us—especially Emma and me—for what seemed like hours, but nothing new came to light.

The numbness of shock had worn off. Exhaustion took its place. My eyes felt grainy under heavy lids. I lacked the energy to hold up my head.

"I'm going to fall asleep right here." I yawned; "Before that happens, please let me show you to your rooms."

I escorted my guests to their bedrooms, bid them goodnight, and passed out in my unmade bed. I was dead to the world for the next eight hours.

Chapter 20

In daylight the next morning, the world outside my window was white. And still. And quiet. The blanket of snow muffled every sound including the occasional crack of snow-laden pine branches. The snowstorm had left behind drifts of snow that the early morning freeze had coated with ice crystals. The sun hidden behind pale gray clouds had just enough strength to sparkle off the ice and make the light dance through the vents of the storm shutters.

The remembered events of the previous day had to have been a bad dream.

"Anyone want coffee? I've got a fresh pot in the kitchen." It was Manny's voice down the hall.

The aroma of coffee enticed me out of my warm bed. I splashed water on my face, washed the sleep from my swollen eyes, and slipped into my quilted robe and slippers.

Manny greeted me with a cup of coffee already sweetened and creamed.

"Did you sleep okay?" He was unshaven and dressed in yesterday's clothes.

"Like a log. How'd you do?" I sipped the strong brew.

"Fine."

"Did I sleep through any excitement?"

"Very little. Rosalind caught a snowplow ride back to the Big Bear Station. She called to say she would be in touch after the lab opens tomorrow. She asked me to thank you for your hospitality." Manny's warm brown eyes narrowed as he sipped the steaming liquid. "The two deputies that arrived last night have been relieved by fresh guards. There will be two men here as long as you are."

"Thank you."

Manny nodded. "Thank Rosalind."

"What would you like for breakfast?" I remembered my hostess duties. "Eggs? Toast? Waffles?"

"I made some toast." Manny pointed to the plate with a crumb or two left on it. "I need to get back. Rosalind had the plows work on your road first thing this morning, and I need to call on Mr. Chaffin in person."

I didn't envy that horrible part of Manny's job. "Will you please let me know what you learn?"

"I'll tell you what I can. Especially anything that might help you think of a clue as to what this is all about. What are your plans?"

"I think we'll rest here today and drive down tomorrow. I'm going to make a list of everyone I know who might have been in touch with Honey recently. And then I'm going to contact them."

I had to find out why Honey's body had followed me and brought violence into our lives.

146

"Good. I'll arrange with the LAPD for some protection at your Los Feliz house.

"Thank You."

"But I'm thinking the kind of security your father has might be more effective. It's your stepmother's house that has the gates and security guards, right?"

I nodded.

"Consider spending some time with your father—until we find out who is threatening you."

"Skip returns to school Tuesday. Emma and I will take him up to Berkeley." I pondered schedules for a moment. "We could spend a few days in the City with Dad. I have some people near there to talk to. Emma can work from Dad's." I heard soft footsteps behind me and turned around to see Emma enter the kitchen. "Speak of the devil."

"Oh, the coffee smells heavenly." Emma took a mug off the shelf and filled it. "I'm staying with Grandpa?"

"That's the plan. We are."

"I'm not in danger. It's Mom who's been threatened." Emma directed her remarks to Manny.

"We don't know yet who's in danger." Manny handed Emma the cream.

Jeff spoke as he walked down the hall. "Emma! Sweet cakes. Let's don't take chances."

Emma sighed.

"Manny, thank you for coming up yesterday. I'm grateful that you were here—even if it wasn't just for our sake." I held out my arms.

"I'm glad I was here too." Manny gave me a very quick

hug. "Stay in touch. I expect a phone call when you leave here tomorrow." Manny looked pointedly at Jeff.

Jeff nodded. "Is it safe to open some of the storm shutters?"

"During the day should be okay," Manny answered.

Emma and Jeff said goodbye to Manny.

"Hold on dude. I'll help you with your car." Skip walked down the hall and through the kitchen to the mudroom and pulled on boots and outerwear. He took a window scraper off the shelf. "Let's go."

I excused myself. "Emma, Jeff, will you please fix some breakfast? I've got some phone calls to make. Emails to send. Lists to write." I shuffled my slipper-clad feet back to my room.

I sat at my desk in front of the window and lost myself in the snow-covered view. Could danger really lurk in the undisturbed branches in the peaceful white scene? Despite the gunshot that had shattered our window in the middle of a blizzard, despite the two sheriffs guarding our house, my habit of denial came easy in that setting. But I refused to have my children endangered.

I opened my laptop and wrote my list of names:

Nancy Beck

Lily Taylor

Phyllis Ralston

Eleanor Martin

Patricia Van Sloane

Linda Howard

Mary Louise (Muffy) Kelly Lawrence

Katherine Cowles Van Sloane

I entered my login and started with the first name on my list. Our alumna directory had phone numbers and only snail mail addresses for most of the "girls". I dialed Nancy's number.

"Allo," A soft voice with a Spanish accent answered.

I identified myself and asked to speak with Nancy.

"Hold please."

"Cissy! Darling. So wonderful to hear from you. How are you?" My heart filled with nostalgia at Nancy's melodic voice.

"How are you?" I responded. We exchanged some chitchat, and then I got down to business. "Nancy, have you been in touch with Honey Nickels in recent years?"

"We see each other occasionally. Why do you ask?"

Mindful that Manny was enroute to Marty's with the bad news, I realized I should have given some thought to what I would say before I got into this conversation.

"I saw her the other day—at the PDC. She seemed upset about something and wanted to speak with me, but we never had a private moment. Now I can't reach her. Do you have any idea what is going on with her?" All true, if twisted.

"I've heard some things—but you know how I hate to pass on gossip."

"Like what?" Oh yeah, she really hated it.

"She and that TV person she's married to—looks like the end of marriage number—what is it? Number five?"

"What happened?"

"She should never have gotten involved with those entertainment people."

"What do you mean?"

"Oh Cissy, I know you work with some of those movie people, but you'd never marry one. Of course, this is the second time she's done so. But Hayward wasn't just a movie person . . . if you know what I mean."

I did know what she meant. Thanks to generations of his family on Mrs. Astor's 400 List, Hayward had enough social standing that his poor choice of profession could be overlooked by even those of the generation who still thought that actors, entertainers, and vaudevillians should be classed with gypsies and other itinerants. I thought it best not to debate the issue in the same conversation as I was trying to get information.

"Nancy, do you know if Honey has had any concerns for her safety?"

"Oh that."

"Oh what?"

"I'm sworn to secrecy."

"Come on. Nancy, it's important."

"I won't discuss this over the phone." Her melodic voice had turned cold.

"Where are you going to be for the next few days?"

"Right here. I have no plans."

"I'll give you a call. I'd like to stop by." We said our good-byes.

It was clear that email and phone would not yield the information I needed. As long as this threat went unsolved,

I would go wherever necessary. I added the locations of their principal homes to the list of names.

Nancy Beck, Montecito

Lily Taylor, San Francisco

Phyllis Ralston, Hope Ranch

Eleanor Martin, Saratoga

Patricia Van Sloane, Carmel

Linda Howard, Pebble Beach

Mary Louise (Muffy) Kelly Lawrence, Atherton

Katherine Cowles Van Sloane, Piedmont

Next, I planned my route through the list of the most upscale old money communities from San Francisco to Santa Barbara. But as long as this threat went unsolved, I would go wherever necessary.

I'd drop off Emma at my father's and call on the women in the Bay Area. Then I would head down the coast starting with a short drive down highway 280 to Atherton.

I would be heading into some of the drawing rooms of my youth—a world far removed from the one I now lived in. The thought of Atherton reminded me of hearing the adults complain about the downward slide letting "people like that" into the neighborhood would start.

Like the Bing Crosby story. I was pretty young. I didn't know who Bing Crosby was, but later I thought him to be a charming, talented gentleman. Still, when he bought a house in Atherton, it started an uproar of neighbors trying to block the sale. My own grandmother apparently chose to disregard the fact that the very length of her California lineage spoke of shady characters with far bigger crimes than being in show business. She voiced the most ferocious opposition, but of course, never in public. Ladies' names and ladies' faces never appear in public places.

Chapter 21

On Monday morning we canceled Skip's return flight reservation. We made a quick stop in LA to exchange dirty laundry for city clothes, to drop off Lulu with Addie Mae and to pick up Skip's duffle bag. After a speedy, five hour drive up the Central Valley, Emma and I dropped Skip off at Unit 2, his high-rise Berkeley dorm on College Avenue, between Durant and Channing. These twelve story buildings, each set of four filling a city block and surrounding a large interior courtyard, had been continuously upgraded since my days as a student here. The seismic handling that had precipitated the work added a sculptural aspect highlighted by stylish deep tones of tan, rust brown and mustard-colored paint.

Skip turned down our offers to help him carry his bags to his room. He stuffed his iPad, cell phone, laptop, and jacket into his backpack and slung the pack over one shoulder. The duffle bag full of his clean laundry—lovingly washed, ironed, and folded by Addie Mae—went over the other shoulder. He leaned into my window for a final kiss goodbye.

"Goodbye, darling." I drew his face close for an extra cheek hug. "Take care. If there's the slightest hint . . . , or if anything happens that makes you think you're in any kind of danger, please call me, or your grandfather, immediately."

"Aw, Mom. You know I'm fine." He walked around to the passenger side of the car and reached through the window to mess his sister's hair. "Make sure you two go directly to Grandpa's. He's expecting you in no more than forty-five minutes. Call him if you hit traffic so he doesn't freak out."

"Skip, Grandpa isn't even there," Emma reminded her brother.

"I'm calling him as soon as I hit my room—as agreed. And his security will call him to announce your arrival at the Seacliff house. Promise to go straight there."

"Yes sir," both Emma and I answered. "Love you."

His response was a grunt that sounded much like "Love ya too." Skip waved and climbed the steps to the courtyard entrance.

I pulled out of the drop off zone, maneuvered into traffic and through the steady stream of young people walking, biking, laughing and greeting one another.

"Mom, you are going to stay with me at Grandpa's, right?"

"Tonight." I stopped for the pedestrians at Telegraph Avenue.

"Just tonight?"

"I'm going to make some calls tomorrow morning. I've made a list of friends who should be able to tell me more about Honey." I turned right onto Telegraph. While we sat at the light to turn left onto Bancroft, we watched the multi-ethnic, but-uniformly-denim-clad students, strolling past Sproul Hall and under Sather Gate. "I'll stay at Dad's place in the City while I interview the women who live nearby. But I think you should stay down at Sandy's." I referred to the walled estate on the peninsula that belonged to my father's wife.

"Mom, I'm not the one in danger."

"We don't know who was being shot at, do we? But I think the security at Grandpa's is probably fine." I thought of Manny's order to seek refuge at my father's and remembered that Manny was thinking of Sandy's estate, not my father's place in the City. "But I'm sure Manny had in mind the security of the gated community together with the guard shack at her own entry."

"Seacliff has plenty of security . . . it's just not so in your face." Emma referred to the quiet, exclusive residential district on the ocean side of the Golden Gate. My father and his neighbors had very effective, nearly invisible private security that befit the elegant neighborhood.

"Right. And I think it's better for actually catching bad guys than just keeping people out of the area."

"So, we're agreed? You'll stay at Grandpa's?"

"For a night or two."

Emma answered my compliance with a sigh.

We were busy with our own thoughts while we drove over the Bay Bridge into the City. I worried that perhaps I was wrong about Honey's death.

What if it *was* connected to Jamie's disappearance?

What if our entire family was in danger? We had no idea who was being shot at. Could have been any one of us.

Why was anyone shooting at us?

But that damn body was obviously following me around. I couldn't stand it. I had to know why.

We pulled between the massive white square pillars with 'Seacliff' carved into the capital marking the entrance to the neighborhood, lowered the car windows and enjoyed the briny aroma of the breezes off the ocean. China Beach, the one beach in San Francisco safe for swimming was below the cliffside site of the house. "Safe," that is, if one didn't mind water temperatures that barely hit sixty degrees on the warmest summer day.

After I'd married, my parents down-sized from six thousand square feet in Pacific Heights to a four-bedroom, six-bath Italian Renaissance villa in the only San Francisco neighborhood adjacent to the ocean and reduced the household staff to day help. Contrary to logic, such down-sizing was more a wish for privacy, not an economical move—houses on Seacliff sell for ten to twenty-five million. The spectacular mansions on Pacific Heights attract some tourist traffic, but Seacliff seems a better-kept secret, in spite of a few famous residents.

The first house on the cliff had been built immediately following the 1906 earthquake by a family that relocated from Van Ness Avenue. The Brown family had had the misfortune to be on the wrong side of Van Ness, the side of the avenue that was dynamited to create a firebreak in the inferno that followed the quake. Philip Bronstein, former husband of Sharon Stone, now lives in the Brown's Seacliff house.

Like most of the mansions along the avenue, my father's was built in the 1920's. I considered the fun the young architect named Bertz had had designing many of the homes drawing on elements from English Gothic, Spanish Colonial, Italian Renaissance, and French Country to create a splendid assembly of city homes, all stuccoed in soft pastels. Well-mannered lollipop-like trees line the quiet street, considerately maintaining a height blocking no house's view, and symbolizing the perfect order that marks the graceful neighborhood.

Emma punched in the code that opened the heavy, wood planked garage door. We parked in the dim alcove reserved for guest cars and carried our bags up the interior, dark terra cotta stairs that led from the parking area to the kitchen, where I dropped the keys on the marble counter. We didn't stop to enjoy the view of the sliver of beach below or of the ocean side of the Golden Gate Bridge.

A spacious master suite shared the second floor with three additional bedrooms, each with its own en suite bath and sitting area. Emma and I had long since laid claim to the guestrooms we preferred. We banged our rolling bags up the stone stairs and moved into our respective rooms. I lifted my bag onto the upholstered bench at the foot of the queen-sized bed. From my window, I heard the foghorns announcing the mist had already obscured the view. Typically, March and October are the two months one can hope to catch a spectacular sunset off land's end, but we wouldn't be enjoying a sunset that March night.

Emma's voice from downstairs interrupted my enjoyment of the fog. I walked down the stairs and took pleasure in the décor that had been my mother's last design work. She died within a few short years of completing these timeless interiors of Venetian plaster, glowing limestone, smooth granite, and lustrous marble, all in warm golden tones to offset the constant gloom outside the windows. Bittersweet chocolate-colored wood, velvets, and leather cozied all the main floor, even the grand sized living room.

Entering through the garage, we had bypassed the formal entry hall, which opened off the gated courtyard and contained a gracious, curved-mahogany-and-limestone staircase. To the right of the hall, I walked through an arched opening and turned on a lamp in the formal living room where two pairs of French doors opened onto a terrace overlooking a garden below and the trail down the cliffs. From first the limestone terrace and then the dining room, I watched the fog creep under the bridge and fill the air until the entire house felt cocooned in grey clouds, calling for a retreat across the entry hall into the cozy, wood paneled study warmed by a corner fireplace.

We met in the kitchen and inspected the wine cooler set beneath the golden-brown marble counter. "Grandpa has this Coppola Pinot Noir. You'll like that, Mama."

I left Emma to open and pour the wine while I lit the logs laid in the study fireplace by the day maids. Emma joined me in that snuggery and handed me a glass filled with a burgundy colored wine so dark it was nearly black. We settled into down-filled bergere chairs and rested our feet on the raised hearth. I rubbed my hand over the silk chenille in the bittersweet chocolate brown that covered the chairs, appreciating once again my mother's brilliance. We studied the dancing flames in the arched opening of the brick fireplace and sipped our wine in silence.

"Mama, I . . . ," Emma began and then stopped. Instead of continuing, she raised her glass to her mouth and licked the edge.

"What is it, darling?"

"I'm scared."

"We're safe here. There are cameras on every approach to the house and constant surveillance by security patrols."

"I don't mean . . . . That's not what I'm worried about." She stopped fooling with her glass and looked me in the eye. Her blue eyes filled with tears. She looked away and returned to studying the blaze.

"What?"

"I don't think you're being careful enough. Oh Mama! You just aren't taking the danger seriously."

"But I am, darling. That's why we're here."

"But you aren't planning to stay here. You're going to go out and see your school friends, and Grandma's friends."

"During the day."

"Why can't you just let the police handle this?"

"Emma, I know these women. All of them are very conscious of their positions in society and they attach a great deal of importance to maintaining decorum. Privacy is an important issue. Remember how your great grand-mother was shocked by the middle-class desire for publicity. These women have the same attitude. They are not going to talk freely to Manny, or any other stranger."

"They won't do anything illegal. You know, like 'im-pede an investigation,' right?" Emma used her fingers to form the quotation marks.

"They won't lie." I tasted the poignant, pinot noir and relaxed into the plush cushions of my chair. "But they won't offer information that isn't specifically asked for. And they won't repeat what they consider to be gossip. Let me tell you a little story that makes my point."

Emma settled back in her chair.

"A few years back, there was a jewel thief operating in Pacific Heights—"

"I never heard about that."

"Nobody did. It never made the newspapers. A great deal of effort insured that." I sipped my wine before I continued. "I was at a luncheon welcoming Katherine Van Sloane home after a lengthy 'vacation' in Switzerland." Now it was my turn to use finger quotations. "A 'vacation' better known as rehab or recovery."

"Drugs or alcohol?"

"We never discussed it, but I assumed both. Eight of us lunched in the conservatory, an intimate enough group that the conversation got rather frank. Katherine mentioned she had discovered she was missing several pieces of jewelry while she was dressing that morning."

"While most of the women commiserated with her, Nancy and Patricia were strangely quiet. So, I asked them, 'What's with you two?' At first, they gave the usual, 'Nothing,' but they finally coughed up that they were also missing jewelry. It seems their husbands had ordered that they not report the losses to either the police or the insurance companies."

"Why not?"

"I asked the same question. I mean, I could understand not calling the police. That would mean publicity and strangers poking around in one's house. But not to be reimbursed?"

"So?'

"Well, Katherine was having no part of the cover up. She and her husband were not on the best of terms—she said they hadn't had sex in nine years! She didn't bother to tell him. And she'd called her insurance company before she came to lunch. The insurance company insisted on a police report. Patricia and Nancy were beside themselves. They immediately got on their cells to their husbands. The cat—or the cat burglar—was out of the bag."

"Why didn't the men want the insurance companies involved?"

"Most of their jewelry pieces were gifts from their husbands."

"So?"

"The jewelry wasn't what the women thought it was.

Those new synthetic diamonds are pretty damn good!"

"I don't get it. Why did the husbands skimp on their wives jewelry?"

"A husband can hide the expense of buying jewelry for a girlfriend by buying jewelry for his wife at the same time. The girlfriend might have the piece checked, so wives don't get the real thing."

"That's terrible!" Emma said. "Were there just three of them burglarized?"

"It's hard to say how many altogether, but before the week was out, I found four more silent victims and suggested they talk to Katherine, Nancy, and Patricia."

"Did they catch the guy?"

"The San Francisco police didn't, but a private investigator did. Some of the better pieces were recovered. And the thief was paid to move his operation elsewhere." I enjoyed a new sip of the pinot noir. "The investigators followed the thief to his new location and called in the police when he was seen breaking into a mansion. He was opening a safe in BevHills when the police arrived."

"Wow." Emma smiled at me and raised her wine glass in my direction. "And you think these women'll tell you the juicy stuff?"

"I won't give up until they do."

Chapter 22

Late the next morning I strolled down the path to the beach. The fog was beginning to burn off, but now a brisk, cool wind whipped through my hair and blew sprays of moisture off the water.

As I walked, I called my mother's friend Lily Taylor. Lily had married into *the* Taylor family, a branch of the de Youngs, one of the oldest and wealthiest families in San Francisco.

"Lily? Cissy Huntington."

"Cissy, how are you dear?" Lily spoke slowly, carefully enunciating each word.

We exchanged pleasantries for a few minutes. Then I broached the purpose for my call.

"Lily, you've kept in touch with Honey Chaffin, right?"

"Oh, dear. I've just heard from Marty's assistant. They haven't scheduled a service yet. Some complication with the medical examiner. They don't know when the body will be released."

"Lily, I'm sorry. Would you like to talk about it?"

"Oh, we weren't that close."

"What are you doing for lunch?"

"I have museum committee meetings today. In fact, I'm running late for one now."

"Dinner?" I asked.

"That would be lovely."

"Meet at the Tadich at 7:00?"

"Oh, they are so tiresome about reservations. One simply has to wait."

"In the bar," I reminded her, "Their cosmos are great."

"See you there at 7:00."

Next, I called Katherine in Piedmont. Katherine and I had been at Catalina at the same time, but her mother had been in Honey's class. I hoped Katherine could fill me in on Honey's life over the last twenty years. And we were close enough that she wouldn't hesitate to tell me all the gossip.

"Come for lunch?" she asked.

"I'd love to. See you in two hours."

I scrambled back up the path, climbing the railroad tie steps set in sand and shoving aside the overgrown bushes. I hurried to shower and dress for both meetings and get to Piedmont.

Surrounded by Oakland, Piedmont is a small, hillside community of thirty-five hundred homes with it's own services: police and fire departments, a city hall amidst a park, and schools. Schools are the main attraction for new buyers, but I've always loved the lush greenery of tree-canopied streets and the incredible views of San Francisco and the bay.

164

Katherine's house has perhaps the best vantage point of all. The best houses such as Katherine's never go on the market. They are passed from generation to generation. Katherine lived in the house she grew up in; the house that had passed to her when her parents made their penthouse apartment in the City on Nob Hill their primary residence.

I was struck anew by the incredible beauty of Katherine's estate. Behind wrought iron fence and double gates, two enormous oak trees framed the view of a cobblestone drive encircling an equally oversized dark stone fountain shooting water in front of a view of the City, the bay, and a perfect shot of the Golden Gate. Tucked into the foliage, a Bavarian castle designed by Beaux Arts architect Julia Morgan turned its side to the view and faced the fountain.

I parked the Prius on the cobblestones on the far side of the circle so as not to mar the scene just as Katherine opened the massive front door and stepped onto the broad porch. She came down the dark stone steps to greet me. The sun glinted off her strand of pearls and the white in her shoulder-length, bobbed hair that was now more gray than black. She lifted her still black eyebrows, and said, "Good choice of car. My children are insisting that I trade in all of my monsters for hybrids. Do you like it?"

"I love it. I can drive all the way from LA without stopping for gas."

We slipped our arms around each other's waists and strolled back into the house.

"I'd forgotten how beautiful your place is. That view."

"I'm afraid I've gotten so used to it . . . . Well, the sunsets still get my attention." Katherine sighed. "We're always so damn busy. It's a miracle I had time open today. My tennis partner twisted her ankle yesterday. Honestly, I felt bad to be so relieved at having an open day."

I stopped walking when we reached the entry hall. "God, I love the details in Julia's work." Julia Morgan, architect primarily to the Hearst family, was best known for Hearst Castle in San Simeon, but I loved her Bavarian style the best. I drank in the ambience of the redwood entry with its combination of Art Noveau and gothic carvings. Julia's brilliant designs escaped the cloying common to Bavarian style by the use of symmetry and local rustic materials. The wood had turned a deep, dark grey brown over the years, making the hall startling dim after the bright sun. The antler chandelier did little to light the elaborate stairs.

In the shadows I failed to recognize Cameron Wells as he walked down the stairs, but I knew his deep voice. "Hello Cissy. How are you?"

"Cameron, good to see you. You must be busy these days, with the upcoming wedding festivities." As my eyes adjusted to the dark, I could see that his dark temples were graying, but his body looked as though he still worked out daily.

"Ah, Joan and Poppy have taken care of all of that." He looked me up and down in a manner that I hadn't noticed as a happily married woman.

I continued to force my smile at him and wondered why he was at Katherine's house, until I remembered that Katherine's mother was Cameron's grandmother's much younger half-sister. In spite of the fact that Cameron was a couple years older than Katherine, she was his aunt.

Cameron continued to speak, "You know, I tried to tell Jamie he was making a big mistake with that fly-in development. I guess he learned that he's not smarter than everyone else after all."

While I stood with my mouth open trying to come up with a brilliant come back—I mean I don't care if Jamie should have known better, I wasn't going to let this prig insult my husband—Cameron leered and turned to go out the door.

"Good to see you. Gotta rush off. Late for lunch in the City. The traffic getting to the Pacific Union can be impossible." He had to squeeze in a mention of his membership in the prestigious club even though we had spoken for less than a minute. Cameron kissed Katherine on the cheek, rubbed my arm, and hurried out the door. "Ciao."

I wanted to ask Katherine what he was doing upstairs in her house, but I couldn't think of how to frame the question. "What's Cameron up to these days?"

"I'm not entirely sure." Katherine scrunched her face. "He said his grandmother had some diaries and family trees that he thought might be in my attic. I told him there wasn't any such thing up there, but he insisted on looking anyway. Probably trying to establish a connection to the royal families of Europe."

I laughed.

"Well, he is the most pretentious prick I've ever

known," Katherine said by way of defending her catty remark. "I suppose that's the result of people fawning over him all his life. It's possible to be too damn good looking."

I had to agree with her. "Can't choose your relatives." I hugged her.

"Come out to the sun porch. Even though it's warm now, the ocean breezes could reach us by early afternoon. I thought we should eat inside."

I wasn't disappointed to be ushered into the sun porch. Diamond-patterned latticework framed large windows over looking the view. Two comfortable armchairs were drawn up to a round table set for two.

Katherine poured ice tea into goblets and waved me into one of the chairs. An African American maid quietly deposited salads on the chargers. Katherine opened the napkin covering the whole-wheat rolls and offered me warm bread.

I placed a roll on my butter plate and enjoyed the view for a few more seconds before I asked, "Tell me everything you know about Honey Chaffin. Especially anything I may not have heard."

"I hope I haven't gotten you here under false pretenses." Katherine's fingers fiddled with a heavy silver fork. "I loved the thought of reminiscing about the good times from years ago, but now that you're here, I find that I'm uncomfortable about discussing Honey. I get choked up every time I think about the fact that they—that is, her generation, including my parents and aunts—are all gone now."

168

"I know what you mean. But usually talking alleviates some of the pain." I really believed that, but I could also see I would have to proceed more gently. "Just tell me what you are comfortable with."

Katherine started to speak, but then covered her mouth with a linen napkin, stood, and walked over to the windows facing the bay. Her shoulders shook with silent sobs. "It's hard," she said after a long silence.

"Katherine, I'm sorry to make you feel bad."

I couldn't help but think that this woman needed some real problems. My mother had died. Katherine's mother had been gone for several years, also. The whole world had to deal with older generations dying. It occurred to me something more current might be upsetting Katherine and I needed to be more compassionate.

"Tell me whatever you can," I said."

"Cissy, do you swear not to repeat anything I say?" Katherine responded.

"I don't know if I can promise that, but I can agree not to say where I got the information."

Katherine's tear-filled turquoise eyes studied my face for what seemed like a full minute. "That works."

Chapter 23

"I'm convinced she was trying tell me something before she died," I said. "And then her killer was trying to tell me something by dumping her body near me, twice."

"So, it's true." Katherine's eyes widened, her black eyebrows raised. "Rumors have been flying since Sunday that she didn't die of natural causes, but Marty has gone into seclusion, and his assistants claim to have no information."

"They might not."

"But the press—the media has been strangely quiet." Katherine frowned.

"Probably don't know who she is. It's been a while since she was a media darling. I'll tell you everything I know about her death, but then you'll owe me. Agree to reciprocate?"

Katherine stared at me, apparently considering her options, but finally sat back down at the table and nodded her agreement to my terms.

I filled her in on the bare bones of what I knew about Honey's death, leaving out the shot fired into the cabin and any danger that I—or those close to me—might be in. No point in starting the rumor that I was dangerous to be around.

"So, I'm trying to figure out what connection Honey might have to me."

"I don't know if I can help you with that. I'm trying to think if any of what I know could possibly tell you that . . . but I . . . ." Katherine held back a sob and toyed with her butter knife and bread roll.

"Tell me what you know."

"Well, as you know, my mother and Honey Nickels were close. They grew up together in the City. And the Nickels and Cowles estates were next to each other at the Lake. As you must know, my mother was a Cowles."

"The Lake" to which Katherine referred is Tahoe. The two estates had at one point been one very large compound with football-field-sized lawns rolling down to the water. Somewhere in the family feud of the Nickels and Cowles dividing Henry Minner's fortune—probably during the height of the upset—the two branches of the family spoke only long enough to split the Tahoe property into two twenty-acre parcels.

"Did they go to Catalina together?"

"No. They started out at Katharine Delmar Burke as day students, but then Honey was sent to board at Catalina. They remained in constant contact. Honey was bored out of her mind in Monterey. She sat in class and wrote my mother long letters." Katherine smiled and looked at the Golden Gate. "As adults, they spoke every day, and Honey was with my mother until the end of her long illness. Honey distracted my mother with stories of Honey's many wild adventures. I admit, I listened at the door more than once. What a life she led." Katherine shook her head and again gave me that beautiful-sadness-of-it-all smile.

"I've heard about Honey's trips to Palm Springs. She was quite a tennis player?" I picked up my fork and tasted the salad.

Katherine chuckled softly. "It wasn't the tennis. She was barely eighteen when she married that film director . . . Hayward. Yet she had an abortion in the first few months of their marriage."

"Did he think she was too young?"

"I don't know what he thought, but it seems, . . . Honey wasn't sure whose child it was." Katherine stuck her fork into a chunk of chicken.

"Oh."

"Unfortunately, abortions back in the late forties were furtive matters, and presumably not the safest of medical procedures when done in some back room. I don't know the details, but my mother and Honey always held that aborted pregnancy responsible for the multiple miscarriages that kept her from ever having children. At least that was the theory they came up with after every husband produced the same lack of result."

"Back up a bit. I'm still trying to understand my connection to her. Remember, besides attending Catalina, the other thing I have in common with her is the Monterey Cotillion." I raised my eyebrows and smirked at Katherine.

"If Honey was from San Francisco, why did she make her debut in Monterey? Wouldn't the San Francisco Cotillion have been much more prestigious?"

"It would have been, . . . if Honey had been invited to participate."

"Certainly, a Nickels—"

"Mrs. Taylor was still alive then. Remember Honey's grandmother was a Spreckels."

"Oh." I giggled. " 'I just don't think your daughter—' "

" '—would be happy as a debutante,' " Katherine finished quoting Mrs. Taylor and then ate a bite of her salad.

Mrs. Phyllis de Young Taylor had revived Ned Greenway and Eleanor Martin's Cotillion in the forties. Mrs. Taylor was very strict about participation, limiting the debutantes to the so-called upper crust of San Francisco society. The Nickels family was usually included, but not if a Nickels had married a Spreckels. The de Youngs and the Spreckels had a long running rivalry.

Although Honey's wild child act probably had much to do with her lack of an invite, too. Not that Mrs. Taylor would have been asked to explain herself. Those not in the know, the nouveau riche foolish enough to ask why their daughter was not invited were humiliated by Mrs. Taylor's stock answer, "I just don't think your daughter would be happy as a debutante." Somehow that phrase was used to explain every rejection in Bay Area society as in "I just don't think your daughter would be happy at Delmar Burke's school." Or, "I don't think your daughter would be happy as a Kappa."

"So, it was either the embarrassing, inferior San Francisco Debutante Ball of the Cotillion rejects—"

"That would never do."

"Or start your own tradition."

"You got it." Katherine touched the tip of her nose. "Why did *you* come out in Monterey?" Katherine leaned forward looking as though she had always wanted to ask me that.

"I didn't want to do it at all. Remember, being a debutante was very uncool in my day. My parents and I compromised. Monterey was so simple, laid back. Not a season. No long white gowns. Just a simple dinner dance. I could pretend it never happened. My father liked the price, and mother didn't have to apologize for my lack of cooperation. Besides, it had a certain cachet of its own."

"Because it was so quiet . . . no unsuitable middle-class publicity." Katherine supplied. "And one had to have family dating back to when Monterey was the capital of California."

"That wasn't actually true." I scrunched my face and shook my head. "Probably a rumor started by a participant who wanted to give Monterey Cotillion more prestige than Mrs. Taylor's Cotillion. Can you think of any way that the cotillion could tie into Honey's death?"

"That's pretty out there don't you think? As in *Death of the Antique Debutante*? I don't think so."

I tried another subject. "Who could have been the father of the aborted child?"

"Well, I never heard that information specifically stated.

But there were mentions of weekends on Errol Flynn's boat, rides in Clark Gable's fancy cars and trips on Howard Hughes's planes. Apparently young Honey had numerous affairs while visiting that aunt of hers in Palm Springs." Katherine ran a manicured finger over the rim of her glass.

"But she couldn't have been more than seventeen."

"Sixteen and seventeen, to be exact. She started going down there as soon as she got her driver's license and her father bought her that white convertible with an interior that matched her honey blonde hair."

"Was statutory rape not an issue in those days?"

"Apparently not in some circles. Honey's father certainly wouldn't have . . ."

"Right. So, she married Hayward already pregnant? Did he know about the abortion?"

"I'm pretty sure not. The Palm Springs aunt. She would have . . . you know."

"Did she continue to have affairs after she married Hayward?"

"I don't think so. At least not at first. Despite rumors about Clark Gable, she spoke of the first few years of their marriage as the happiest, most romantic time of her life. They were the glamour couple of Hollywood."

"And then they moved back East." I sipped my tea and buttered a roll.

Katherine nodded. She chewed a bite of salad.

"Why did they do that?"

"Hayward wanted to try his hand at theater. And he had lots of family there. His parents were getting elderly . . .

and there was a sizable estate."

"Honey wasn't happy there?"

"She was used to being the center of attention. In Newport, she was nobody. She had acquired enough glamour by then that she would have done okay in Manhattan if she had stuck it out, but she accompanied Hayward on a European shoot and opted to stay there. She divided her time between Paris and London with recuperation in northern Italy, at Villa d'Este, at Lake Como."

"When did she start having affairs?"

"I think on that trip. She was fascinated by titles. Told mother she had always wanted to marry a prince. She almost did, too, but instead she married one of the largest fortunes in the world."

"Randolph. What happen to him?"

"She only lived with him for a matter of months, but never divorced him. He died five years later and his wealth was evenly divided between Honey and his two children from a previous marriage."

"So, Honey ended up with her father's money and lots of Randolph's. Whew!"

Money being a forbidden subject in the Bay Area, Katherine barely smiled at my gaffe. Probably put it off to my manners having been tainted by those transients in LA. Abortions, statutory rape, murder—all safe subjects—but never money.

I brazened on. "Did she still have all that money when she married Chaffin?"

"Oh, you've forgotten one of the husbands, and a string of lovers. She only made the mistake of marrying one of them."

Katherine studied the view out the conservatory window while her fingers toyed with her butter knife.

I almost apologized for my gauche behavior, but then she continued.

"The countess title cost her a lot. After that she just took lovers . . . until Marty. But I imagine a prenup handled any worries she had about that."

"A prenup wouldn't necessarily keep him from inheriting. But he wouldn't get the Nickels's money."

Again, Katherine just smiled, but I got her message.

"Oh, right. He's loaded from all those successful TV shows. So, it wasn't Marty arranging her murder for her money." Besides, what would Marty have to do with me? "Katherine, do you have any idea why someone would kill her?"

Katherine frowned and shook her head. "Maybe if I think about it for awhile."

"What about why her killer would dump her body on me?"

She shook her head again.

"You'll call me if you think of anything that might remotely . . . , could one of her string of lovers been jealous? You know the old 'if-I-can't-have-you-nobody-can' routine."

"She's been married to Marty for twenty years. They would all be terribly old . . . if they are even still alive."

177

"Oh yeah. There's that." I put my elbow on the table and my chin in my hand. "Maybe Marty's been having an affair and the other woman wants to get married."

"Have you seen Marty lately? He's not exactly sprightly. And he's—since the day they met—only had eyes for Honey. He worshipped her."

I remembered seeing Marty hobbling around in his walker. "Pretty unlikely, huh?" I gave the puzzle another moment's thought. "Who are her heirs?"

Katherine shrugged her shoulders.

"What about the Nickels's fortune? Is it still intact?"

"Remember the stories from when we were children?" she reminded me.

The Henry Minner estate had been fought over for 47 years. When it was finally settled in 1965, the Nickels branch was outraged.

"My family carefully avoided discussing it, since my branch of Nickels changed their name to N-I-C-H-O-L-S and cut themselves off from the rest of the tree," I reminded Katherine.

Katherine stared at me for a full minute before she looked around the room, and even peeked into the adjoining rooms as though someone would overhear her breach of etiquette before she whispered, "Years ago, I overheard Mrs. Mein, the former Sarah Minner Nickels, complaining bitterly that she only got five million when her cousin Henry Minner Cowles was awarded six by the court."

"That was a lot of money in 1965 when you could still

buy a house in this neighborhood for under fifty thousand. I bet you can't touch even the smallest for under three million now." I got a perverted thrill at Katherine's wince that acknowledged that I was correct.

I knew that much of the wealth of the San Francisco Bay Area was involved in the venture capital that backed promising start ups. I braved another scandalous question. "How did she fare in the Great Recession?" I took a bite of the chicken curry salad.

"I really wouldn't know." Katherine's guilt got the better of us.

I swallowed the chicken. "Come on. Please."

"No, really. I don't know. That happened after my mother died, and she was my contact with Honey," Katherine held her napkin up to her mouth while she spoke.

"One hears little tidbits here and there. But I don't think any of the so-called old money lost serious amounts.

I frowned at Katherine and raised one eyebrow. "Did she invest in the Tech start-ups? Any that went wrong?"

"I doubt she had reason to touch the Nickels's money." She drank from her iced tea.

I patiently waited to see if she would continue.

"Ancient history isn't that? Katherine whispered "Even the so-called Great Recession didn't affect many of the old families seriously. At least not that anyone is admitting." Katherine sighed. "But the new 'start ups' are mostly 'up starts.' "

I knew that many of the new batch of tech people made more than the old guard ever dreamed. I'd heard the whispered criticisms of "those people" that I believed were the result of resentment. The most popular criticism of the new money was their lack of decorum. I found it amusing, considering the backgrounds of the old money.

"Who would know about Honey's finances and her heirs?"

Katherine studied the upper corner of the ceiling for a minute. "Lily Taylor. She was part of their circle."

Ah, my 7:00 pm dinner date.

Chapter 24

I left Katherine about 4:00 o'clock. I doubted it would take more than an hour to an hour and a half to drive to Tadich Grill and park. Not enough time to accomplish much at the house. I had time to kill before heading over the Bay Bridge to the City.

I pulled out of the gates and waited for a black BMW to pass the driveway. I used the Bluetooth to check in with Emma as I drove away from Katherine's. "How's it going?"

"Okay. I've been checking stock and placing orders for the fabrics for Sally. I'm going to run out of things to do online pretty soon though, Mom, I really don't see any reason not to go over to the design center."

"Sweetheart, please humor me.

Sigh. "Do you think we'll still be here on Thursday?"

"I would be more comfortable if you stayed at Grandpa's until Manny knows who was shooting at whom. And next week Poppy's wedding festivities start. Rehearsal dinner, bachelorette party, shower—you're going to be busy."

Emma sighed again. "Jeff is flying up on Thursday night then."

"That'll be nice. The two of you can have a romantic weekend with the house all to yourselves."

"Mom," Emma whined. "Please!"

"Did you find food for dinner?"

"There's plenty here. Maria went shopping."

"Have a nice dinner. I shouldn't be too late." I turned the car into a sharp right turn and drove down the winding Hampton Road to Grand Avenue.

I thought about stopping at Fenton's for ice cream, but I really didn't need it. Besides it would "ruin my dinner." I could drive over to the campus and check out the latest exhibit at the art museum. Go up to Tilden Park. Check out the view from Grizzly Peak. In the end, I opted for a walk around Lake Merritt.

My car started making funny noises and stuttering just past the Grand Lake Theatre. "What the hell?" The car had never given me any trouble, but it was acting strangely enough that I decided not to chance taking it on the freeway.

I found a convenient spot in the Lakeside Park and maneuvered the Prius into a space. I got out and closed my door before I noticed a black BMW with two passengers behind black tinted windows pull into a nearby space. Was that the same black BMW that had been in front of Katherine's gates, or was I being overly suspicious?

I opened the hood to see if there was some obvious detachment, but as soon as I did, I realized I had no idea what it was supposed to look like under there.

 I took a deep breath and reminded myself that I had plenty of time to get to the City before my dinner appointment.

I called AAA. "I'm in the parking area of Lake Merritt Lakeside Park. My car is stalling whenever I take my foot off the gas. But it's a hybrid so it shouldn't have an idling problem."

"Someone will be out in about 45 minutes."

"Forty-five minutes," I groaned. "Can't they come sooner?"

"Sorry ma'am."

I climbed back into my car and looked around for the occupants of the BMW. I could see the car. The passenger seat appeared to be empty. Thanks to the black glass, only the silhouette of the driver was visible. The angle of his baseball cap reminded me of something—or someone.

Where was the other guy? The lid of the trunk was open. I saw the top of another baseball cap. A black cap. What was he doing in the trunk? What if he was getting out a gun?

Shit, I was a sitting duck.

Or my imagination was running away with me.

I called AAA back. "Look, I just want you to have my car towed to the Toyota dealer on Van Ness in San Francisco."

"No problem, Mrs. Huntington, but we need you to

show your card and sign for the service when the tow truck driver arrives."

"I'm not waiting here, so how do you want to do this?"

"Is there someone there you can leave the keys and the card with?"

"No, but I can leave the card and the keys with the car."

"Wouldn't recommend that."

"Neither would I." Where the hell did the other guy go now? I couldn't see any part of him, but the trunk was closed. "The key—which is actually a black plastic thingie—will be behind the left front wheel, on the ground. The card in the console between the front seats." I hung up.

Act like everything is normal. I told myself. Set off for a brisk walk. The path around the lake was three and a half miles. Act like you are getting some exercise. Surreptitiously, I dropped the key on the ground and kicked it under the back of the front tire.

Canadian geese were thick on the lawn sloping down to the water. A nice breeze blew across the lake, rippling the surface. Even though the City across the bay was fogged in, on this sunny side of the Bay, blue skies and sunshine reflected off the water and the windows of the tall buildings ringing the south and west edges of the lake. I headed toward the Tribune Building and downtown Oakland on the far side of the park.

I'd gotten nearly a third of the way around the lake when I allowed myself to look back at the black car. A man in a black hooded sweatshirt over a baseball cap leaned against the car while he used binoculars to study a flock of gulls. I turned around and walked faster. I entered a group of redwood trees that were between the black car and me. I snuck a glance between branches and thought I saw the binoculars trained on the trees I had just entered. He *was* looking for me. Shit!

Think. Think.

What does this mean? Who are they? If they wanted to shoot me, they easily already could have. I called my father.

"Dad, you didn't by any chance ask someone to follow me, did you?"

"What do you mean, follow you? Aren't you at the house?" His voice got tighter with each word.

Oh shit, shit, shit.

"Not exactly."

Great, now I've got him worried. The last thing I ever wanted to do was to stress him out. "Never mind, Dad."

"Cissy, I'm coming up in the morning for a meeting in the City. I plan to come over for lunch after the meeting, and you can tell me what the hell this is all about."

"Right. Sure. See you then."

That is if I'm still alive.

Manny wouldn't have anyone following me. Who were they?

I remembered there was a stop at Lake Merritt for Bay Area Rapid Transit train. Of course, the BART station wasn't right on the lake. Where was it?

At the next clump of trees, I turned off the path and walked across the lawn perpendicular to the line of trees. I crossed the street and made for a building that I could duck into.

Predictably there was a Starbucks in the bottom of the high-rise. I slipped past the line and looked out the window. The black car pulled out of the parking lot and headed in my direction. Damn.

One of the doors of the Starbucks opened into the lobby of the building. I spotted an information desk at the entrance manned by two men in security uniforms.

I pushed past an elderly couple. "Excuse me. Where is the nearest BART station?"

The heavier of the two men pointed northwest. "It's just down Madison at 8th. Two blocks that way."

I pulled off my navy blue Max Mara jacket uncovering my white blouse and raced out the main entrance, taking care to hug the building and stay inside the pedestrian traffic. I hoped to make myself harder to spot.

I got lucky. The train going under the Bay pulled in just as I reached the platform. I jumped in, watched with satisfaction as the doors closed, and took a huge breath.

Whoever the hell they were, I had to have lost the two men.

Only one other time had I ridden the train beneath the Bay, and that excursion had been for the experience of going through the tunnel under the water. I had been disappointed that it felt no different than any other tunnel. Now I leaned back in my seat and tried to relax for the twenty minutes it took to arrive at the Market and Montgomery station, but my heart kept racing. I fought down the panic.

Taking the BART made the trip faster than if I'd driven over the bridge, so despite my stroll, I was early. I thought about the cosmopolitans at the Tadich and headed directly there. At five o'clock the financial district was emptier than Market Street, but there was still enough pedestrian traffic that I felt safe in the crowd. I hurried along California Street.

I hadn't been to Tadich this early in the day. It was just as crowded as it is later in the evening. I ordered a cosmo, told the bartender I would be right back, shoved through the raucous crowd and down the restaurant aisle that ran in front of the wood paneled alcoves to the ladies room behind the noisy kitchen.

After using the facilities and washing up, I put my jacket back on, smoothed my hair, and freshened my lip-gloss then made it back to the bar. I was lucky to find an empty seat.

The tall, dark-haired bartender winked as he set the cosmo in front of me. "Welcome back, Mrs. Huntington."

So much for anonymity. But the first sip of the pale red drink did much to calm my nerves.

Being in the familiar environment helped, also. The Tadich Grill is the oldest restaurant in San Francisco. It's been on California Street as long as I can remember. Before that it had been just around the corner for a hundred years.

The massive dark mahogany bar, more than fifty feet long, was jammed with customers. Behind the tables on the left ran a row of private alcoves lined with dark wood paneling and faced with arched wood openings. Tables covered with starched white cloths were crammed into every possible inch. Diners were elbow-to-elbow, back-to-back.

The atmosphere was, as always, loud, casual, and jovial. Names of patrons whose tables were ready were shouted out. When the line for those waiting snaked out the door—as it often did on weekend evenings—customers would pass on the name to anyone who was waiting on the sidewalk.

I loved Tadich Grill. To me it well represented the City I loved with its lack-of-pretension mixed with tradition. I loved how the menu of grilled meats and fish seldom changed, and the never-ending supply of sourdough bread on the tables always tasted great.

I let the sound of laughter and happy chatter wash over me. Half way through my cosmo, I felt the tension drain from my body, and I realized that I had been scared beyond belief. I started to call Manny to ask for advice, but then I remembered that I was supposed to be safe at my father's estate.

How would I explain? I took a gulp. Oh, fuck it. I'd just have another drink.

The tall, dark-haired bartender stood smiling in front of me like he had all the time in the world. Like he didn't have thirty customers all trying to get his attention at once. How did he remain so calm in this madhouse? He raised his eyebrow and I nodded. Before I had even downed the last sip of the drink in my hand, a second appeared on the bar in front of me.

I chatted with the couple sitting next to me. Well, she was sitting next to me. He was standing between the two of us. I glanced over her shoulder and realized the man behind her was Cameron. What a coincidence—twice in one day.

"Must be fate." His smile was much warmer than it had been this afternoon. His pale blue eyes had nice crinkle lines from years of outdoor sports. "I think I upset you . . . talking about Jamie earlier. Sorry."

The couple left for their table and Cameron slipped onto the stool next to me. He was still smiling and looking at me as though we weren't both married. His looks were the kind that had never appealed to me. He was too perfect with too broad shoulders, too narrow hips . . . . It was easy to imagine the tanned washboard abs. Whoa girl, get a hold of yourself.

The bartender set the third Cosmo in front of me, glanced at Cameron, and asked, "Mrs. Huntington, is anyone joining you for dinner?"

"Oh, yes. Mrs. Taylor." I needed to lose Cameron. Lily would clam up with him around.

Cameron looked a bit surprised when I told him to shove off. Bet hunks don't get that treatment often.

The bartender grinned as he leaned on the counter. "What time would you like your table?"

"Let's have it when she arrives. Just after seven." That'll handle her snotty attitude about waiting here being so tiresome. I giggled. "Oh, and let's have her Cosmo ready when she sits down. I'll signal you like this," I waved my pinkie finger at him and giggled again. "When she walks in the door."

I would have, but I was busy getting rid of Cameron and then I got immersed in a very interesting conversation with a woman who writes a column for the *Chronicle* and didn't see Lily until she was standing right next to me. I greeted her by spilling my third, or was it my fourth, cosmo down the front of her winter white cashmere blazer.

I hadn't seen Lily in several years. Perhaps not since my mother's funeral. She looked a lot better since she had let her hair go natural. The white was much softer around her eighty-something face than the dyed brown had been.

"You look great." Second faux pas. Not supposed to act as though anything else was possible. Then I tried to wipe off her jacket with my napkin. Of course, I hadn't been exactly pristine in the manner in which I had been setting my glass down on the bar. Okay, so the napkin was as soaked in the pale red drink as was the front of her jacket. Third faux pas. I smeared red all over her jacket and managed to yank on her triple strand of opera length pearls. Shit. I realized I better chill or I'd not get one bit of info out of the woman who was now looking at me with disdain.

"Cissy, whatever is the matter with you?"

"I got here a little early. I needed a drink."

"Ladies, your table is ready."

Rescued by the maître d'.

Lily followed my rescuer to a booth on the far side of the restaurant.

When I got off the barstool, I swear, the floor moved.

Earthquake? No. No one else seemed to notice. Shit. How many of those damn drinks did I have?

I had abandoned my Cosmo, but the bartender, who was following me with Lily's drink, had picked up mine as well.

As soon as I squeezed into the alcove containing our table and sat in my chair, I pounced on the breadbasket. I slathered on the butter. Had to soak up the alcohol.

My charming bartender set the fresh cosmo in front of Lily who shoved it away and asked for white wine. "Sauvignon Blanc, please." Lily placed her elbows on the table and stared at me as she removed her gloves one finger at a time.

Oh, shit. This wasn't going well.

"Cissy, I know you've had a very rough time of it recently. But truly dear, there is no reason for a public display of—"

I didn't wait to hear a display of what. "I'm fine Lily."

I stuck my head in the tall menu. What was I thinking? Shit. Shit. Shit. What counteracts alcohol? Grease. I ordered fried oysters.

Lily ordered a small salad with dressing on the side and grilled salmon. "You know, dear, even if you don't need to watch your weight, there's the cholesterol to consider."

As soon as the waiter exited our little alcove, I dove into my topic. "Lily, do you know much about the circumstances surrounding Honey's death?"

"I heard that you were the one to find her body. Found that to be rather strange. I didn't realize you were close."

"We weren't," I admitted.

"The papers didn't mention you, or even where she was found."

"I think Marty is working hard to keep the papers from sensationalizing her death."

"That's admirable of the man. For someone with his . . . background, he can be a gentleman. Honey would have hated any publicity other than the small, tasteful obituary."

"I don't think much has gotten out." When I thought about the frozen body being carted all over the southland, I realized it was just a matter of time before the paparazzi got hold of the story. Oh, the shit would really hit the fan then.

"Lily, I need to have a really frank discussion about Honey. About her finances."

Lily put a hand to her mouth and stared at me in horror. "Cissy!" she gasped.

The thought struck me that the reason that the subject of money was an absolute no-no in polite society in San Francisco was because there were so many skeletons in every family's closet on exactly that topic.

Take the Taylor family for example. Lily had married Michael Taylor, son of Phyllis deYoung Taylor, one of the four daughters of Michael de Young. Michael de Young began life as Meichel De Jong, the son of a Dutch Jewish immigrant. Even though the de Young family never mentioned their Jewish ancestry, it wasn't a topic of particular concern to the citizens of San Francisco.

What was of concern, but no longer publicly mentioned, was the persistent rumor that the source of the de Young fortune was blackmail. Michael de Young, as owner and editor of the *Chronicle* newspaper, discovered that more lucrative than selling papers was offering to refrain from printing certain scandalous information, for a price.

Sometimes a very big price. Such as the Crocker mansion that sat just up the hill on California Street. In the 1880's, William Crocker built a mansion for himself on Nob Hill. The Crockers moved in, but a month later hurriedly moved out. When the de Youngs immediately moved into the mansion, it was widely assumed that de Young had something on Crocker, and that the residence was the price of silence.

"Lily, this is strictly between us," I whispered.

Lily continued to stare at me. "Your mother . . . she would be so . . ."

"I know, I know. I haven't completely forgotten my manners, but Aunt Lil, I have to know just a couple things." I hoped reviving my childhood endearment for her would soften her resolve.

"Cissy, this is not a conversation I'm comfortable with. I'm shocked that you would . . ."

"I think . . . , it's possible that my family maybe in some danger. You have to help me." I motioned to the waiter to refill Lily's wine glass.

The waiter poured the wine, and Lily immediately drained the glass. "If you ever let on to anyone . . ."

The waiter refilled the glass and discreetly backed out of the enclosed alcove.

"I promise, I promise." I grabbed her hands and held

them in mine across the table. "Who is her heir?"

Lily pulled her hands away and smiled at me. She took a sip. "Now that's an interesting question." Lily glanced at the tables outside the alcove and nearby. I assumed she was checking for familiar faces to reassure herself her breach of propriety would not be noticed by anyone who mattered.

I raised an eyebrow, shoved another piece of bread in my mouth, and waited without taking my eyes off her face.

"The money she got from Randolph is nearly gone. What's left will go in the form of bequests to those who have cared for her. Her stylist. Her trainer. Her personal maid."

"What about her Nickels's money?"

"That's a different matter. That capital has been in a trust since 1965. She never touched even the interest or the dividends."

"So, it's a lot."

"Her father got five hundred million. She had no siblings. What do you think?"

"So, who does it go to?"

"Per the terms of Henry Minner's will, the one that was fought over for fifty years, his money can only go to his biological descendants."

"So? What am I missing?" I downed the third piece of bread, or was it the fourth? Talking with my mouth full, discussing money, and eating bread with butter. I knew I was horrifying Lily. But she kept talking.

"Honey's cousins, Sarah's children—all adopted. Honey had no children. Neither did her cousin Henry. Two Nickels were killed in a small plane crash without ever having any children." Lily stopped the rundown of the Nickels lack of offspring to sip her wine.

"Sarah's children will break the will."

"Fifty years." Lily smiled into my eyes.

"It was actually forty-seven years that the estate was tied up in legal battles. But I get your point. No one will try again to break the entailment." I forced myself to slow down on the bread. "Not to mention that Sarah's children have all that Mein money." Poor things.

Lily nodded her agreement.

"Okay, there are no Nickels left." I decided not to mention my family's connection to Henry Minner. "But there are plenty of Cowles."

"No Nickels estate plan would ever allow Nickels's money to pass to a Cowles."

"So, a museum will end up with it." I picked up the cosmo meant for Lily. Hell with it. I had to take an Uber home anyway.

"Henry Minner had no desire to compete with the Spreckels and de Youngs in what he called 'the great bullshit Museum war'. His money cannot be given to a museum." Lily sipped the sauvignon blanc.

"So—bottom-line here is, Honey had no known heir. And therefore no one would be thus motivated to kill her." I gulped the red stuff.

"I think so." Lily stared at the salad that had been placed in front of her.

"What do you mean, you think so? Aunt Lil?" I reached

across the narrow table.

"Honey had some wild idea that at least one possible heir existed, but she refused to say who it was."

Chapter 25

The next morning, I woke up with the flu. Or I'd eaten some really bad food. My head throbbed, my stomach lurched, and my mouth had this strange greasy feel. Then I remembered the night before.

I couldn't get any more info out of Lily. I ate the damn oysters, but since I washed them down with cosmos, they did nothing to alleviate the amount of alcohol I had consumed. In the light of day, the grease-versus-alcohol theory wasn't holding up.

I was planning to take a taxi or Uber out to Seacliff, but when we came out of the grill—I thought I saw a black BMW sedan parked across the street.

Instead of my planned escape from Lily, I allowed myself to be ushered into Lily's car and her driver brought me home. All the way to the house I was lectured about my drinking, my eating, my lack of a car and driver, my sloppy appearance—the wrinkled jacket I had jammed in my bag, and on and on. Even hours later Lily's rebuking voice, "Cissy, what would your mother think?" reverberated through my damaged brain.

The promise of coffee lifted me out of bed. The aroma of a powerful brew wafted up the stairs. In spite of the blinding pounding inside my head, I'd made it as far as the top of the stairs when I heard my father's voice in the study. Shit. Another lecture.

"Cissy. Where the hell is your car?" My father came out of the study and watched me fumble my way down the stairs. "Are you okay? What is going on with you?" He walked over and helped me down the final two steps. "Are you sick?"

"Honestly, Dad, I've got a doozey of a hangover."

He chuckled. "It's finally getting to you, huh?"

"What?" I shoved the hair back from my face, stood up straight and looked him in the eye. "What do you mean?"

"Sweetheart, you've had one hell of a year. I've been wondering when it was going to hit you." He gently placed his arm around my waist and guided me into the kitchen.

He sat me down in the window seat behind the breakfast table. I glanced at the window. A typical March morning, the bright sun mirrored off the ocean and struck me painfully right in the eyes. I placed my hand on my forehead to shield away the intense light and turned toward the dark room.

"Here." Dad handed me a glass of what I thought was tomato juice until I tasted it. A bloody Mary.

"Dad, I can't drink today. I've got so much to do."

"Just a hair off the dog that bit you. You'll be fine. Drink up."

I dutifully downed the fiery liquid. I did immediately

feel better. Was I turning into an alcoholic?

Next, he handed me a latte. He filled a mug with coffee for himself and sat down across the table. My dad is still a very handsome man. Tall, still slender—three days a week at the gym supplemented by golf, tennis, and skiing—gentle blue eyes, a full head of white hair, and the most comforting smile. Even in my disheveled, uncomfortable, pain filled state, I returned that smile.

"Dad, I think I'm in big trouble." I'd already told him about Honey's body following me around and the shot fired into the cabin. Now I filled him in on the black BMW and what I had learned from Katherine and Lily. "Dad, have we ever officially divorced ourselves from the Minner estate?"

My father scowled and looked at me. "Cissy, my grandmother wanted nothing to do with any Minners, Nickels, or Cowles. Not only did she resent the fact that no one in that family offered to help her when she desperately needed it, but she also felt that their constant battles were a terrible waste of one's life."

"Yeah, I know. A lot of years of litigation," I murmured between sips of the comforting warmth of the latte.

"Not only the forty-seven years of legal battles. Those years were preceded by many years of fighting among themselves—even trying to kill each other. A lot of shots fired, attempted murders—nasty business."

"Yes, I know all that. But what—"

"Nana was a very wise woman. She believed that self confidence, a belief in the ability to take care of one's self was far more valuable than any fortune." My father paused and sipped his coffee. "She did not want to see her children, or her grandchildren, or her great grandchildren spend their lives fighting with their own over money. Family is far too important."

"Dad, I understand that philosophically we have detached from the battles, but what if we are the only biological heirs on the Nickels side?"

"Cissy, we are not N-I-C-K-E-L-S. We are N-I-C-H-O-L-S."

A word game. What's in a name? I drank my latte.

Five hundred million. Could be that much. I could get my life back with that. Maybe I could get my husband to come home.

But it was my father and his sister who would inherit, and they wouldn't go against the orders of the Nana they both worshipped. I wished again that I had known her. I've been told I'm like her, but I couldn't imagine myself turning my back on that kind of money.

"My car is parked at Lake Merritt." I sipped the latte. "Or maybe AAA delivered it to the Toyota dealer on Van Ness."

"You hope it is. Oakland? Not the best place to abandon your car. I'll send Sandy's drivers for it."

"I could get it. You could drop me off there . . . or drop me at the BART station."

"Are you out of your mind?" Dad shook his head. "Have you forgotten the men who followed you yesterday?"

"If they wanted to shoot me, I gave them the perfect opportunity yesterday."

He shook his head again. He walked over and refilled his mug. He sat down across from me, touched my chin with his finger to direct my gaze into his eyes. "Cissy, this is foolhardy behavior. If you have no fear for yourself—think of your children. Don't play reckless with their futures. They still need you."

"I'm sorry Dad. It's just . . . it doesn't seem possible that I'm really in danger. I can take care of myself. I lost 'em yesterday." I rubbed my forehead. "Speaking of my children—where's Emma?"

"She's walking on the beach."

"Is that safe?" I didn't mention my stroll on the beach the day before.

"I've asked the security guys here to be extra alert to anyone they don't know. They've put on an extra man for each shift. The extra man is concentrating on this house."

"What's that costing?"

"Cissy, you've got to stop worrying about money. I don't care what its costing if it'll keep my girls safe."

"I'm sorry Dad. I'm sorry to be such a pain. I've caused you so much trouble lately."

My father reached across the table and took my hand. "Sweetheart. You are my only child. There is nothing in this world that means more to me than you and your children. I don't have anything better to spend my money on. And I won't be able to spend what I've got before I die, so you have to stop fretting over money and just let me help you."

I returned the hand squeeze and tried to smile. I couldn't

hide the tears running down my face. "Excuse me. I have to find a tissue." I stood and walked toward the powder room.

"Do you want to come down to Sandy's?" Dad called down the hall.

"No thanks. Poppy's wedding is next week, and Emma and I will both be involved in that here in the City." I remembered the tall wall around Sandy's estate and the two security gates one had to go through to enter the property. A revision of my plans to avoid any danger might be wise. "On the other hand, I did want to see what Muffy can tell me about Honey. She lives pretty close to Sandy, doesn't she?"

"Not too far. When were you going to see her?"

"I have to call her. Not today."

Dad came to the door outside the powder room. "I need to go if I want to avoid traffic on the 280. I have a meeting tomorrow afternoon here in the City. How about coming back to Hillsborough with me after that? You and Emma can spend the night and then see Muffy the next day. I'll have your car waiting for you there."

Minus a car for two days. As if reading my thoughts Dad said, "You don't need a car here. Maria will pick up anything you need."

"Dad, Cameron made a crack yesterday about Jamie not taking his business advice. Do you know—"

"Sweetheart, Cameron has no business giving anyone business advice."

"What do you mean?"

"Rumor has it . . . look, he's no genius. He's having to

do some liquidating himself trying to settle a couple suits against his company before the media gets the story and he's faced with a class action suit."

A quick hug and he walked out to the garage.

How was I going to find any answers without leaving here? If only the pounding in my head would stop. I needed to think straight. Who could tell me who Honey thought was her heir? Marty. I could call Marty. But first, maybe a nap would help my head.

Chapter 26

"Mom, are you okay?"

I looked out of my cocoon of comforter and pillows. My daughter was standing by the bed looking at me with worry plain on her face.

"Just a little hungover."

I was embarrassed to admit it. But a nap helped. I thought maybe I could eat something. I threw back the covers and reached for my robe.

"Come down to the kitchen, and I'll fill you in on what happened yesterday."

"Where's your car?"

I explained. I explained everything until Emma was completely up-to-date on my activities and information.

"What now?" Emma asked.

"I'm going to call Marty. Then I'll make a list of everyone I know who might have some clue about the unknown heir."

"Do you think it might be you? Is that what she wanted to talk to you about?"

"I wondered about that, but it doesn't make sense.

Grandpa and Aunt Tootie would be heirs, not me."

Escaping the bright sunny kitchen, I carried a bowl of yogurt, granola, and fruit into the dark relief of my father's study and found the number for Marty's private line in Dad's brown leather Rolodex.

"This is Cissy Huntington calling for Mr. Chaffin."

"Mr. Chaffin isn't taking calls, Madame."

"Please tell him it's me. He might be willing to talk to me."

"Please hold."

I was exposed to some horrible elevator music while I waited for Marty to pick up.

"Mr. Chaffin will have to get back to you. May I please have a number?"

Damn. I left the Seacliff number and my cell number.

The phone rang almost as soon as I replaced it in the cradle. Oh God, it was so loud.

"Hello."

"Hello, Cissy. So glad that you and Emma are in town this week. There are so many parties in addition to the shower and spinster party that Emma was to come up for next week. Poppy is thrilled."

Poppy's mother didn't even bother to identify herself. I wasn't thrilled—I had hoped it was Marty. And Poppy's mother, Joan was not on my list of possible sources of info.

"Hello, Joan. How are the wedding preparations coming along?"

"All under control. Cecilia's wedding planners are fab. And of course, Philip, as he usually does, takes care of everything."

Joan was referring to her butler Philip who was known for his attention to every detail of the Wells's family life.

"All I have to do is enjoy," she said.

I doubted the truth of that statement. I knew Joan well enough to be certain that she would have her thumb on every aspect of the wedding and the festivities leading up to it. But I let her white lie slide and listened.

"Speaking of enjoy, will you and Emma join us for lunch at the Mural room tomorrow?"

I knew Emma would want to do this and maybe there would be info sources in the room for me. I agreed to a one o'clock date.

The phone rang again. I wondered how to turn that damn ringer down.

"Mr. Chaffin for Cissy Huntington."

"This is Cissy."

"Cissy, thank you for calling. It means a lot."

"I am very sorry for your loss."

"And I'm sorry you had to experience such a dreadful shock. I'm doing everythin' I can to keep the sensational details and your name out of the papers. Honey taught me that a lady such as she was, or you are, never wants her name attached to a sensational media blitz.

"I appreciate that, Marty." I paused. "Look, I know this is a bad time for you, but I was hoping you would be willing to answer some questions for me. But if it's too difficult, please stop me."

I didn't wait for him to answer, didn't want to give him

a chance to say no.

"Honey was trying to tell me something just before she died. It's been driving me crazy trying to figure out what it could have been. Do you have any idea?"

"Hmm," Marty paused momentarily, "Far as I can recall, I never heard her mention you. When I got together with your Dad, she never said a word about knowin' him, or you. Did you know each other?"

I didn't know how to answer his question, so I ignored it.

"I've heard that Honey thought there was an unknown Nickels heir." I held my breath while I waited for his response.

"Yeah, she was goin' on about that. Seemed like craziness talkin'. Mean, how could that be? But once she got that bee in her bonnet she wouldn't give it up. Even hired a PI."

I took a Wild Ass Guess. "Mr. Pelancono?" I picked up the pen on Dad's desk and wrote Pelancono on the note pad.

"How'd ya know that?"

"Just a WAG. What did he find out?" I underlined Pelancono on the paper.

"She didn't exactly tell me. Something about how he proved she was right. That's all I know."

"So, who were her heirs?" I held my breath waiting to see how he would answer.

"Just some small bequests here and there. Not much Randolph money left."

"And the Nickels's money?"

"I suppose it will revert back to the trust. She never touched it anyway. We didn't need that money." Marty hesitated. "Was nice to know it was there, though. I mean it probably made me braver over the last couple decades. More adventuresome in the projects I picked. But hey, it all worked out. I made killin's every time, didn't I?"

"You certainly did."

We shared a soft laugh as I doodled dollar signs on my father's note pad.

"Yeah. It's been quite a life. I'm sure gonna miss that old dame."

"Again, I'm truly sorry for your loss."

"Yeah, yeah."

"Marty, when will her will be read?"

"Well, as you know, there were some complications with the autopsy. I'm hoping we'll be able to have a service this week. Startin' to plan for Saturday. I think it's a nice touch to read the will—especially given the bequests— right after the service while everyone is gathered together."

"Will you please let me know if there is anything unexpected about the will?"

"Sure will. Guess that means you won't be here?"

"Oh. No. I don't think that would be appropriate. I mean, we barely knew each other. And I'm in San Francisco. And besides, my presence might cause more gossip."

"Yeah, that's right."

"Thank you for returning my call, Marty. Even though Dad and I can't be there on Saturday, our thoughts will be with you. Bye."

I wondered if Mr. Pelancono would tell me anything about what he had done for Honey. One way to find out. I pulled out my cell and gave him a call.

"Mrs. Huntington. I don't have anything new to report. I'll call you soon as I do."

"Actually, Mr. Pelancono, I . . . . Can you please tell me about the work you were doing for Honey Chaffin?"

"Now, Mrs. Huntington, you know I can't talk about another client's investigation."

"You know, of course, that she's dead."

"Doesn't change a thing."

"Does she owe you money?"

"As a matter of fact, there is a final bill outstanding, but I'm sure Marty's good for it."

"What if I paid you?"

"Well . . . I don't see how that would work."

His hesitation telegraphed his willingness to consider the possibility of selling me the info. I bet he thought he could collect from both Marty and me.

"What if I were to hire you to find out why Mrs. Chaffin hired you?"

Pelancono chuckled. "You aren't gonna give up are you. I just got some DNA tests results for her."

"Whose DNA?"

"Tell you what, I'll send you the bill, you pay it and I'll send you the results."

"Okay. email me the bill. I'll give you a credit card and send it back. Then you email or fax the results."

He chuckled again. "Fine, fax is probably more secure."

I swiveled the desk chair, looked at my father's old fax machine on the credenza, and read off the numbers.

I hung up, punched the air with my fist, and let out a yell. "Yes!"

Emma poked her head around the study doorframe. "What in the world, Mama?"

Chapter 27

The first fax took two hours to arrive. I signed it and returned it in under a minute, but the next fax did not arrive. I called Pelancono's office after an hour, but by then it was after six and I got a voicemail. There was nothing to do, but wait.

When I finally went to bed, I had a hell of a time getting to sleep. Honey's penetrating stare popped into my mind every time I closed my eyes. We had only distant familial ties. What was she trying to tell me?

Was it about a mutual friend? But if so, who?

Did it have to do with the parallel lines of our personal histories: the attending the same school? The same debut?

I couldn't turn off my thoughts. I imagined conversations with each person who might be able to give me some clue. The worst conversations I imagined were with people who refused to help me.

Of course, I overslept the next morning. And the damn fax had yet to arrive.

Emma woke me with a latte in her hand. "Mama, we

need to leave pretty soon. I know you're really tired, but I don't want to be late meeting Poppy." She handed me the latte.

"And, no, the fax hasn't shown up. I called the number on the fax you got yesterday, and the woman said it would be sent 'soon.' Whatever 'soon' means."

I downed the latte and rolled out of bed. I let the shower run on my head washing away the cobwebs. I got into my ladies-who-lunch Chanel suit, added the pearls, and slipped on Jimmy Choo sandals. Mural Room, here we come.

The Mural Room had been the scene of dances and society lunches at the St. Francis Hotel since 1908. One's social standing dictated at which table Ernest, the maître d'hôtel, seated "his ladies." The "best ladies," meaning the most socially prominent women, sat at tables along the center aisle. Those with less standing were relegated to Siberia along the outer edges of the room under the faux balconies held up by white and gold columns.

Ernest smiled at us warmly as Emma and I entered the room whose walls were painted with a trompe l'oeil Italian garden of cypress trees, latticework and statuary.

"Good day Mrs. Huntington, Miss Emma. So good to see you here again."

Emma greeted Ernest affectionately, like the old friend he was. Lunching here followed by a matinee at the Geary Theatre around the corner, or shopping around Union Square had been Emma's favorite treat as a little girl.

"You are lunching with Mrs. Cameron Wells, correct?"

Emma and I had arrived right on time, but Poppy and

Joan were already seated at the center table on the center aisle. I raised an eyebrow at Ernest who responded with, "It is Thursday, after all. And the Cameron Wells wedding will be . . . well, it seems that everyone is to attend."

After all, it was Thursday. Monday had been the fashionable day for lunch at the Mural Room since 1935. Presumably, had it been a Monday, the four of us would have been seated under the balconies in Siberia.

Slender and golden-haired, mother and daughter, Joan and Poppy stood to greet us with hugs and air kisses. Emma was to be an attendant at Poppy's wedding. As soon as we sat down, the girls chattered about their dresses and wondering if they still fit properly, since it had been some months since the last fitting. Poppy had been taking the pill in preparation for married life, and the prescription had done wonders for her bosom.

"We didn't have to worry about you filling up the cleavage in your dress," Emma said with a giggle. "You've got some to spare."

Poppy laughed too, but then grew serious. "Do you think it will be too . . . déclassé?"

I was certain that it was her father Cameron's influence that made Poppy concerned about cleavage. Cameron was such a hypocritical tight ass.

"We can have a bit more lace added at the décolletage," Joan assured the worried Poppy. "We'll take care of it this afternoon."

"Did Cameron mention that I ran into him at Katherine's a couple days ago?" I asked.

Joan gave me a quick, startled glance, and then studied the silverware at her place setting.

Poppy said, "Really. I thought Father was at the Lake."

"Would you ladies care to start with a cocktail?" asked the bent, white haired gentleman who had waited for a break in the flow of conversation to star our service.

"Definitely not for me, thank you." I thought back to how awful I felt yesterday . . . and how wasted the day had been. "I'll have the iced tea, please."

We ordered the signature chicken curry Waldorf salads, and in consideration of those tight-fitting gowns, had the bread removed from the table. A server poured iced tea for each of us.

Once the waiter was out of earshot, Joan said, "Cissy, I have a rather delicate matter to discuss with you. I'm sure I can rely on your discretion?" She looked at me questioningly for a second, but when I returned her gaze, she glanced down and smoothed the crisp white linen tablecloth with her long, slender fingers.

Alarmed, I wondered what was coming next. "Of course, you can." I replied.

"It's about the wedding. As I assume you know, I, of course, included Jack Trevor and his lovely wife, Nikki Howe, on the guest list."

I, in fact, had no idea who all was invited to this wedding. Even though Joan was sure it was all anybody who was anybody in California was talking or thinking about, I had somehow failed to miss out on all the gossip. I'd been a little preoccupied. I tried to think if Nikki had ever mentioned the wedding. Meanwhile, I nodded encouragingly.

Joan continued, "I know you and Nikki are friends," she hesitated, "and Jack is such a lovely man . . . ." She played with the compostable straw in her tea. "But it seems as though Jack will still be on location next week and unable to make it."

"That's too bad," I sympathized.

"So, here's my problem. Nikki RSVPed weeks ago that they would attend. Then when the movie thing . . . the shoot ran over schedule, she called Tuesday to say that she would bring Sally Abbey as her companion instead of Jack. I was at a loss what to say." Joan fiddled with her straw and avoided eye contact with me.

Aah, now I understood the sudden lunch invitation. But I didn't know what to say either. "Sally's lots of fun," I offered.

Joan raised an eyebrow at me, but gave no explanation for her concern. I knew what it was. Whereas Jack and Nikki were always the perfect gentleman and lady, and were from an acceptable background, Sally—wild, loud, unpredictable Sally—was another matter. And I figured that Cameron would never forgive Joan for allowing anyone to embarrass him.

"Joan, what would you have me do? Speak to Nikki?"

"Oh no, I wouldn't want to discourage Nikki from attending."

There is a certain cachet in having a number of well-behaved celebrities in attendance at a social function. But not ones who were liable to drink too much, or swear too loudly, or dance too suggestively—all of which we both knew Sally was capable of doing.

Joan looked at me imploringly. "Would you consider speaking to Sally?"

"And what? Ask her to tone it down? That could just make her worse."

"Would it work to ask her to change her mind about coming?"

"If she doesn't come, Nikki won't either."

Joan sighed. I could see her weighing the possibilities. "What do you think?" she asked.

"Joan, how many guests are you expecting?"

"About eight hundred."

"The odds are pretty good there will be a few drunks in that large of a crowd. Maybe she'll get lost in the crowd."

Joan looked me and faked a smile. A memory of a gossip magazine with a photo of Sally drunkenly slut-dancing splashed across the cover came to mind. We both knew that was an absurd statement.

"Let me think about it. I'll come up with something." I made a mental note to call Nikki and Sally on the cab ride home and invite them to stay with us next weekend. "I'll take care of it, even if I have to monitor her drinking myself."

Joan placed her hand on top of mine and smiled into my eyes. "Thank you very much."

As we dug into our salads, I changed the subject. Perhaps Joan had heard something about Honey's death

216

that would be useful.

"Are people here talking about Honey's death?" I ventured.

Joan turned pale and choked on her greens. Poppy spoke up. "Abso-freakin-lutely. Mother was really annoyed that so much time was spent discussing Honey's death, not to mention her life, at the shower my godmother gave me at Monday's lunch."

"What are they saying?"

"She was the original wild child. And that she had more money than God," Poppy said with relish. "I would have never dreamed either of those things. I mean, she seemed just like all of Gran's friends. You know: very well preserved, perfectly groomed and dressed. And she never paid all that much attention to me, so I was hella shocked when she sent me this necklace." Poppy opened the collar of her jacket revealing a beautiful double strand of pearls with a sapphire and diamond studded gold front clasp.

Now that was a revelation. "Wow!" Emma and I said in unison. "Beautiful, gorgeous."

"Did she say why?" I asked.

"Just a note that said she was looking forward to seeing me as a bride, and this was a family heirloom that she would have given her daughter to wear on her wedding day."

"Are you related to Honey?" I addressed my question to both Joan and Poppy.

Joan had some color and her voice back. "Well, San Francisco being such a interconnected society. Everyone is someone's cousin. Who knows?" Joan considered the question for a moment. "It's more likely on Poppy's father's side. The Nickels, Cowles, Meins and Wells are all intermarried." Joan was married to Cameron Wells.

"Joan, do you have any idea why Honey would give Poppy such an exquisite piece?"

Joan lowered her eyelids over her pale blue eyes and shook her head as she picked up the china teacup and lifted it to her lips. She studied and poked at her salad through the rest of the meal while the girls did most of the talking—and giggling. Poppy teased Emma about marrying Jeff. I squirmed while I waited to see if Emma would bring up her absent father, but the luncheon concluded without any further drama.

"Mama, do you mind going home alone? I want to go with Poppy to the dressmaker."

I didn't want to mention my fears for my daughter's safety in front of the Wells women, so I merely gave my daughter a look that she correctly interpreted.

"Mama, I'll be fine. Poppy has her bodyguard with her." Emma motioned to the hefty looking man standing just outside the door of the restaurant. "I'll come right back to the house right after."

As we stood to leave, Joan interceded, "Cissy, I'll send her back to Seacliff with my driver."

We reached the door and Joan motioned to the black town car parked just behind the taxi zone. The bodyguard walked alongside the vehicle as it glided to where we stood.

I air-kissed and hugged the three women good-bye. "See you soon."

The doorman opened the door to a cab and I slid into the back seat.

A quick wave and I began scrolling to Nikki's number while I told the cabbie the Seacliff address. "Hello darling. I hear that you and Sally are coming up for the Wells wedding."

"Yes, at least I planned to do so, but Joan sounded a bit hesitant when I spoke with her."

"Don't worry about that. She just has some concern about Sally's . . ." I struggled for the right word, "flamboyance."

Nikki chuckled.

"I told Joan not to worry. Between you and me, we can, you know?"

"Maybe." Nikki laughed.

"I would like for the two of you to stay with Emma and me at my father's house here in the City. But I have to warn you that being with me may have some danger." I went on to explain all of the dramatic events of the days since we last spoke.

"Wow. Exciting. Sally will love it. And me, too. We planned to come up on Thursday. We can do a little shopping on Friday. Does that work for you?"

"Great." I gave her the address. "Maybe by then this matter with Honey's death will be resolved and we won't have to worry about getting shot at."

"I guess that would be okay too." Nikki sounded disappointed at the prospect of missing out on the excitement. "Do you want us to come sooner and help out?"

"I don't know what I would have you do." I thought about it for a moment. "I'm not sure what I'm going to do next. I'm hoping that by the time I get back to the house the fax about the DNA will have arrived."

We said our goodbyes and I promised to call if I thought of something she could do to help.

For the remainder of the cab ride I pondered the facts I knew. I thought about Honey's gift of the necklace. Was Poppy—Penelope Olivia Priestly Wells, the unknown heir? How could that be?

Chapter 28

The fax had arrived. My hands shook with excitement as I tried to decipher what it meant. I slumped into the dark leather desk chair in disappointment. There were no names identifying any of the subjects, but, if I was reading the papers correctly, the documents definitely showed a genetic relationship between Honey and two other people. Two? What two?

I called Pelancono's office. "Who are the people whose DNA matches Mrs. Chaffin's?" I asked as soon as his secretary put him on the line.

"Don't know. She sent us hair samples labeled A and B. That's all." There was a click as he hung up the receiver.

If Poppy was one of Honey's relatives, how or when would Honey have gotten a sample of her DNA?

No mention had been made by Poppy or Joan of having seen Honey recently.

I called Emma.

"See if you can find out when Poppy last saw Honey without making a big deal out of it."

"Sure, Mom," Emma said. "Poppy, when did you last

see Honey?"

I could hear Poppy in the background. "Let's see, uhm, at Gran's funeral, I think. I have a vague recollection of having seen her someplace else since then, but I'm not sure. That's why this necklace shocked me so much. I mean, I barely knew the woman."

I sighed in frustration. "Get her to remember where else she saw her," I ordered Emma.

"Poppy, think, where was it that you saw her recently?"

"Oh, I don't know. I'd have to ask my mother."

"Come on, P. You can remember. What were you doing when you saw Honey?"

"I was trying on a hat. Must've been in Saks." Silence for several seconds. "I know! Mother and I were looking at coats in the January sales. And Mother started talking to this woman. Turned out it was Mrs. Chaffin. She, that is Mrs. Chaffin, asked me to try on a hat. She said something about she was considering buying it for a niece. Emma, what do you think? Is this too tight? Too much boob showing?"

Giggle. "Definitely add some lace."

"Emma, get her to tell you exactly what happened when she tried on the hat."

"Yes, Mother. So, P, what was this hat like?"

"What hat?"

"The one you tried on in Saks."

"Why do you care about the damn hat? Okay, it was this stupid, complicated thing with all kinds of feathers and shit hanging off it. I told her before I even tried it on that the

222

only reason someone my age would wear it would be to a costume party. Then my hair got all tangled in it. Really annoying."

Bingo. Hair tangled. Pulled out by the follicles. Perfect DNA sample. That's how Honey did it. Maybe she follow-ed them to Saks and waited for her opportunity.

"Thank you, sweetheart. That's what I needed. By the way, what is mtDNA?" I asked.

"Stands for mitochondrial. That's the DNA that's passed down in the maternal line. Oh."

"What?"

"Just a sec, Mama. P, I'll be right back."

I heard the muffled slam of the dressing room door. It took ten more seconds for Emma to speak.

"You only need a piece of hair, not necessarily the follicle to match mtDNA."

"That works doesn't it?" I asked. "So, a match in DNA that is beyond the immediate parents would have to be in the maternal ancestry? Any link between subjects would have to be from one's birth mother?"

"That's right, Mom. Whoever those pieces of hair be-longed to had a mother or a grandmother or a great grand-mother in common with Honey."

"So that means that Honey and the two other subjects shared a mother? Or, if the subjects are female, a grand-mother is possible?"

"So, it's that, or Honey was their mother. Gotta go. Joan's driver is downstairs."

I leaned back in the chair, rolled my shoulders, and tried

to make sense of the DNA data. If one were to theorize that Poppy was related to Honey . . . or, shit, maybe it was Joan that was related . . . then that mtDNA info eliminated the possibility of Poppy, or her mother, being the product of a Nickels male's out of bounds liaison. Would have to have been one of the Nickels women. But who? Eleanor, Joan's mother, was not related to Honey. They didn't have a grandmother in common.

I punched the speed dial button for my father.

"Dad, who could tell me Honey's Nickels family history?"

"Are you still on that? Maybe Muffy. I'll be there to pick you up a little earlier than I planned. My meetings are nearly complete."

"What time? I need to get Emma home."

"Where the hell is she?"

"With Poppy, trying on wedding gowns and dresses."

"Oh, for Christsake. You both should stay in secure places. Where exactly are they? I'll send my assistant for them."

"Joan's driver is already there to pick them up. I'll make sure they come directly here and we'll be ready to go when you arrive."

I called Emma and told her to have the driver bring her to Seacliff straight away.

While I waited for the two of them, I repacked our bags and thought about this DNA info. It seemed that Honey was either trying to find out if the other two subjects were related to her, or she was establishing proof of the biological relationship. She obtained hair samples from each of them and sent the samples to Pelancono for testing. Instinct, and the hat incident, told me that Poppy was one of the two subjects.

So, if Poppy was the unknown Nickels heir, whose child was she? Evidently not Joan's, or that would make Joan the heir. I tried to remember Joan's pregnancy. We had to have been pregnant at the same time. Poppy and Emma were born just weeks apart. We introduced them when Emma was two weeks old. Poppy was three weeks old. I remembered that occasion, but not Joan's pregnancy. Huh?

Joan announced her pregnancy at a luncheon. I had just learned I was pregnant too, but not far enough along to tell anyone other than my husband. In those days, we waited until we had passed the danger of miscarriage, past the third month, before making any public announcements.

What I didn't recall was seeing Joan showing.

I called Pelancono's office. "Who is the person whose DNA matches Mrs. Chaffin's?" I asked him as soon as his secretary put him on the line.

"I told you: don't know. She sent us a hair sample. That's all."

Chapter 29

"Sandy let Muffy know that you want to see her while you're here. She invited Muffy for drinks tonight, but Muffy said she would prefer that you came over to her place. She doesn't get out much these days," Dad explained as he pulled onto the 280 freeway. "She's in the older section of Atherton. Not too far from us."

"I've been there several times. With Mom." I remembered the columned colonial that resembled an oversized Tara.

"Grandpa, is Muffy related to us?" Emma asked from the backseat of Dad's Jaguar sedan.

"Good question. Somewhere along the line, it's possible, but not that I know of. Just long-term family friends. She was the younger sister of Annabelle, who was, before she died, a very close friend of your grandmother's."

I relaxed into the comfy, self-warming seat. "Dad, it turns out that Honey did find an heir, someone who was re-lated to her via her maternal line per the DNA report. I'm thinking it was Poppy Wells."

"Really. Her biological mother was a Nickels? How

could that be?" He glanced away from the road long enough to see if his daughter had completely lost it. "How in the world did you come to that conclusion?"

"Have you seen the pearl, sapphire and diamond necklace that Honey sent to Poppy?" I asked my father. "That's some amazing trousseau shower gift!"

"Yeah, Grandpa. It's freaking outrageous."

"As a matter of fact, I've heard about it. Nick Montgomery, Poppy's grandfather had it appraised for insurance purposes, as Poppy insists on wearing it every-where. That's why Nick hired that bodyguard."

"And?" I prompted.

"Rumor has it that it is first rate, magnificent stones, and an antique to boot."

"And?"

"A quarter of a million."

"Oh, my God!"

"Freaking cool!"

"So, do you think Honey would give such a gift to just anyone?" I asked my father. I also wondered why Poppy's grandfather and not her father arranged for the insurance and the bodyguard.

"Not just anyone. Remember that Poppy's grandmother, Joan's mother, was Honey's most loyal friend. Stood by her through all of her adventures even when others thought to cut Honey off. And Eleanor—" My father looked in his rearview mirror and directed the next to Emma. "Eleanor was Poppy's maternal grandmother," he explained. "She had such impeccable social standing that she got away with forcing Honey on the would-be snobs. They were very close."

"So, you think the generosity of the gift was Honey's way of standing in for Eleanor since Eleanor didn't live to see Poppy's wedding?" I asked.

"That's exactly what I think. And so does everyone else with whom I've discussed it." Dad checked his rearview mirror again.

"I suppose it's possible, but then who else could it be? Who does the second DNA belong to?"

"That's why I think you ought to speak with Muffy. She was close to both of those women. She might have some idea. We'll just swing by and pick up Sandy. I'll give you a minute to freshen up, and we'll head over there."

I thought over the plan while appreciating still another bright yellow clump of daffodils set in lush green grass on the roadside. "Don't you think Muffy might be more gossipy if I went over by myself?"

"You're probably right about that. But I don't like the idea of you going anywhere by yourself. Either I drive you, or Sandy's driver could, I suppose."

"Dad, don't you think some bad guys would be rather conspicuous driving around Atherton, or Hillsborough?"

"A black BMW? Would fit right in, wouldn't it? I'm driving you. I'll wait in the car if you prefer."

"Speaking of being obvious."

"Then George will drive you."

At Sandy's Shingle style mansion, black wrought iron gates stood open against the cream color brick pillars.

Sandy walked out the glossy black door onto the wide veranda as our tires crunched over the gravel of the circular drive.

Sandy leaned her blonde head in the car window. "Hello. Do you want to freshen up before we head over?"

"Darling, Cissy was thinking she ought to go to Muffy's by herself."

Sandy married my father barely a year after my mother died. My father felt that at his age he had no time to waste being lonely, and I agreed with him that a long mourning period was unnecessary after Mother's long illness. I felt very lucky that my father had gotten involved with some- one as lovely as Sandy, and there was no doubt that she hadn't married him with money in mind, as she had twice as much as he did.

Sandy and her previous husband had completed the renovations to this estate and moved in three months before her husband had died of a sudden heart attack.

That was two years before my mother died.

Sandy and Dad had known each other for decades, having moved in the same circles. She was ten years younger than my father, but having always taken excellent care of herself, she could have passed for even younger. She had no children of her own and was thrilled to finally have grandchildren. She tried her best to spoil my children and if love, affection, and generosity could actually spoil a child, the five years she had been grandmothering my children would have rotted them beyond belief.

Sandy's housekeeper and her assistant appeared as soon

as we exited the car and carried our bags inside. I walked through the grand entry hall where the cream and black color scheme continued in a curved black-railed staircase above traditional black and cream marble floor tiles set in alternate squares. I ducked into the tiny powder room below the stairs and applied the lipstick that was a requirement to arrive at the home of any of Mother's friends. To have arrived bare lipped, thus disrespectful, would have barred any possibility of gaining the info I sought.

George waited at the front door. He escorted me to the black town car, opened the door behind the driver's seat, and held it while I slid onto the cream leather seat.

It was a quick drive to Muffy's. Her butler must have been on alert as the dark green door opened just as I stepped onto the columned brick porch.

"Good evening, Ms. Cissy. Please follow me. Mrs. Lawrence is on the rear terrace."

The rear terrace was a conservatory filled to the glass ceiling with palms from the far reaches of the tropical world. Muffy stood up from a wrought iron chaise lounge and brushed her silver hair streaked with white, off her forehead.

"We'll talk in here, my dear."

She led me away from the echoes of the fountain off the metal and glass and into floral chintz-covered sitting room whose pink and green coordinated with her pink cashmere twin set and grey-green flannel slacks. Muffy eased herself onto a wooden chair with a needlepoint covered seat, and waved me into the chair opposite the tea table set with all the accouterments needed for martinis.

Muffy gave the shaker a quick jiggle and poured the clear liquid into the awaiting olive filled glasses. "You didn't drive, did you?" She handed a glass to me.

I shook my head and took the first sip. I was really glad I hadn't driven. That swallow went straight to my head.

"I thought if we were to have a good gossip, it would be a martooni occasion. My husband loved his martooni— drove my mother mad that he insisted on calling the drink martooni. Mother thought it terribly middle-class to nick-name one's drinks."

She stopped to sip from her icy glass. "So nice to have a guest for cocktails. Cheers." Muffy raised her glass to mine. After swallowing a good-sized sip, Muffy said, "Now, dear, you want to talk about Honey."

This was going to be easier than I thought, if I kept a clear enough head to ask the right questions. I was careful to take very small sips.

I gave Muffy a quick run down on the past week. I tried not to be too shocking, but I shouldn't have bothered. She seemed to enjoy the more dramatic, even gruesome events. She quizzed me with particular relish.

"So, you want to know who could be this mysterious heir?"

"Exactly."

"I wish I could say that Honey told me all about it, but no such luck. Have another?" Muffy poured the martini concoction into my half full glass without waiting for an answer.

"Do you have a guess?"

"Here's what I do know: Poppy was adopted. It was a private, quietly done matter, but a few of us did know about it."

"Adopted? Really?" I tried not to look too surprised. Poppy looked so much like Joan, and there had never been even a hint of adoption.

"You see Joan had one miscarriage after another. She had an operation that was supposed to correct whatever the hell it was that kept going wrong."

"Tipped uterus?"

"Maybe. I don't remember that part." Muffy stared at Annabelle's portrait over the fireplace as though her older sister would supply the answer.

She shook her head and continued. "She was barely three months pregnant and very excited. So excited that she started to tell everyone about the pregnancy, even though she wasn't past the danger point. Eleanor and Honey decided they needed to keep her quiet and off her feet so they took her to Eleanor's house at Tahoe. It was off-season and quiet there. But it didn't do any more good than the operation had done. At nearly five months, she miscarried for the fifth time. Needless to say, she was devastated." Muffy frowned and slowly shook her head. "And so was Eleanor."

"So, what happened then?"

"The story I heard was that Honey found some girl who was 'in trouble', and brought her to stay with the three women until her baby was born. The baby was Poppy. But

I can't imagine what Nickels she could possibly be the daughter of."

Muffy sipped her drink and stared into space.

"No, I really have no idea how that could've come about."

"What are the possibilities?"

"There were only two Nickels women of childbearing age at that time, both in college. One was studying abroad in Florence, one at Stanford. Sarah was at Stanford, and she couldn't have children. She adopted that crew she has."

"Who was the other one in college? I mean, 'studying abroad' sounds like a possible excuse for staying hidden at Eleanor's place on the Lake, doesn't it?'

"Well, yes, but that young lady, Cassandra and her brother were both killed in a small plane crash about twenty years ago." Muffy finished off the last of her drink and poured another. "I just can't think of who we could ask."

"How about Joan? Could I just ask her?"

Muffy held the silver shaker in her hand until she saw that my glass was still full. She set the container back down on the pink marble topped table. "You could try it, but I don't know if she'll tell you. You would have to find the right moment this particular week."

"Are you saying, 'be discreet?' "

"Exactly."

My cell phone rang. I looked at the caller's number. It was Emma. "Please excuse me. It's my daughter calling."

Into the phone I said, "Hi, sweetheart."

"Oh Mom, Poppy called. She was sobbing so hard I

couldn't really understand her, but I think that their butler has been arrested, and her mother has been taken in for questioning."

Chapter 30

I rushed back to Sandy's. With Emma on the library extension and me on the phone in the entry hall, we spoke to Poppy. But what she was telling us still made no sense.

"Philip has been with us all my life. I can't imagine he would do anything bad. He's always so correct." Poppy sniffled.

By the time you are my age you realize there's a big difference between correct and good, but at twenty-five, Poppy still thought that Philip was blameless.

"Poppy, tell me exactly what happened."

"When I got home from dropping off Emma, there were three strange cars—including a police car—in the drive."

I imagined the front of the palatial Wells mansion on Pacific Heights. Their lot was one of the few wide enough to have a circular drive.

"I was so scared. I thought maybe something awful had happened. And it had. But not like I thought. Philip was in handcuffs and being led out the front door. And as soon as Max walked in the back hall, he was arrested too."

"Your bodyguard?"

"Yes." Poppy sobbed.

"Then what?"

"The police put Philip and Max in a car and then started asking Mother if she would please come down to the station. I heard Mother say they could talk to her right there in the privacy of her own home, but shortly after I walked in the room, she seemed to change her mind. She stood up and said she would have her driver follow them back to the station."

"Poppy, where is your father?"

"I don't know . . . . Maybe at the Lake?"

"Has anyone called him?"

"Don't know. Should I?"

"Yes. And make sure he sends his lawyer over to the station to be with your mother."

"Okay. I'll call him."

"Call us back as soon as you've spoken to him." I hung up.

"Mom. What the hell is this all about?"

Sandy, Emma and my father all looked at me as though they thought I knew all the answers. Too bad I had no idea what was going on either.

"Sandy, is it alright if I invite Poppy down here? I hate to think of her all alone," I asked.

"Of course. Shall we send George for her?"

"Thanks, that's great. But I think she can drive down. Or Joan's driver can bring her. Unless he's waiting at the police station. When she calls back, I'll work it out with her."

"In the meantime, how about some dinner?" Sandy waved her hand towards the end of the hall.

The four of us walked into the sun porch that overlooked a magnificent, romantic garden. In the far corner, the square table for four had been set for dinner. We each took a seat in black Chippendale chairs cushioned with cream silk upholstery. We picked at the baby lettuce leaves and sipped Pinot Grigio.

My father broke the silence. "The butler did it?"

I shook my head. This development surprised the hell out of me. I had no idea what to say.

Emma's phone rang before I felt obliged to answer. Emma said hello and handed her cell to me. "Cissy, I called my father. He and his lawyer are on their way to the police station. What do I do now?"

"Get in your car and drive down to Sandy's. You know where?"

"My aunt has a house just down the road from Sandy's. But I want to do something to help my mother."

"Do you have something in mind?"

"Uhm, no," Poppy admitted.

"Come down here and we'll strategize." Poppy no longer sounded on the verge of hysteria. It didn't seem necessary to send a driver for her. "We'll expect you in an hour. Drive carefully."

I handed the phone back to Emma who took it to the opposite end of the porch and coaxed Poppy into her car. "Don't worry about clothes. You can wear mine. Nobody here cares if the boobs are tight."

While Emma spoke with Poppy, my father grilled me. "What is going on?"

"I wish I knew. It seems that I asked the very man who had been threatening us to watch over Emma."

"What?"

"This afternoon, I let Emma go off with Poppy. I thought that Cameron had hired a bodyguard for Poppy and thought Emma being with her . . . damn." I explained what Poppy had told me about the butler and her bodyguard being arrested and her mother being questioned.

"Philip has been with the Montgomery's for forty something—maybe fifty years." My father paused and appeared to study a row of English tea roses in the garden. "I remember him working at Joan's parents' when I was in my twenties. He was put in charge of Cameron and Joan's first house." Father looked puzzled. "He would never do anything to endanger that family."

"Maybe he thought he was protecting them," I mused. "Maybe it's all a mistake."

Chapter 31

We were still lingering over our coffee when Poppy arrived at the house. Sandy sat her down next to Emma and had dinner brought to her. We allowed her a few minutes to eat, but as soon as she set her fork down, Emma and I both quizzed her.

She froze like a deer in headlights, and I immediately regretted having said anything that reminded her of the events of the day. As she unsuccessfully fought back tears, I announced, "Okay, sweetheart. We won't discuss this tonight."

Actually, I doubted that Poppy had any idea what was going on in her household. I changed the subject to wedding plans, but that brought another flood of tears.

"Oh, Mother is going to be so unhappy. This is going to wreck all of her plans. She's worked so hard to make everything perfect. This is shit." Poppy daubed her eyes with her napkin, smearing black mascara onto the creamy white linen.

Emma hugged Poppy and frowned at me over Poppy's shoulder.

I mouthed, "I'm sorry." And resisted the urge to speak any further.

Emma and Poppy wandered into the garden. As soon as they closed the glass door, Sandy pounced on me. "What is this all about?"

"I'll tell you what I know so far, but I may have gotten this all wrong because I never dreamed that Joan had anything at all to do with this murder. I'm sure the reason that Joan agreed to go down to the station was because she didn't want Poppy to find out she was adopted. I imagine that Joan realizes she would have to tell her now, but overhearing the information while her mother's being questioned by police is not the best way to break the news."

Sandy and my father were staring at me in silence.

"Please excuse me. I've got to get a hold of Manny. Perhaps he can explain. What possible reason would Joan have to murder Honey?"

I walked over to the black wicker seating group in the far corner of the sun porch and speed dialed Manny's cell.

"Hi Cissy. What took you so long to call me?"

"What the hell? The butler?"

"Chill. Philip's confessed."

"To what?"

"He and the bodyguard poisoned Honey and then the bodyguard stuck her in a freezer when they panicked. He thought Honey was blackmailing Joan."

"Blackmailing Joan? That's ridiculous. Honey had more money than God. Why would she do something like that?"

"Don't know. But the butler claims he got rid of Honey.

240

He couldn't explain why he tried to scare you off, or why the body was frozen—a fact he pretended not to know. He vehemently denies it, but we're pretty sure he acted at Joan Wells's request."

"Joan! No." That made no sense. Why would Joan then turn around and invite me to lunch if she wanted me to butt out? Not to mention that Joan was so obsessed with orchestrating the perfect wedding, she would never dream of screwing it up with a murder.

"He slipped up. Admitted he has a note from Poppy's mother. We're on our way to his apartment to find it."

"Really! A handwritten note?"

"I'll let you know when we have it." He hung up before I could protest or explain how wrong he was about Joan.

Poppy's mother. Maybe Manny didn't know that Joan was not the only possible person who could be described as Poppy's mother. Who was the biological mother? Was she alive?

Chapter 32

The guestroom I occupied at Sandy's house couldn't have been more luxurious. Deliciously soft, smooth sheets over a pillow-topped mattress strewn with down pillows and duvet, cashmere throws, and heavy quilted wool curtains at the windows: everything was perfect. But all the luxury in the world wouldn't have helped me sleep that night.

Manny hadn't called back. Or answered my calls. Nor had we heard anything from Cameron or Joan.

Fortunately, Poppy had stopped sobbing. I even heard giggles coming down the hall from the suite Poppy and Emma occupied.

The two girls had been introduced as infants when Joan and I placed them next to each other on a bed at a birthday party for a one year old. Emma, who was seven days the younger, let out a shriek of delight at the sight of Poppy. Three-week-old Poppy immediately began to cry. Joan fortunately decided not to pick up Poppy to comfort her, but rather decided to see if she would realize she had nothing to fear from Emma. Poppy stopped crying after a minute or two and stared at Emma.

The two girls had celebrated their birthdays together every year with a day set aside for the two of them to do marathon movies, attending one showing after another and eating movie theatre food until they were sick. The summer they traveled in Europe together, they had continued the tradition with subtitled movies in Venice.

I was happy to hear their giggles, but it didn't stop me from tossing and turning, worrying about Joan and the wedding plans, and Poppy's future. Joan had a dinner party planned for Saturday night following the wedding rehearsal. And Sunday afternoon was a kitchen shower. And Monday at the Mural Room was the lingerie shower. On Thursday were both the spinster and bachelor parties. Friday night was a gathering including dinner for all the out of town guests. And the wedding was Saturday at two in Grace Cathedral followed by a reception at the Palace Hotel. What if Joan was in jail? Who would make it all happen?

The last time I checked, it was just after four in the morning. I awoke to the smell of coffee at nine. Somehow, someone had managed to leave a carafe of my favorite latte next to the bed. I hadn't heard a thing. Sandy has fantastic staff.

I poured the steaming hot liquid into the porcelain mug and enjoyed the first sip. Nothing in the world could be all that bad. What a grand way to start the day! I luxuriated in the latte and the comfort of the bed for a few minutes before I remembered the events of the previous evening. Shit.

I pulled on my robe and located my cell on a table in front of the fireplace. I hadn't missed any calls. I punched in Manny's number. My "What's happening?" was greeted by a grumbling groan. "Ooops, sorry I woke you up. It's after nine. What's up?"

"Not me." Manny groaned. "We searched the Wells's mansion until six this morning."

"Sorry," I repeated. "You're in San Francisco? So, what was the story with the note? Did it exist? Was it hand-written? Did you check the writing for authorship?"

"Whoa. Which question do you want answered first?"

"Come on."

"Okay, there was a note. It was a computer printout. It wasn't signed."

"But it said it was from Poppy's mother?"

"Hold on a sec. I'll tell you exactly what it said." The sound of rustling, presumably of clothing came through the phone. "Okay, I wrote it down. Here it is. 'I am very con-cerned about my daughter. Honey Chaffin is threatening to reveal information about my daughter's ancestry that will destroy our relationship and my daughter's future happi-ness. I know that you love her like a daughter. I pray that you will help me.' "

"That's all? Hey, she never said, 'Kill the bitch.' That note certainly wouldn't be the basis of suspecting Joan of anything, would it? Read it again."

Manny read it again. I had him repeat the few lines as I

244

wrote down what he said.

"Thank you for that. So what's happening now?"

"Mrs. Wells left the station with her husband and attorney late last night. We didn't have enough to hold her, but once we build a case—"

"You do realize that her daughter's wedding—to which eight hundred of who's who not only in San Francisco but in all of California are invited—is next week?"

"She should've thought of that before she hired her butler to kill people."

"That's just it. She wouldn't have done anything to jeopardize the success of this event. That's how I know that she didn't do this."

"Cissy, who else could've written the note?"

"Anyone could've—to frame her maybe? Or here's something else to consider . . . if I wrote this down correctly, the note doesn't actually say the daughter referred to is Poppy. And help doesn't mean murder. That butler knew Honey and Eleanor when they were young. Maybe someone thought he had some influence with Honey."

"Hmm." Manny was silent for a moment. "Well, we'll see. The butler's not talking. He got confused—Christ he's in his late eighties—clammed up when he realized he had said something that implicated Mrs. Wells. But I think the butler truly believes that Joan Wells asked him to get rid of Honey Chaffin."

"You could've jumped to the wrong conclusion. He is in good shape for his age, but . . . . Are you assuming the bodyguard did all the . . . ? Do you have any evidence besides Philip's statement that points to Joan being involved?"

Manny ignored my question, as I knew he probably would, and said, "I gotta get some sleep."

"I assume if you'd had evidence she would be in jail now?"

"Goodnight Cissy. We'll talk later."

"Wait! Wait—so does this mean that Emma and I are no longer in any danger? Did the butler and the bodyguard say why they shot at us?"

"No, he didn't say. Probably just to get you to butt out. Guess they don't know you very well, huh?'

"So we don't have to worry about our safety?"

"It seems not. Bye."

Manny broke the connection before I could ask him anything else.

I called Joan. I wanted to make sure she knew that Poppy was safe and with us in Hillsborough.

"Hello. Joan, it's Cissy."

"Hello. Thank you for having Poppy stay with you last night." The ice queen's tone was frostier than usual.

I didn't mention that I knew the police had been at Joan's house all night searching for evidence. "Just checking to make sure you knew that she's here."

"She left messages." Her tone said her daughter wouldn't make her worry. The social veneer was very thin that morning. "Is she awake yet?"

"I haven't heard anything from their suite this morning. Hopefully, they're sleeping in." I hesitated for a second.

"Poppy was very upset last night."

Joan sighed. "Oh, God. How did this happen? And right now—"

"Joan, let me help."

Silence.

"Joan. We love Poppy, too. And I know you had nothing to do with this murder."

"I wanted this week to be lovely—to be magical for her."

I was sure I heard a sob, was the ice cracking?

"Cissy, what am I going to do?"

"I don't know what we can do, but I'm going to do everything I can to help you . . . and to get to the bottom of this. When the girls wake up I will bring them to your house, okay?"

"Thank you." She was crying noisily.

Chapter 33

"Come on girls, I want to get into the City before the Friday traffic gets too bad." I motioned to Poppy and Emma. I kissed Sandy and my father good-bye. "Thank you for your hospitality, Sandy."

"We loved having you. I was hoping it would be for longer." Sandy hugged Emma to her side and we all walked toward Poppy's car in the drive.

"Dad, I hope you don't mind, but I've asked Nikki Howe and Sally Abbey to stay at your house in the City next weekend. They're coming up for Poppy's wedding."

"No problem. Sandy and I were just planning to come up for the day, anyway. We have a golf tournament starting the next morning."

The two girls and I got in the car, Taylor Swift's latest CD was turned up full blast, and Poppy drove out the gates and onto the winding road that led onto the 280 freeway. Both girls were uncharacteristically quiet. Perhaps because one would have to yell to be heard over the music. I settled into my back seat and enjoyed the views of green rolling hills scattered with architectural wonders lit by sunny skies.

In the distance, a heavy mass of gray fog loomed over the City.

At the Pacific Heights mansion, we found Joan's mood matched the gloom. Even Poppy's tearful but enthusiastic hugs seemed to do little to brighten her frame of mind. Nor did a cheerful blaze burning in the fireplace set between two plush window seats with unobstructed views of the bay and all three bridges.

Despite the lack of the butler who had kept the household running smoothly, the staff seemed to be coping well. A scrumptious tea had been laid out on the table between the sofas and the fire.

As we sunk into the down-filled cushions, I asked Joan if she would like to have time alone with Poppy before we spoke.

"Why?"

I widened my eyes and looked at her meaningfully.

"Poppy, please take Emma to your room. Show her your trousseau." The frosty tone was back.

Joan and I both concentrated on our tea as we waited for the girls to pick up their teacups, and walk to the top of the stairs and into Poppy's rooms.

I heard the door slam.

"Joan, you're going to have to tell Poppy."

"Tell her what?" The veneer of ice had refrozen.

I shook my head and frowned at her. "That she's adopted," I whispered.

Joan stared at me in silence for two full minutes.

My affection for her grew. I realized for the first time in

all the decades that we'd known each other that her cold manner was a mechanism for hiding a vulnerable heart.

I finally spoke, "Look, it's bound to come out. You don't want her to read it in some headline, do you?"

Joan continued to stare for a few more seconds, and then she burst into tears. "Oh, Cissy. What am I going to do? My mother and Honey were the only ones who knew. Not even Cameron. We were a bit estranged at the time. He was told that Poppy was born prematurely while I was with Mother and Honey at the Lake."

The idea that someone could actually keep such a huge secret from one's husband startled me into momentary silence. "Whew. Hmm. Well, you'll feel better when you've come clean."

Joan sat up straight. "But I didn't have anything to do with Honey's murder."

"No, I mean about Poppy. Who was her mother?"

"Honey's cousin Henry's daughter, Cassandra."

"Please explain."

I was pretty sure I knew what happened next, but I waited to hear Joan say it.

"Cassandra was ostensibly studying in Florence that year. Cassandra was in Florence when Honey stopped by to visit her. Honey called Cassandra from her hotel and left message after message for her without hearing back. Honey even stopped by the pensione where Cassandra was supposedly living. She couldn't find her." Joan stopped to blow her nose. Tears were free flowing from her pale blue eyes.

"I'm guessing she didn't give up?" I used the dainty porcelain teacup to warm my hands.

"The Helvetia Hotel was lovely and more than comfortable so Honey stayed a few more days. Then one night, Honey was enjoying her after dinner gelato and the street musicians in the galleria of the Uffizi when she spotted Cassandra in the crowd. And she saw why she hadn't heard back from Cassie. She was visibly pregnant—nearly seven months along. Honey caught up to her and insisted that Cassie explain."

"She didn't want the baby?"

"Cassie hadn't decided what to do at that point. She was living in an apartment owned by the child's father, but she had finally realized that he wasn't going to divorce his wife."

"I guess she didn't know much about Italian men." I sipped the tea from the delicate cup.

"No. Definitely not. And she had just learned the apartment that she had once found to be so charming had been occupied by a long string of mistresses for generations. Honey didn't have too much trouble talking Cass into returning to California and joining my mother and me at the Lake."

"And then?" I was pretty sure I knew what happened next, but I waited to hear Joan say it.

"They had been with us for almost three weeks when I miscarried. The four of us, then the five of us, stayed in the houses there for another seven weeks. In fact, I had just returned to the City the day before I placed Poppy on the

251

bed next to Emma."

"So, Poppy's father is some unknown Florentine?"

"I know who he is—or at least I have the information somewhere—but I don't think he knows anything. Unless Cassandra told him before she died."

"Could he possibly be behind this?"

Joan shrugged. "What possible gain would there be in it for him?"

"I don't know." I considered the possibilities. "I guess none. Unless he has some reason that he doesn't want it known he has a daughter. Do you think that's possible?"

Joan shook her head.

"Yeah." I thought about how casual Europeans are about parentage and marriage. "Doesn't seem likely, does it?"

Joan was busy wiping her eyes and nose.

"Do you think Cassandra told anyone else?"

"Probably her brother. They were close, but he died in the same plane crash."

"There must be someone. Honey, Eleanor, Cassandra—all dead. The Florentine father—no motive. What about your father?"

"Oh, please. What motive could he have?"

"But he does know?"

"Yes, Mother never kept anything from him."

Funny, Joan didn't follow her mother's example. "Could he have told someone else?"

"It's possible. But why would he?"

Good question. My chance to quiz Joan ended when Emma and Poppy returned.

"Mom, you should see Poppy's beautiful clothes, her trousseau." Emma plopped on the seat next to me and pounced on the scones and jam.

"I'd love to, but now I think we should head for Seacliff. Poppy and Joan have lots to talk about." I fixed my eyes on Joan's face until she acknowledged me with a slight nod.

"My driver will take you. Thank you for taking Poppy in."

The four of us exchanged hugs. "See you tomorrow," Poppy reminded Emma.

Chapter 34

"Sweet. Mom, we've an evening to spend together. Want to go to the movies?"

"I'm kinda tired sweetheart. I didn't sleep too much last night. When are you picking Jeff up at the airport?"

"Not until tomorrow morning. He had some work stuff and might not even make it then. Shall we pick up some Thai and watch DVDs in front of the fire?

Given the heavy mist, a cozy evening in sounded good to me. Joan's driver dropped us at the car dealer. We arrived just in time to collect the Prius. The receptionist in the service department was closing her window when I stopped her. "Do you know what was the matter with my car?"

"Something tampered with in the electrical system. Disconnected is what I heard."

"Could it have fallen off?" I asked.

"Not that I know of."

"May I speak with the mechanic?"

"If you call on Monday. They've all left for the day."

I plunked down my credit card and collected my receipt

and keys. The car was parked just outside the service area. We climbed in and headed to our favorite Thai place, six short blocks from my father's house. I called ahead for our usual curry and satay chicken while Emma drove.

The loading zone in front of the restaurant was full, so Emma dropped me off to grab the food while she circled the block. The food wasn't quite ready. I waited just inside the entrance and studied the colorful effect of the heavy mist on the lights of the traffic and the neon signs.

Emma circled several times. Something like the third, maybe fourth time she went by, I noticed the black BMW following her. Damn. I pulled out my phone and called Manny.

"There's still someone following us," I said without preamble. "A black BMW, just like before."

"Where are you?" Manny groaned.

I explained and gave him directions to my father's house. I had just hung up when the waiter handed me the white bag full of food.

I watched for Emma, then rushed through the damp to hop in the car. "There's someone following you."

"I thought so. Black BMW, right?" Emma checked the rearview mirror. "What do I do?"

"Head for the house. Manny's on his way. Is the garage opener in this car?"

"Yeah. In the console."

"Good." I held the opener in one hand and pulled my phone out of my coat pocket. Thank God I had thought to put Seacliff security on my speed dial. "This is Cissy

Huntington. My daughter and I are about to arrive at my father's house and there's a black BMW following us, potentially a threat."

"An officer will be waiting for you in front of the garage. Pull right in and he'll deal with the BMW."

Not one but two security officers were standing at alert when we pulled into the drive: one at the front door, one next to the garage door. But there had been no car lights behind us once we had passed between the white stucco pillars marking the entrance to the Seacliff neighborhood.

I waved at the officers. Emma and I exited the car in the garage and ran up the interior stairs to the kitchen. The security officers were both at the front door by the time we got to the first floor. I let them in, and they searched the house for intruders. Emma and I waited in the family room adjoining the kitchen.

Ten minutes later the two men reported, "No sign of anyone, ma'am."

"Thank you." I wondered if I should explain, but what was there to say.

My debate with myself was interrupted by the doorbell. Both men jumped to alert. "Don't worry. That should be a police detective friend of mine."

All four of us walked to the entry hall, but one of the security guards insisted that he open the door.

Chapter 35

Manny chuckled with obvious relief. "You two look pretty safe. You scared the hell out of me."

I looked out the door and saw a squad of police cars, lights flashing and parked in a chain of diagonals six cars long, filling the street in front of the house.

Emma greeted Manny with an enthusiastic hug. "So good to see you. Please come in."

"Where's the black BMW?"

Emma and I both shrugged.

"License plate?"

I shook my head. "It was dark, foggy and I couldn't see it from where I stood. I may have just panicked, but Emma was driving around the block while I picked up the food. And a black BMW—same model as the one that followed me a couple days ago—was two cars behind her every time I saw her go by."

Emma continued to hold onto Manny's arm. "Please stay."

"Give me a minute with the guys." Manny nodded towards the cars out front.

He and the two security guards headed to the street. Several of the police officers gathered around Manny and the guards. Lots of nodding, glances toward the house, kicking and spitting, and then everyone but Manny went back to their car, turned off the flashing lights and drove away.

Manny pulled his car to the curb and walked back into the entry hall. "What kind of food did you pick up?" He grinned. "It smells good."

Emma returned his smile. "Thai. Do you like it? We got plenty."

The three of us walked to the back of the house to the breakfast nook in the family room. I lit the gas fire and hit one light switch that turned on several soft lamps designed to add a glow to the room without distracting from the view of the bay and the bridge. In the deep fog, the lights on the bridge gave an eerie glow that made the room feel even cozier.

Emma unpacked the bag of curry, rice, sate' chicken, and peanut sauce on the round, wood-planked breakfast table. While she placed plates and flatware in three place settings, I got chilled mugs and bottles of IPA from the refrigerator. Manny stood in the bay window and admired the view.

Once everything was in place, Emma and I sat down and invited Manny to take the seat that allowed him the panorama of the misty scene. We piled our plates and each took several bites before we said anything other than have-some and please-pass-the.

Manny took a gulp of ale to wash down the spicy curry and leaned back in his chair. "So, what's the story, ladies?"

"I wish I knew," I said. "I thought we didn't have anything to worry about now that the butler and the bodyguard have confessed, but it sure looked like the same car."

"We need to get the plate number."

"Hey, believe me, I'd like to get it," I protested. "Are we sure the butler did it?"

Manny shrugged. "He confessed. But we may have to let the bodyguard go. No evidence. And he didn't confess."

"So, who's following me?" I asked.

"Maybe they don't have evil intentions." Manny looked at me. "Any chance someone hired them to look out for you?"

"I asked my father. He only asked the Seacliff security to watch us while we're here."

Manny shook his head. "The view from here is killer isn't it? Like to see it in the day."

"Hey, why don't you stay here with us? Where are you staying anyway?" Emma asked.

"Some dump hotel near the Tenderloin," Manny said. "This city is tough on my expense account."

"You could stay here," I offered. "There's room. I'd sure feel safer with you in the house."

"I'll stay tonight," Manny agreed. "But now that the killer is in jail, I have to go back to LA."

"But what about who hired them?" I was sure we hadn't resolved Honey's murder yet. "And what about getting evidence against the bodyguard?"

"That's not really BevHills PD's problem. The DA's office and the SFPD can handle that."

"Aren't you curious?" Emma asked.

"The mother seems a good bet." Manny rubbed the frost off his beer mug.

"It's not Joan," I said.

Manny raised an eyebrow at me.

"I talked with her today. I'm sure she didn't have anything to do with this. And she's not actually Poppy's mother."

"Mom?" Emma looked at me in astonishment.

I explained the story of Poppy's origins to both Emma and Manny.

"Wow. How cool. Poppy's Italian." Emma slapped the tabletop. "Does she know?"

"That's what I wanted Joan to tell her about this afternoon."

"That doesn't change much. Joan's still the only mother who's still alive," Manny said.

"It doesn't have to be a mother," I said. A father could have written that note. Could be Joan's father. Could be Poppy's father."

"Why?" Manny asked before taking a drink of his beer.

"I don't know . . . yet." I tried to think of who else I could ask for information. I decided to call Joan's father in the morning. As soon as I had some sleep. Maybe he had a clue, and he certainly would want to aid in any effort to clear his daughter's name.

Chapter 36

"Mr. Montgomery, this is Cissy Huntington. Sir, may I see you sometime today?"

"Cissy, I'd love to see your charming face, but I've got a rather full schedule."

On a Saturday. At his age. Full of what, I wondered. Golf game, tennis, doctor's appointment? "Mr. Montgomery, it's about Joan and Poppy, and Honey Chaffin's murder."

"Young lady, I can assure you I know absolutely nothing about that."

"I'm sure you don't know about the murder, but I think you may be able to shed some light that might help clear Joan of the suspicion she's under. This would be a terrible time for her to be arrested. I'm sure you agree."

"Do you play golf? Don't remember seeing you on the greens."

"Sure," I lied. "Where are you playing?" I asked hoping I would be lucky enough that he would be playing the course at land's end. That was within walking distance of Seacliff.

"La Rinconada."

Jeez, way down in Los Gatos. "May I join you?"

"As it happens we've just lost Judge Blair. Some stupid papers that had to be looked at immediately." The exasperation in his voice said that Judge Blair had his priorities screwed on backwards. "Care to make it a foursome?"

"I'd love to. What time are you teeing off?" At least I knew the lingo. Never mind that the golf pro had asked my father not to bring me for any more lessons halfway through the series of twenty Dad had paid for in my teenage years. I'd been on various courses with Jamie. I knew the etiquette. I could hit the ball. It was just a bit unpredictable as to which way the damn thing would go after that.

"Ten o'clock."

Shit. Could I make it down there by then? "It's a date. Are the renovations to the clubhouse completed?"

"The place is looking beautiful. Meet you at the 19th hole for a little warm up shot." Montgomery chuckled at his cleverness.

I forced a polite giggle and hung up.

I made a dash for the shower and tried to think what I could wear while I lathered up. I thought there might be a pair of Mom's golf shoes on a shelf in the garage. Let's see, if there's not I could call ahead to the pro shop and have a pair waiting for me to pick up at the club. Club! Shit, what was I going to do for clubs? What was I thinking? I suddenly realized what I had to do.

I wrapped myself in a towel and called Sandy. "Sorry to bother you so early on a Saturday morning, but I need some help. Could I possible stop at your house for some golf gear?" I explained my predicament.

Sandy must have heard the stories of my golfing antics because she immediately burst out laughing. "I'll have everything ready for you." She continued to laugh.

"Emma," I yelled as I past her door. "I'm going to play a round of golf with Poppy's grandfather."

"You're what?" From the sound of her voice, Emma was half asleep, but she was already laughing. "Hey, don't forget the kitchen shower. It's at four."

"We're playing at ten. I'll easily be back in time."

"Mom, it takes awhile to accumulate a couple hundred strokes." Emma laughed uproariously.

I grabbed a banana, poured a cup of tea into a travel mug and jumped in the car.

The City was quiet early on a Saturday morning. The streets were deserted. I was able to make good time down to Sandy's.

A set of clubs and pink shoes were on the front porch when I pulled into the driveway. Sandy opened the door and pulled me inside. "You can't wear black denim on a golf course."

"Still?"

She shoved some clothes into my arms and pushed me into the powder room. Pink culottes? Where the hell do you even buy such things these days? Pale pink polo shirt with the ubiquitous horse on the chest. TSE pink cashmere cardigan. Pink visor. Pale pink anklet socks. Pink driving moccasins. I threw it all on.

As I exited the powder room, Sandy handed me a pair of pink-framed sunglasses with rose-colored lenses. At least the course would look good.

The clubs and shoes were loaded into my car. I gave Sandy a quick hug, and the pink bunny hopped into the driver's seat.

"Good luck." Sandy struggled to get the words out as she doubled over with laughter.

"Hey, I'm not that bad."

I raced back to the 280 freeway, grateful that the Saturday traffic was still light. Minutes later I exited onto Winchester and remembered to slow down once I turned onto La Rinconada Drive.

This neighborhood had changed drastically during the Tech boom. Pleasant middle-class houses on half-acre lots had been torn down to make way for tasteful mansions in Tuscan, Craftsmen, and Tudor styles. The country club had also been reworked with a new clubhouse and the currently required spa.

I hadn't been in the club since it had quadrupled in size, so it took me awhile to find the 19th hole—especially since it was now known as the Watering Hole. I checked my watch as I walked in the room. Five minutes to ten.

It had been a decade since I had last seen Mr. Montgomery, or any of his cronies. I was prepared for the thinning white hair, but not how much even these athletic outdoorsmen had shrunk.

I greeted him with a hug.

"Cissy, I'm sure you remember Bill."

"Hello. Good to see you." I shook Bill's offered hand, grateful for the hint that a handshake was the appropriate greeting for our relationship.

"And Bob." Another handshake.

"I don't believe you've met Lou before. This is Luigi Chiari."

On automatic, I offered my hand and stared into blue-green eyes and dark blonde hair not uncommon in northern Italy.

Could this be Poppy's biological father? If not, what the hell was he doing in Los Gatos playing golf with three men three decades his senior?

Wait a minute. I was to be the fourth.

"That's Lou's new house down near the main gate. The one surrounded by the vineyard and olive trees."

"Oh yes. A piece of Tuscany. Chianti country? Are you Florentine, Lou?"

"You know Firenze, dear lady?"

"I've been there a few times. It's a beautiful city. I'm particularly fond of the gelato at Vivoli."

"The best gelato in all of Italy—in all the world."

"Gentleman, Madame, our tee time." Nick Montgomery picked up his whiskey glass for one last swig and gestured toward the French doors exiting to the first hole. Bill and Bob moseyed outside.

I slipped out of the pink driving mocs, jammed my feet into the two-toned pink golf shoes, and slung the bag of clubs back onto my shoulder. I hurried to follow the three older men.

Luigi took my clubs off my shoulder. "Mrs. Huntington, please allow me. We need to get you a cart."

That's what that foldy thing in the back of my car was. Ignorantly I had abandoned the pieces of metal with wheels in my rush to get into the club. "I left it in my car."

"No problem." Lou placed my bag against a bench near where my foursome was teeing off. "With whom will you ride?"

I pointed at Mr. Montgomery. Lou put my clubs into the back of Mr. Montgomery's electric vehicle. While I sat on the bench and tied my pink shoes, I noticed there were three levels of tee boxes—the top for the championship round, the second plateau for men and pro women players, the lowest for seniors, juniors, and women like me. With relief I saw that they were teeing off at the lowest level.

Two rows of giant dark green redwood trees marked the curve down the lush green grass to the first hole. I saw the red flag between the trunks of the redwoods.

I watched Nick swing at the small white ball on the tee. His club made contact and the ball flew out of sight between two stands of majestic redwood trees.

I could do that. I prayed I wouldn't miss. Or even more embarrassing, divet the lawn. I hated the way that sent shock waves down my arms and into my body.

"Cissy, tee up."

If I could just get past the first few holes, I could get Mr. Montgomery alone to ask him a few questions. Like who the hell was Luigi Chiari?

I tried to remember everything anyone had ever told me about how to stand, how to swing, but it was just too complicated. I stared down at how damn tiny that little white ball was, then closed my eyes, and swung as hard as I could.

To my great surprise, my club didn't hit the lawn, and the ball went sailing between the tall trees much like Nick's had done. I couldn't wipe the grin off my face. Is this why grown men and women spend so damn many hours hitting at little balls with sticks?

No one else seemed to notice that I had done exceptionally well. I guess my reputation hadn't preceded me.

As we loaded into two carts, I tossed my driver in the back and jumped in with Mr. Montgomery. Luigi waved goodbye as we drove down the fairway.

"Who is he?" I asked.

"Who's who?"

"Lou, Luigi Chiari. Who is he?"

Mr. Montgomery shrugged an I-don't-know. "Some Italian. A real estate developer, I think."

"You don't know him?"

"Not particularly."

"So, he's not Poppy's father."

Montgomery slammed on the golf cart brakes jerking us both forward. "What the hell are you talking about?"

"Joan told me about Cassandra and the Florentine."

Mr. Montgomery slowly started the cart rolling again. "What about Cassandra?"

"She told me the whole thing. About the miscarriage and Poppy, and even how Cameron doesn't know he isn't Poppy's father."

"Why the hell would she go and do a damn fool thing like that?"

"I'm trying to help her. I know she didn't have anything to do with Honey's murder, but the police have a different idea. I think you can help me help her."

"I sure as hell don't know how. I didn't have anything to do with the damn arrangements those silly cows made." Mr. Montgomery groaned. "Don't think there was a damn thing about it that was legal."

"What do you mean?"

"There were no documents, nothing in writing. If Cassandra had changed her mind, there wouldn't have been a damn thing Joan could've done about it."

"But of course, Cassandra died just a couple years later in that plane crash. How did that happen?" I wrapped an arm around the side pole of the cart as a distracted Mr. Montgomery bounced the cart over bumps in the rough.

"No one really knows. Cassandra and Charles crashed into the side of a mountain on their way to Eagle Lake. Both died on impact. Not enough left of the charred remains to know if there was a mechanical problem, or if it was pilot error."

"And there was no doubt that both of them were on board?"

"Two bodies identified from dental records. Between them they had inherited hundreds of millions. Great care was taken to insure proper identification."

"Who inherited?"

"The bulk of their estates went to Honey, in keeping with old Henry Minner's will. Funds never left the trust."

That reminded me. It was Saturday. The day of Honey's service. And the reading of her will.

"What will happen to that money now?"

"Good question." Nick Montgomery let the cart roll to a gentle stop on a plateau over looking the putting green. Miraculously all four balls were on the green.

"You know, I suppose it's possible that Poppy could end up with it. As far as I know she's the only one left with Nickels's blood." He sat in the cart, elbows on the steering wheel, head resting on his hands.

"Joan's not going to like this development. My God, what have those women done?" He seemed to consider his own question. "We'll have to do DNA tests."

"Honey already did that."

Montgomery sighed. "The whole damn sordid mess is going to come out now. The tabloids are gonna love it. Bad timing, huh?"

I nodded. Poor Joan.

Bob and Bill had climbed out of their cart. They knelt on the grass studying their shots. Once that task was out of the way, they ambled towards our cart.

"I don't want to talk about this in front of them. Bill's wife has a big mouth and she's no doubt going to the shower this afternoon." Mr. Montgomery cautioned me.

I nodded my agreement. I knew it was just putting off the inevitable especially as that very afternoon the reading of Honey's will would most likely give the whole story away.

Now I had to hit the damn ball again. At least putting's not as scary as driving.

Nick Montgomery, even as shook up as he had to be, managed to get the ball into the hole in two strokes, placing him one under par.

I couldn't remember which club to use for putting. I snuck a look at the putter Mr. Montgomery used. Looking over the collection of clubs in my bag I choose one that looked similar.

I looked at the hole and gently pushed on the ball. It moved less than three inches.

The next time I swung harder and missed the ball entirely.

The next swing made contact and sent the ball flying past the hole and into the rough. I dug around in a mess of eucalyptus droppings to find the freaking thing.

The sixth time, the little white piece of shit went whizzing by the hole, Bob and Bill gave up on controlling their laughter.

"That's some fourth you brought, Nick," Bob snickered. "Need a mulligan?" Bob and Bill both doubled over with laughter.

Nick picked up my ball and motioned me back into the cart. "Cissy, how long do you think we can keep this quiet?"

"I spoke with Marty. He was hoping to have the service and the reading of the will today."

"Fucking hell! Excuse my French." Nick rubbed his forehead and started the cart. "I don't really know Marty. Do you think there's any way we could talk him into waiting until after the wedding to make that will public knowledge?"

"I could ask. But Joan promised she would tell Poppy the truth. And I'm assuming that means she'll tell Cameron."

"I'm glad to hear that, but don't you see? Once this gets out, we'll have paparazzi climbing all over us the whole time we're trying to have a nice, simple wedding."

Eight hundred guests in Grace Cathedral and the Palace Hotel. Not everyone's idea of a nice, simple wedding.

But I agreed that the prospect of tons of media coverage was daunting. And would the press and TV ever love this story! A previously unknown, newly made billionairess's wedding complete with celebrity attendees. Definitely all over us.

"Mr. Montgomery, I'll speak to Marty. But I need your help. We need to figure out who benefited from Honey's death. I know Joan didn't do this. She's too smart. She would've had to realize that Honey's death would bring the whole damn story to light, and I doubt that Joan even wants Poppy to have that kind of money. Thank God, Poppy found a good husband before anyone knew she's a bil-lionaire," I rambled.

Montgomery looked at me thoughtfully. "Bottom line, Poppy is the only person who stands to gain from Honey's death . . . and she doesn't know it."

"What about her father?"

"Wells?"

"Yeah, that one."

"He's well set up. And he doesn't know, either."

"What about her biological father?"

"The Italian? I don't know who that is, I think Joan knows his name. But what are the odds that he would know anything?"

"He presumably knew something about Cassandra."

"Do you think if he knew she was worth hundreds of millions he would've let her go?"

"He may not've been given a choice. Honey may have rushed Cassandra back to California without telling him she was leaving. And then they disappeared on to Eleanor's family's gated estate at the Lake."

Mr. Montgomery turned to look at me. "You've got a point there, young lady. Were you ever at that place? Several houses behind gates. No guards in those days, but a good hideaway nonetheless."

Our cart had been at the next tee for several minutes. Bob and Bill were looking at us intently. "They're probably wondering what we're talking about." I bobbed my head in their direction.

Mr. Montgomery jumped out of the cart. He took a quick swing and drove his ball into the rough. I'd definitely thrown him off his game.

I tried the closing-my-eyes and imagining-the-ball-sailing-onto-the-green routine again. The second time I swung, it actually worked. My ball stayed out of the rough, although it kind of dribbled along the fairway.

We headed back to the cart, rudely ignoring the other two golfers. Mr. Montgomery was already on the phone by the time I climbed in.

"Joanie, sweetie, I'm with Cissy. You had a talk with Poppy, right? . . . Good, good. How 'bout Cameron? . . . Well, you gotta do that."

I tugged at his sleeve. "Joan knows Marty. She should call him."

Montgomery nodded. "Okay sweetie, there's one more conversation you need to have right away. Call Chaffin and get him to postpone the reading of the will. Or to find some way to keep the contents from becoming public knowledge."

I whispered. "Ask her what the father's name was?"

Mr. Montgomery repeated my question. "Don't worry sweetie. Cissy and I are on this. It's gonna work out." He pushed a button and put the phone back in his jacket pocket. "She's gotta look it up. She thinks Giovanni was his first name, but she's got it written down. She'll tell you after the shower."

"So now that we are 'on this', what are we going to do?"

"We're gonna get out of this golf game. You suck at it." He smiled at me. "And I'm not playing so well myself."

"Guys, Bob, Bill, I'm sorry. That call was Joanie. She's got all kinds of problems with this damn wedding. I gotta see what I can do to help out. I had to promise to get her to quit her bawling." Montgomery pounded his friends on their backs and got back in the cart.

He drove directly back to the parking lot, bypassed the Watering Hole, dropped me at my car and told me to follow him to his house.

"We're gonna get to the bottom this."

Chapter 37

Nick Montgomery's house surprised me. Two blocks from the club, the starkly modern residence sat on a high plateau overlooking the Santa Clara Valley—these days more commonly known as Silicon Valley. Glass walls framed killer views in three directions.

"Cool place. Sort of in the style of Philip Johnson," I said as I climbed out of my car.

"Not 'in the style of.' It is his work. I picked it up some years ago for a song—the dot-commer who'd had it panicked."

"It's really different than the last house of yours I was in." I recalled the large, traditional Montgomery mansion of a few years earlier.

"I decided to give this a shot. Eleanor would've never considered living in a place like this. Kind of a nice change for me right after she died," Mr. Montgomery explained as he walked me into the atrium entrance. He stuck his thumb on a pad and the front door clicked open.

We entered the spacious great room and he headed directly to the bar. "Whadda ya having?" Montgomery asked as he poured whiskey into a tumbler.

"Do you have Pellegrino?"

"Somewhere around here." He ducked down and opened cabinet doors in the base of the bar.

I could hear doors being slammed. "A diet coke, or club soda would be fine."

Relief replaced the frustration on his face. He poured a diet coke into a glass with ice and handed me the glass and the can.

I sat on a modern Italian sofa covered in ivory-colored leather.

He hoisted himself onto an Aldo barstool and swiveled to face me. "I figure we gotta find out what the story is with the natural father. Soon as Joan gives us the name, I'll get my guy on tracing him."

"That would be great."

"The only other thing I can think of—there's some papers of Eleanor's." Nick paused, studied the view for a moment. "I've never managed to get through all of them. Tell you the truth, makes me too damn sad to read 'em. I could be wrong about the 'nothing in writing'. I don't think those women used a lawyer, or made sure anything about what they did was legal, but there could be something."

I nodded encouragingly.

"Eleanor also had all these family tree papers. She got really into researching that crap the last few years of her life. Maybe, maybe she's got some info on Poppy's family tree. You know, for the day that she and Joan finally fessed up." Nick said. "Might be possible to find out if there is anyone else around who would inherit. It's just possible that whoever it was who tricked that damn fool Philip into killing Honey had no idea that Poppy was Honey's heir."

That concept twisted my head around. But it made sense. Only a handful of people knew Poppy's relationship to Honey. And we'd pretty much eliminated everyone in the know as possible suspects. That left the possibility of another heir thinking he, or she, would inherit Honey's millions. "Who could that be?"

"That's what I'm thinking could be in her papers."

"Where are the papers?"

"Follow me."

Mr. Montgomery led me to what looked like a vault door in a wall in the center of the house. It was the one part of the house that was windowless and presumably contained all the mechanical units. It also contained an eight feet by ten feet room lined with metal shelves. The shelves and the floor were filled with banker's boxes with lids askew and papers tumbling out.

"All of that? That's all Eleanor's papers."

He pointed to a section of neatly arranged boxes, lids taped in place, sides labeled. "That stuffs mine." A quarter of the boxes.

"The rest of it is all Eleanor's." Montgomery grimaced. "Nobody's really done anything with it other than to dump it in here."

"Didn't she have a personal assistant?"

"We called the girl she had a social secretary. That's who boxed all this stuff up."

"You want me to go through all this stuff?"

"Maybe you could get some help?"

I stared at the boxes trying to calculate how many man-hours it would take to sort through it. "Wow."

"If you want to see if you can find some discreet help to do it, I'll pick up the tab," he offered.

"Where do you want us to look at it? Here?"

"Oh, no. I'd like to get it outa here. I kept thinking the day would come that I could handle going through it myself, but . . ."

I thought about who I could get to help. "Okay, have it delivered to my dad's place in Seacliff. In fact, I'll take as many boxes as I can fit in my car with me now."

I went out to my car, put down both of the back seats, placed the bag of golf clubs on the floor in front of the passenger seat, and left the rear hatch open ready to receive boxes. I went back into the vault.

Mr. Montgomery stood in the doorway, staring aimlessly at the contents of the windowless room.

"Were the boxes placed in here in any particular order?"

"I don't think so, but I wasn't actually here." He ran his fingers through thin white hair and rubbed his scalp. "Nothing was ever said about an order."

To play it safe I started with the box on the top shelf closest to the door, then took one box at a time and filled the back of the car with twelve boxes.

"That ought to keep us busy until the remainder are delivered."

"My man can bring them up this afternoon."

"Just make sure he get's there before three. Better yet, can he bring 'em tomorrow?"

"No problem." Mr. Montgomery started to speak, then stopped. Then he said, "Look, can we agree that if you find anything shocking, or important to the case, you'll discuss it with me before you take the info to the police, or to Joan, . . . or anybody?"

"You mean anybody other than the people I have help me? I'll swear them to secrecy. Don't worry. I'll make sure that anyone who comes close to these is someone I trust."

Montgomery patted me on the shoulder. "Thanks."

Chapter 38

Once I was back on the freeway headed for Sandy's and my familiar black clothes, I turned on the Bluetooth phone and asked to be connected to Nikki Howe.

"Hello, darling. How is it going up there?"

I filled her in on the latest developments. "So, I've got these boxes. I remembered your offer of assistance. Would you and Sally like to come up early next week? Or maybe even tomorrow?"

"Awesome. Sounds like fun. I love digging in other people's secret papers. I'll call Sally and see if she wants to fly up with me. Call you back. Tootle loo."

At Sandy's, I rushed to the powder room, tore off the pink, and reclaimed my black jeans before I said so much as hello. Sandy was waiting on the settee in the entry hall when I had finished redressing.

"That was a quick round. Did you only play nine holes?" Sandy smiled at me.

I checked my watch. It was just after one o'clock. "We played two holes. Well, actually one and a half."

Sandy pressed her lips together, biting down to suppress

her giggles. She nodded and awaited further explanation.

I placed the pile of neatly folded pink clothes on the round table in the center of the hall, then grabbed the golf bag, clubs, and the folded cart out of the front seat of my car and brought them into the hall.

"Thank you very much for the use of this stuff. And for organizing it all so that I made to the club right on time."

Sandy gently placed her arm over my shoulders. "Cissy, did you get kicked off the course?"

"Not exactly."

She smiled sympathetically. I could tell she expected a wild tale of my golf antics. Avoiding the temptation to satisfy her with a made-up story, I told her the same version of the truth that Montgomery had told Bill and Bob. "Joan needed Mr. Montgomery, uh, Nick's help with some wedding details she's worried about. And we'd had the conversation I wanted to have, so I left with him."

Sandy looked at me with one eyebrow raised. My father must have told her some humdinger stories about golf and me.

"Really. No dramatics. I didn't hit anyone with a ball . . . or a club. I didn't play through without permission. No sand traps. No loud swearing." I failed to mention the eight putts on the first hole. Why give my ridiculers any more fuel?

"Got things to do before the shower this afternoon. Will I see you there?"

"Of course," Sandy said.

We hugged and I continued my drive back to Seacliff.

Nikki called to say that she and Sally had some schedule rearranging to do, but they would be arriving the next afternoon. She'd call when she knew the exact time, but not to worry about picking them up. A car had been arranged.

By the time I arrived back at Dad's house, I itched to go through the boxes. Emma and I carried the load of papers to the dining room table. As soon as the last box landed, I took off the lid and pulled out a party book. On one page was a diagram of a table with names written at each place. On the opposite page was a series of menus. Handwritten and signed by Eleanor, it was the meal plan for a weekend house party from 1952. Oh, my God, had they saved every piece of paper she ever touched?

I dug through the box. It was packed with party books. All menus and meal plans with a few instruction notes for what particular guests preferred on their breakfast trays. I pulled out the book for 1961. The book fell open to a reception following Joan's christening with a list of guests and a plan for the ceremony. Honey was Joan's godmother. Amazing how much time Eleanor had spent during her pregnancy with menu plans. I wondered why she bothered when she and Honey seemed to be the only people at the Tahoe house for months before the christening. At a glance, there did not appear to be any family trees, or adoption papers. At least that box seemed to be organized by subject. Hopefully they all would be.

The second box contained nothing but correspondence and receipts for Junior League charity events. I wondered why the league didn't keep those. And what was the sense of keeping receipts from fifty years ago?

The next box I opened contained photos: snapshots, Polaroids, some color photos, but mostly black and white. I pushed that box aside to deal with later.

Emma reappeared in the dining room. "Mama, we need to leave pretty soon. What are you wearing?"

"Emma, do we have any Post-its here? I want to label these boxes as I identify them." Leaving the box of photos on the table, I took the other two boxes I had looked at and stacked them on the floor next to the sideboard.

"I'll get the post-its if you promise to get ready to go."

I held out my hand, thumb up, signaling that she had a deal. I was disappointed when she returned with the post-its before I understood what the contents of the next box were. Some pages were in loose leaf notebooks, some in spiral notebooks, some in binders. Most were handwritten, a few were typed. It might have been a manuscript for a book, or even several manuscripts. I scanned one of the pages. Hot damn. It looked like a memoir. That would explain why Eleanor had saved all these papers.

"Mama! Get dressed!" Emma stood at the end of the table tapping her foot. She had on an embroidered Nanette Lepore dress and jacket. Her hair was in a chignon with blonde wisps framing her face.

"Okay, okay." I would've loved to spend the remainder of the day with that box, but it would have to wait until after Poppy's kitchen shower. "Emma, what did we buy for Poppy?" I yelled out as I ran up the stairs.

"*The Joy of Cooking* and Julia Child's *The Way to Cook,*

his and her aprons, matching hot pads, towels, spatulas—I had it all wrapped up in a basket."

"Sounds good."

My Chanel suit was seeing a lot of use this week. I put on a different camisole, black pumps, and my usual pearls, I touched up my make up and ran a brush through my hair.

"I'm ready." I called out to Emma and dashed down the stairs. I found her in the garage loading an enormous, beautifully wrapped basket into the back of the car.

Chapter 39

We were less than ten minutes late to the shower, which meant we were among the first to arrive at the China Basin loft.

Joan greeted guests and introduced her friends to Poppy's friends. We exchanged hugs and air kisses. "We'll talk later." Joan said with a cautious look.

I smiled, nodded, and gave her hand a gentle squeeze. "Of course." I had no intention of bringing up the Italian at Poppy's shower.

Across the polished concrete floor, in front of a huge forty-foot tall factory window, Emma and Poppy hugged and giggled. The young hostess joined them.

I scanned the room for women I knew, especially women of Honey's generation. I waved to Katherine whom I had visited in Piedmont. Muffy was deep in a conversation with Lily. I was a little sheepish about approaching Lily. She had been so critical during our dinner date. Not that I hadn't deserved it. Disparaging my choice of food was a bit overboard, but I had downed cosmopolitans way too fast.

I joined their circle in spite of my embarrassment. "How are you, ladies?"

"Aah, Cissy pull up a seat." Katherine waved at the Philippe Stark molded armchairs. Very chic, only slightly uncomfortable seating. I pulled one over to the molded sofas where the women were perched. Lily's daughter-in-law excused herself to sit with the younger set who had congregated near the bar sipping lavender cocktails garnished with skewers of tiny orchids, raspberries, and blueberries.

"What are those beautiful drinks called?" Muffy pointed to the cocktails. The lavender was nearly same color as her St. John suit.

"Lavender Ladies. Made with Chambord Liqueur and Raspberry vodka. I'm going to try one. May I get one for any of you?" I avoided eye contact with Lily.

"Yummy" Muffy clapped her hands together.

"Yes, please," Katherine said.

Even Lily was tempted away from her usual white wine. I walked across the vast room to the bar and asked the waiter to bring us a tray of Lavender Ladies.

When I returned, the three women had been joined by three more of my potential interviewees. Nancy Beck, from Montecito, and Phyllis Ralston, from Hope Ranch, had flown up from Santa Barbara together. Linda Howard had arrived from Big Sur. I headed back to the bar and added three glasses to the tray and a pitcher of Lavender Ladies. I figured if I plied them with enough alcohol, I could get more info.

I hugged the newcomers. "Did you come up for the weekend, or will you be in town until after the wedding?"

Nancy answered for herself and Phyllis. "We'll stay and do some shopping this week. Maybe even make it up to the Lake for some skiing. Ooh, these look nice." Nancy took one of the cocktail glasses.

"Did you ever stay at Eleanor's place at the Lake?' I lifted a glass off the tray and saluted my fellow drinkers.

"Once or twice in ancient history, but once Joan was born, one had to be issued a formal invitation to even stop by there," Phyllis cackled. "Honey was the only one who spent a lot of time there after that.

Muffy turned to Phyllis. "Oh, yes. Remember that time when you and I stopped by without calling first? We no more than tried to get the gate open when the housekeeper came out and shooed us away."

"She was very polite about it, but she said Eleanor was napping—she must've been eight or nine months pregnant then—and Honey was also napping. She made it clear we were never to appear unannounced again. Of course, we would never have stopped by unannounced in the City, but everyone was always so casual at the Lake in those days. Sometimes one would just be out for a walk and drop in for a drink."

"I hate being chastised by the help. That housekeeper's husband, the butler, would really let you know about if you did anything he considered to be improper.

"Always had the idea he was looking down his nose at us. Didn't think we were quite good enough to associate with his precious Eleanor—or especially with Joan."

"Strangely he didn't seem to have a problem with Honey, but surely he must've been aware of her wildness?" Linda quizzed the older women.

"Did you go to her service today?" I asked in what I hoped sounded like a casual tone.

"No, we were not invited. I only found out it was today from my brother last night." Nancy sounded miffed. Linda shrugged her shoulders.

"Does one have to be invited to a funeral?" Phyllis follows proper etiquette.

"You do if it's private and held on Marty's gated estate," Nancy explained.

"Before Eleanor got pregnant with Joan, did all of you hang out together at the Lake?" If these women couldn't supply info about Honey's service and will, at least I could get a better understanding of the relationship between Eleanor and Honey.

"Oh, yes. We had some wild weeks there both before and after we were married," Phyllis smiled.

"Once we became old married ladies, we'd spend the afternoons by the pool, playing bridge and drinking salty dogs. Our husbands came up on the weekends." Nancy said.

"Did Eleanor have trouble with miscarriages like Joan did?" I asked.

"Even among close friends we didn't talk about things like that too much, but I vaguely remember an operation for female trouble. Was it a tipped uterus?" Nancy asked the others.

"No silly, it was Joan who had that operation." Muffy held up her empty glass and I filled it with lavender concoction.

"It wasn't both of them?" Nancy suggested.

"Maybe. Like mother, like daughter." Muffy took a generous drink of her cocktail.

"These purple things are really delicious. Pour me another please." Nancy passed her glass to me.

"So, Eleanor had to be careful while she was pregnant too?" I poured the mix and handed the glass back to Nancy.

"Very much so." Nancy sipped the drink. "She went to bed at six months. Didn't go out at all."

"Yeah, no one saw her for months." Phyllis held out her glass to me. "And then, when Joan got pregnant, she had to do the same thing."

"I guess that had something to do with why each of them only had one child."

Muffy had finished off her drink already. She twirled the empty glass for a moment and then handed it to me.

"Honey never had any children?"

The pitcher was nearly empty, but I didn't want to interrupt the conversation. I filled Muffy's glass half full and held the pitcher aloft in hopes that a waiter would notice. I felt sheepish about being rude to him, but priorities are priorities. "Was she sterile or something?"

"There was a story about a botched abortion when she was seventeen." Phyllis drained her glass. "I think Eleanor might have helped her with that. In fact, I think that might have been when they got so close. Eleanor was a few years older—an old married woman."

"Did Eleanor try to have more children?" I poured what was left of the lavender mix into Phyllis's glass.

"She never mentioned it."

"What about this cousin of Honey's? Cassandra?" I asked.

"The one who died in the plane crash?" Muffy's glass was empty again.

"Yeah. Did she hang out with you up at the Lake?" I hoped she wouldn't hand me the glass. I held the pitcher higher in the air.

"I remember her being around with Honey right after Poppy was born. Beautiful girl. I think she and Joan were close." Nancy sipped her cocktail.

"Did Cassandra have children?" I felt the pitcher lifted from my hands and turned to see that Emma had noticed my dilemma. She carried the tray and pitcher to the bartender.

"She was really young when she died." Nancy shook her head. "Only twenty . . . maybe twenty-one and never married."

"What about Honey's other cousins? Didn't any of them have children?" I finally took a small sip of my cocktail.

"No. It'll be interesting to see what happens with Honey's money," Nancy whispered.

All the rest of the women nodded in agreement.

Emma returned with a tray of drinks and a full pitcher.

"Thank you, darling." I patted my daughter's arm before

she walked back to join the young set.

"Let's hope this tipped uterus problem, or whatever it was, wasn't inherited by Poppy," I said. "Emma says Poppy is planning a large family."

I doubted that Poppy would actually have the problem, since Poppy was not Joan's biological child.

"Well, of course adoption is so much more the done thing now." Phyllis poured her own drink.

"It wasn't earlier?" I continued to carefully nurse my beverage.

"It was the kind of thing one didn't talk about, since the child was often the product of an inappropriate liaison. It was considered shameful, even for the child." Nancy took a new glass from the tray.

"Thank God, we're past that now." I hoped they'd all consumed enough alcohol that I could be more direct with my next line of questioning. "Who do you think had Honey killed?"

All five women froze and looked at me as though I had just dropped a poisonous snake on the cocktail table. No one answered, or even moved for a full minute. Then they all spoke at once.

"Obviously, not Joan."

"Definitely, not Joan."

"This ludicrous nonsense about Joan being involved."

"Ridiculous."

"Damn fools to think that Joan had anything to do with it."

"Maybe the butler took it on himself. He always was

bossy as hell."

"Yeah, very much like he knew more than anyone else."

"He was very protective of Joan and Poppy."

"Definitely. It was entirely the butler's idea."

"Why would he blame Joan?" I asked.

"He must've been being pressured," Nancy said.

"Makes no sense." Phyllis put her glass on the table and twisted her hair in her fingers.

"Who else could it have been?" I asked.

They shook their heads. Nancy spoke for the group. "There is no other possibility. End of discussion. Oh look, the gifts."

The gift opening had started in the circle of twenty-somethings in front of the wall of windows that faced the bay.

The consensus: the butler did it.

I wasn't going to get any more info out of them. I walked over to stand behind Emma. She turned around and looked up at me with one eyebrow raised. I smiled, nodded, and placed my hand on her shoulder.

I fixed a smile on my face and pretended to watch the gift unwrapping while I mentally sifted through the information I had just gotten. So, Eleanor and Joan had both had difficult pregnancies. Both stories of confinements that lasted months seemed suspicious.

Was it possible that both Joan and Poppy had been adopted?

What was the deal with the butler? He couldn't be the father, could he? I was pretty sure the butler had dark brown eyes; Joan's were pale blue. So were Poppy's. Joan and Poppy looked quite a lot alike.

I was missing something.

I waited until Poppy opened the gift Nancy brought, then I took Nancy aside. "On the phone, you mentioned that Honey was concerned for her safety. What was that about?"

Nancy looked around the room. No one was paying attention to the two of us. "She said she had been threatened because she intended to name new beneficiaries to the Nickels trust."

"Threatened by whom?"

"She didn't say . . . but I know she was shocked to have them speak to her in such a manner."

"So, it was more than one person?"

"That was the impression I had."

"You said you were sworn to secrecy. About what?"

"That she planned to change the beneficiaries. She said that she wanted to be certain that the money would be used wisely and philanthropically. She was worried. Said it was a terrible responsibility, and she wasn't sure if she was doing the right thing. Honey hoped that she wasn't harming the new beneficiaries. Apparently, they're people she loved. That's all I know." Nancy finished speaking and rejoined the party in front of the window.

The gift part of the party was followed by food and gossip. To my ear, the gossip seemed carefully edited to avoid any mention of Honey—or of Joan's legal predicament.

My impatience to talk with Joan grew by the minute. Finally, the guests began to depart. I took Joan aside.

"Cissy, not here."

I pulled her into the one fully enclosed room in the loft and shut the bathroom door. "What was his name?"

"I haven't had time to look for it. I don't see what it matters now what his name was. That was twenty-five years ago."

"He's a potential suspect."

"I don't understand what—" Joan's phone rang. She took it from her Hermes handbag and looked at the incoming number. "I have no idea whose number that is. I'm not answering."

I looked over her shoulder at the phone screen. "I think that's Marty Chaffin's house line."

"What? Why is he calling me? I already talked to him this morning." Joan continued to ignore the ring.

"It probably has to do with Honey's will."

"Cissy, what are you talking about?"

"I asked Marty to avoid making the contents of Honey's will public until after the wedding for fear that it might fuel a paparazzi frenzy. Your father asked you to call him, remember?"

"And I did call him," Joan said. "But he said it was too late to hold off the reading of the will. He promised to ask the lawyers to handle the trust separately. In a private session. So, you think Honey's left the Nickels's money to Poppy?"

"Seems pretty likely, doesn't it?" I said. "At least listen

to the voicemail."

"Not now. The girls are going to wonder what the hell we are doing in here. Come home with me. If we have to talk about this, I want to do it in private."

Joan and I exited the bathroom. One of the waiters walked past us pushing a dolly loaded with cartons of glassware. The caterer and bar staff loaded glasses, dishes, and bottles into cartons and carried them out a rear door to an awaiting van.

In the seating area in front of the enormous windows, Poppy, Emma, and the two young hostesses were dissecting the gathering, sharing gossip, and giggling about the funnier presents.

"I don't know why we had a kitchen shower. I guess it means I have to learn to cook something besides take-out."

"You mean—learn to make your own dinner reservations." Emma giggled.

Joan interrupted the fun. "Poppy, Cissy and I are going to our house. Shall I send the driver back for you?"

"The girls can use my car." I handed Emma the keys. "Bring Poppy home and pick me up." I leaned over and whispered in Emma's ear. "Don't hesitate to call for help if—"

"Mama, I know what to do."

I thanked the two hostesses, hugged and kissed all four girls and followed Joan to her waiting car and driver. We slid into the back seat.

"We'll continue our discussion when we reach the house," Joan dictated, nodding meaningfully at the driver.

She immediately launched into a speech about how stressful the whole mother of the bride thing was. What Emma and I call "bragging disguised as complaining."

I listened politely, enjoyed the views of the City from the car windows, and, as the car climbed the hill to the Wells's mansion, wondered why Marty was calling Joan.

The driver pulled into the driveway in front of the house but stopped the car short of the entrance. A long white Hummer limo sat in front of the steps to the entry.

"Who does that thing belong to?" Joan's disdain referred to the fact that no self-respecting San Franciscan would be seen in such an ostentatious vehicle.

We climbed out of Joan's discreet black town car and up the steps to the entrance. The housekeeper opened the door just as we reached it. "Ms. Joan, there are two men here to see you." She motioned toward the living room. Standing in front of the window seat, studying the view of the Golden Gate and the bay were two gray haired men clad in three-piece dark suits.

Joan looked at me as though I might have some idea who they were. I shrugged, and we both entered the room.

"Mrs. Wells, I'm Stanton North. This is my associate, Kenneth Bratton." Stanton North turned his attention to me, held out his hand and waited for me to offer my name.

Joan identified me.

"Mrs. Huntington, would you excuse us please? We have a personal matter to discuss with Mrs. Wells."

"It seems that I am to have no secrets from Cissy, we may as well have her stay, but should I have my lawyer present?" Joan's voice shook, her body swayed.

I put my arm through Joan's to support her. "Shall we sit down?" I guided Joan to a nearby sofa and sat her down. I sat beside her and continued to hold her arm.

The two men sat down on the opposite sofa. "You may have another attorney present if you wish, but in point of fact, we are your lawyers. We represent the trust of which you are the beneficiary."

Joan and I were puzzled. "But Poppy is an adult." Joan said.

Now it was the two men who looked puzzled, but Mr. North continued. "Regarding the estate of Honor Chaffin and the Nickels trust, Mrs. Chaffin has named you and your daughter, Penelope, as beneficiaries."

"Why me? I mean, I've always understood that the Nickels trust, per the terms of Henry Minner's will, was limited to his biological descendants."

"That is true. You understood correctly."

Chapter 40

Joan sat perfectly still. Her mouth was open but no sounds were coming out of it.

No one spoke.

My mind raced. My suspicions had to be correct.

Joan was Honey's child. So much for the supposedly botched abortion. Joan was Honey's child. Poppy was Cassandra's. Joan's grandmother was Poppy's great grand-mother. Thus, the strong resemblance between Poppy and Joan.

Perhaps, when I read Eleanor's papers and memoir I would find, in Eleanor's own words, an explanation of how she and Honey had substituted Nickels heirs for first a Montgomery child, and then for a Wells child. They had done it twice!

"Mrs. Wells, there is a substantial sum involved in this trust. We would like to meet with you and your daughter, and any legal or financial advisor you wish, as soon as Monday. But we understand from Mr. Chaffin that Penelope is to be married in a week, and that the publicity that would no doubt accompany an announcement would not be welcome at this time. Thus, we thought it best to meet in private. We know from unfortunate experience that the more individuals who are aware of the inheritance, the greater the chance of the media getting—" He looked at me as he hesitated over the last words.

Joan continued to stare out the window, unaware of the insult that had just been dropped at my feet.

I ignored the affront. "Gentlemen, does this mean that you are in possession of proof of both Joan's and Pop— Penelope's biological connection to Mr. Minner?"

"Mrs. Chaffin supplied us with both, as well as an affidavit before her death."

"Are you aware that Mrs. Wells is under some suspicion in regards to Mrs. Chaffin's death?" I asked.

Mr. North squirmed, then cleared his throat. "Of course, if Mrs. Wells were to be convicted of murder, she would not, by law be allowed to remain a beneficiary, but Ms. Penelope's benefit would in no manner be effected by such a circumstance. Except that it would increase."

"That's not why I brought it up. I'm more concerned that the fact of her benefiting from Honey's death will increase the suspicion, and this would be a very bad time for Mrs. Wells to be caught up in a legal matter."

Both men nodded.

Joan, her eyes round with shock and fear, moved closer to me and grasped my hand.

"Mrs. Wells will consult with her attorneys. In the meanwhile, you are to keep this matter quiet." I gave each man in turn a stern look. "Who else knows about it?"

"Mr. Chaffin has been informed of the terms of Mrs. Chaffin's will, but the other beneficiaries were informed of their proceeds only. Nothing was said regarding the Minner Trust."

"So, it's just you two and Marty?" I asked.

"One or two of the clerical staff of the trust," Stanton North said.

"And Mr. Chaffin's attorney," Bratton added.

I looked at them both. They studied their feet. And your wives I thought. Possibly a mistress, or two.

"If Poppy and Joan had not qualified to inherit the trust, who would have done so?"

The two men exchanged looks, avoided my eyes.

"Would the trust have reverted to the Cowles family?"

"No," North said without hesitation.

"So?"

"Mrs. Huntington, our conversations with Mrs. Chaffin are to remain confidential, but as you and your children were the subject of one discussion, and as Mrs. Chaffin intended to speak with you regarding the conversation, I think it would be her wish that we relate what she planned to tell you."

North looked at Bratton for confirmation.

Oh my God, was I about to find out what Honey wanted with me?

Bratton nodded and North continued.

"Mrs. Chaffin wanted to be assured that you and your children would not contest her will. She was aware that your financial circumstances had changed recently, and she was concerned that, without an explanation as to why Mrs. Wells and Miss Wells were the beneficiaries, you—or, more likely, one of your financial advisors—would feel that you had a more legitimate claim. She intended to tell you the facts with the hopes that the details of—that the information would not have to be made public."

That's what Honey wanted to talk to me about!

Why would she be killed to prevent that conversation?

Or was the timing of her murder an unfortunate coincidence?

I tried not to think about the implication that, perhaps if not for our recent financial difficulties my children and I might have been the beneficiaries, but my heart sank anyway.

I understood Honey's intent. Leaving the dynasty trust assets to wealthy heirs meant no attempt to break the terms perpetuating the trust would occur and the proceeds would likely go to charities.

Emma and Poppy entered the adjoining entry hall laughing and shrieking. Their high spirits contrasted sharply with the solemn mood in the living room. They peeked in the doorway and hesitated before bursting into the room.

"What's up, Mom?" Emma said.

"What's happening, Mother?" Poppy glanced at Joan and then glared at the two men she must have assumed had upset her. "What's the matter, Mother?"

"Nothing's the matter. Everything's fine," I said. "These two gentlemen were just leaving." I stood up and motioned toward the door.

Joan didn't move. Poppy took my place next to her mother on the sofa and placed a protective arm around her shoulders.

Emma helped me usher the two men out the front door.

"Mrs. Wells will be in touch on Monday. Meanwhile, we all appreciate your discretion." I said good-bye and closed the door.

"Mom, what in the world?" Emma asked.

"Emma, I'll explain later."

Back in the living room, Joan's silence scared me.

"Poppy, get your mother her favorite cocktail or tea or water or something."

As soon as Poppy hurried out, I spoke to Joan. "What's your attorney's name? Where can I find his number?"

Without a word, Joan stood, took my arm, and walked us both into the book-lined library. She picked up a rolodex from the leather-paneled desk top and opened to a card with a name, address, and office number phone number typed on it. Scribbled in pen across the top was a number next to the word "cell".

I dialed the cell number from the phone on the desk, then handed the phone receiver to Joan but she shoved it back to me.

"Joan, what's the matter?" I heard a strained man's voice over the sounds of a noisy bar or restaurant.

I identified myself, stated that I was calling on Joan's behalf and that she needed to see him as soon as possible.

"I'm ten minutes away. I'm leaving now."

Chapter 41

"Joan. He's coming over." I decided to voice my other concern. "Does Poppy have a pre-nup in place? One that'll cover this?"

Joan nodded. "I think so."

Poppy found us. She had a steaming mug in one hand, a whiskey glass in the other. Joan chose the glass and downed the contents in one long swallow. She collapsed on the library sofa.

"What? Tell us what is going on right now!" both girls demanded of me.

"Joan just got some rather surprising—but good news." At least most people would consider a legacy of billions of dollars to be good news. "I think it's taking her a minute to get used to the idea."

"My mother never told me . . . ," Joan said softly.

"Girls, would you please get me a drink now?"

Emma knew this meant, "Get out of here!" and she ushered Poppy out of the room.

"You only recently told Poppy." I didn't think I had to remind her that she did so because circumstances forced her to do so.

"Are you saying that the situation was the same? That I'm the illegitimate child of a Nickels?" Joan looked at me in wonderment. "It could have been my father who was a Nickels. Oh, my God! This is so awful to even consider . . . that my mother would keep something like this from me, even when I was experiencing possibly the same thing she had. Why wouldn't she confide in me?" Joan's eyes implored an answer.

"I don't know. But unless I have misunderstood what mtDNA is, your link to the Nickels genetic line had to be maternal. So, it wasn't your biological father who connected you to Nickels."

"I thought we were so close. I had no secrets from her."

"Perhaps she was keeping a promise never to tell."

"What do you mean—what's mtDNA got to do with this?"

"Honey had some mtDNA tests run weeks before her death. I originally thought she was hoping to find someone with a genetic link to the Nickels, but, in fact, she was establishing proof of facts she already knew."

"Cissy, what are you talking about?"

Emma and Poppy came in with a bottle of Prosecco and four flutes in hand.

"Joan, do you mind if we let the girls in on the news?"

"I think we have to."

Emma and Poppy seemed equally shocked at my explanation. For once they were silent, not a single giggle.

"Cissy, what were you talking about? About Honey and

304

DNA?" Joan, nearly back to her normal self, demanded an answer.

Sheepishly, I admitted having bribed Pelancono to send me the results of the mtDNA tests. I explained how mtDNA traced genetic links only through the maternal line. Therefore, the relationships had to be between mother and child. I had pretty much told the three of them everything I knew about DNA—which was not much—when the doorbell rang. I heard the housekeeper speaking with a man.

"So, who is my mother?" Joan murmured.

"I think—Honey."

"Mrs. Wells, your attorney is here. May I show him in?" The housekeeper asked from the doorway of the library.

Joan nodded and pulled herself to a sitting position.

"Joan, what is this all about?" said a bald man I recognized. C.K. McGrath had represented several high-profile defendants against murder charges and was frequently interviewed by the media. He sat in the armchair opposite the sofa on which Joan perched.

Joan turned to me. "This is my friend, Cissy Huntington. And her daughter Emma. Cissy, please. Tell him."

Once again, I explained about the two men we had found at the house upon our return. C.K. McGrath's craggy face showed little response. I guessed trial lawyers needed to be good at concealing their emotions. I wondered how much of what I had just said would effect his fees.

Mr. McGrath remained stone faced, but he did speak. "Mrs. Wells, we do need to be concerned with how the police and the DA will respond to this news. Perhaps when we make it clear that you had no knowledge of your biological connection to Mrs. Chaffin—"

"No!" Joan barked. "You will not offer any explanation as to why Honey left me money."

"But Joan, it might clear your name."

"I don't care. This information is to stay between us. If you tell anyone, I'll deny it, and find new representation."

The lawyer stared at his client. A hint of exasperation showed on his face. He sighed.

"Look, C.K. just keep this out of the news, and keep us out of the courts, until Poppy is safely away on her honeymoon. I'll deal with this then." Joan was adamant.

"Joan, for once you have to deal with the real world." C.K. was equally resolute. "Murder—hiring a murderer— these are capital offenses. If the authorities think they have a case, they will not wait a week to arrest you."

Poppy ran to her mother's side and protectively wrapped her arms around Joan. "Oh Mother, please! Who cares who knows what? You can't go to jail." Tears streamed down her face. "We can postpone the wedding."

Joan held her daughter at arm's length. "Postpone the wedding! Do you have any idea what the waiting list for the Grace Cathedral is like? Or for the Palace Hotel? For Peter Duchin's orchestra? Not to mention eight hundred guests." Joan pressed Poppy to her and addressed the lawyer. "C.K., father said you are the best. Do your magic. Hold them off for one week."

"The best way to do that would be to find the real

murderer," I offered.

C.K. scowled at me. "I'm a lawyer. Not a detective."

"Don't you have a Paul Drake type person?" I asked.

He apparently refused to dignify my question with an answer. Instead he said to Joan, "I will handle this as I see fit. I will give the DA's office whatever information I deem necessary to convince them that you are not involved. I will not be hamstrung by your concern for your reputation. Being arrested for murder will do nothing for your repute. Now, what other information can you give me that might keep you out of jail?"

Chapter 42

Joan slumped back into the velvet sofa.

Poppy looked at her with alarm and emphatically said to C.K., "Philip didn't kill anyone. He wouldn't, couldn't do that. There can't possibly be any evidence against Philip therefore there can't be any evidence against Mother."

"He confessed," C.K. reminded Poppy.

"He's protecting someone," Poppy said.

"Your mother," C.K. said. "The police think he did it for your mother—or that he's protecting her."

"Let's assume for a moment that that is true. Joan, why would Philip think you killed Honey?" I asked.

Joan shook her head. "He's been with my family all my life. He's probably the only other person who knew about the babies—the only person besides my moth—other than Eleanor and Honey." Joan's eyes filled with tears. "I don't know why. Could it have something to do with the note the police found in Philip's rooms?"

"I bet he's told Maggie." Poppy moved closer to her mother. "That's Philip's wife, our housekeeper," Poppy told C.K. "She's been here all my life. They're both part of our family."

Not a chance in hell Maggie would say anything to anybody.

"Where were you the day Honey was killed?" C.K. asked Joan.

"I don't know—let me think, what day was it?"

"It was a Tuesday. Two weeks ago," I supplied.

Joan walked over to the calendar on the Eastlake desk. She pointed to the day. "Playing golf with my father at La Rinconada. We ate at the clubhouse afterward."

"When was the last time you were in Southern California?" C.K. asked.

"Last summer we spent a week in La Jolla."

"What about Philip? Did you send him down there for any reason?"

Joan shook her head.

"Where was Philip when Honey was killed?"

"I don't know. He took that weekend off. He left earlier in the week, but Maggie didn't go with him," Joan said.

Poppy said, "His brother, who lives near Auburn, has cancer. Philip goes to see him. I think that's where he was."

"I'm going to question Philip. If he is trying to protect someone by saying he did this, I'll convince him that he's only making matters worse," C.K. said. "When investigators check your bank accounts, are they going to find any large withdrawals in the last few weeks?"

"Lots. I've been paying for a wedding."

"In cash?"

"There have been some cash expenses, tips to wait staff,

to valet staff, the deposit for ceremony musicians . . . I've made sure to carry more cash than usual recently."

"Large amounts for which you have no receipts?"

"No. No large amounts," Joan said. "And the envelopes with cash are here."

"Daddy's very strict about getting receipts for everything," Poppy said.

Speaking of Cameron, I wondered where he was. I hadn't seen him at the house any of the times we'd been there that week.

"What about this note the police found? Was it written on your computer? Are they going to find it on your hard drive?" C.K. fired questions at Joan.

"I don't know anything about the note, but the police did take my computer. And my printer."

"Alright. I'm headed over to talk to Philip. If you think of anything else that might help me—or if you think of anything incriminating the police might find—you are to let me know immediately." He scanned the room looking each of us in the eye. "That goes for all of you."

Chapter 43

"Yahoo! Anybody home?"

Sally's voice outside my bedroom window. The doorbell chimed again, and I realized it had been chiming in my dreams.

Shit! Sunday morning! Sally and Nikki were here already. How late was it?

Emma and I had skedaddled out of the Wells' house soon after the lawyer left. Poppy and Joan had a lot to talk about. They didn't need an audience.

Besides, Eleanor's papers beckoned. We had grabbed mugs of vegetable broth on our way through the kitchen and settled down in the dining room. We each took a box.

When we found anything particularly interesting, we read it aloud. Before I knew it, it was three o'clock in the morning. We had reluctantly pulled ourselves away. It was harder than putting down a captivating mystery novel.

By the time I made it down the stairs, Emma had already opened the front door and she and Sally and Nikki were exchanging hugs. A driver carried more luggage to add to the piles of Gucci, Vuitton, and Tumi bags that already filled the entry hall.

"Welcome girls."

All the hugging and kissing requirements fulfilled, we four women told the driver good-bye and headed for coffee in the kitchen. Emma ground the beans while I filled the water reservoir.

"What a fucking fantastic view!" Sally squealed.

Nikki sank into the cushions of the breakfast banquette in the bay window. "Darlings, I love this place. It's so cozy. Charming."

"So, what's happening in LA?" I asked.

"All anyone can talk about is Honey Chaffin and the enormous trust no one knew about," Nikki said.

"Fuck yes! Ten billion, eight million, four hundred and fifty thousand buckaroos! What the fuck else would they talk about?" Sally said. "The speculation about who's going to end up with the money—Shit, everyone has a theory."

"I thought Marty was going to keep a lid on the contents of Honey's will. How does everyone know the amount?" I was disappointed.

Both Sally and Nikki shrugged and shook their heads.

"So, what are the theories?" I asked.

"Museums, cousins. The most prevalent one is that the money will go to one or several of the charities that Honey has given proceeds to in the past," Nikki said.

"The last I knew, the trust was worth about five hundred million. Not too much of it has been given away. It sounds like a lot has been re-invested," I said.

"Mom, I heard you say it was worth five hundred million back in the sixties. That was a long time ago."

"Yeah. Ancient history," I said. "Sally. What's happening with Bunny and what's-his-name?"

"Engaged. Wedding planning in the works." Sally clapped her hands and grinned.

"Congratulations!" Sally and I exchanged high fives. "Have they set a date?"

"Fuck, do you think my spies are that good?" Sally chortled. "I think it'll be soon."

I poured us each a cup of coffee. After swearing them to secrecy, I told Nikki and Sally everything I had learned about Honey's death, her will, the butler's confession, and the cloud of suspicion hanging over Joan.

"Joan's father gave me her mother's papers. Some are here. The rest will be delivered today."

Nikki leaned forward in her chair. "What are we looking for, darling?"

"Anything that might give us a clue as to who killed Honey."

Sally drained the last of her coffee. "Like what?"

"Eleanor was Honey's closest friend. If anybody knew Honey's secrets, it would be Eleanor," I said. "I'm guessing Eleanor saved all this stuff with a mind to writing a memoir. Finding that memoir could be very helpful. It's just possible that the answer as to who killed Honey—and why—is in these papers."

Sally stood up. "So where are the fucking papers?"

I ushered the ladies into the dining room. Sally's and

Nikki's eyes widened at the sight of the boxes and papers strewn around the table and the room.

"There's a method here. That stack of boxes—" I pointed to the pile against the wall, "are ones that we looked at and decided they may not be as fruitful. Things like menus and stuff. The papers stacked here had some data that could fit with other data. The piles of boxes under that end of the table are ones we've yet to go through."

"Fuck, what fun! Where do we start?"

I explained. "Take a box from under the table and go through it. Try to keep it in order."

Emma handed stacks of white paper and Post-its to Sally and Nikki. "Put a piece of paper where you remove papers. Write on it what you took out. And here are the Post-its to put on the outside of the box. That way we'll know what's in there, and we'll also know we've already looked at it."

"Do you want to put your things in your rooms? Or freshen up before you start?" I asked.

"No thanks, darling." Nikki smiled at me.

"Fuck no." Sally pulled a box from under the table.

"Well, I'm going to get dressed. Look for anything about Poppy or Joan's birth. Or anything about—let's see––1960. Or '61. Or 1994, '95." I started out of the dining room headed for my bedroom. I was climbing over the Mount Everest of luggage in the entry hall when the doorbell rang.

I pulled my robe closed and opened the door. Two uniformed men, each with a pile of banker's boxes in his arms stood on the porch.

314

"Mrs. Huntington?"

"Yes."

"Mr. Montgomery sent—" The deliveryman motioned to the covered truck that sat at the curb.

"Right." I backed up to let them in and stumbled over a pile of Vuitton. I landed with an oomph on the top of the pile.

Emma suppressed a smile as she pulled me to my feet. "Are you okay, Mom?"

Sally snickered from the archway of the living room.

"Oh, Cissy, darling. I'm so sorry. How inconsiderate of us to leave all these bags here! Sally, get in here and help me make a path," Nikki ordered as she walked across the living room. "Here. Take this one upstairs." Nikki shoved a trunk toward Sally.

"I'll show you where to go." Emma picked up one of the bags and walked up the stairs.

Sally grabbed the large Vuitton trunk and pulled it up the first two limestone steps. "Fuck, why didn't we have the driver put these bags in our rooms?"

The younger deliveryman set down the three boxes he had been holding and ran to help Sally. "Here, let me help you, miss."

"Thank you." Sally stood up and let him pull the trunk by himself.

"Miss, anyone ever tell you that you look a lot like Sally Abbey?"

"Thank you very much. That's quite a compliment. I think she's gorgeous, don't you?"

"Oh . . . yes . . . Miss," the deliveryman gasped as he struggled to pull the Vuitton up the curved stairs.

Sally grinned, winked at us, and followed Emma to the master suite. The trunk followed Sally.

I directed the other man to stack the boxes at one end of the dining room and then helped Nikki clear a path.

"Be a darling and move that trunk out of the way, please." Nikki batted her eyelashes at the older man. He dropped the boxes in his arms and complied immediately.

Once the way was clear, the two men filled the wall of the dining room with stacks five boxes tall. I then had them start a new row in the living room. Soon both rooms looked like a banker's warehouse.

Once the entry was clear of luggage and the truck empty, I was free to dress in sweats and settle down at the dining table with tea, toast, and a box of Eleanor's papers.

Nikki lectured Sally, "I know you love that damn luggage more than me, but did you have to kill Cissy with it?"

Sally ignored Nikki. "So, we're trying to find evidence that someone else, not Joan, killed Honey in these papers?"

"I think if we understand better what Eleanor and Honey did—well, yesterday I figured Eleanor could give us some insight into Honey. At that point, I only suspected they might have made a habit of trading babies around. There might still be some info here that would get us new suspects to consider."

"Don't get the wrong idea. I don't mind looking—I'm just fucking nosey enough to get a thrill out of this."

"Excuse me, I saw something in the garage I want to use." I located the blank whiteboard I had noticed on a workbench in the garage, dusted it off, and brought it back to the dining room. I leaned the board on top of the buffet and against the wall between two sconces.

Across the top of the board I wrote Joan, Poppy, Cameron, Nick, Italian father, Philip, Maggie, Unknown bad guy.

Down the left side, I wrote motive and opportunity. Under 'Joan,' I wrote a dollar sign and the word secrets, under 'Poppy,' another dollar sign, and a question mark, under 'Cameron,' a question mark, under 'Italian,' another question, under 'Nick,' 'protect his girls', under 'Philip,' 'protect girls', under 'Maggie,' the same, and under 'unknown bad guy,' nothing.

I turned to my audience. I had their full attention.

"Okay, let's start with Joan." I pointed to her section of the board. "She's going to inherit five billion dollars. *But* she didn't know that. The one thing she did know was that Honey knew her secret of adopting Poppy, something that not even her husband knew. So maybe she killed Honey, or had her killed, to keep her from talking."

"But Mom, Joan wouldn't have killed Honey right before Poppy's wedding. She wouldn't want to take any chances on the truth coming out at such a bad time. Not to mention that she had to realize that Honey's death might bring the whole story to light, given that Poppy is Honey's heir."

"What about that necklace that Honey sent to Poppy to

wear at her wedding? Maybe that gift led Joan to believe that Honey might tell Poppy when Honey came up for the wedding festivities," I said. "And we have no reason to think that Joan knew that Poppy would inherit from Honey.

"Wait a fucking minute. Isn't Joan the one we're trying to clear of suspicion?" Sally asked. "Why don't we just assume she didn't do it and see who else did?"

"Okay, okay. Next is Poppy."

"No way, Mom. Poppy wouldn't do anything like that. *And*," Emma paused, "Poppy didn't know anything about any of this. She had no idea she was Honey's heir."

"Next is Cameron. By the way, has Poppy said where Cameron is? I haven't seen him at the house."

"He's up at the Lake, staying away from all the showers and luncheons and girlie shit until it's time for the rehearsal dinner," Emma explained.

"So, Cameron. Per Joan, he knows nothing about any of this. Doesn't know about Poppy and doesn't know about the money. That leaves him without a motive."

"Unless, he actually does know . . . in which case he would have about a billion motives," Nikki said.

"Now, how the fuck would he know?" Sally asked Nikki.

"Well, dar-ling, I don't know." Nikki glared at her best friend, "but it's possible isn't it?"

"I'm going to leave a question mark there," I said. "Next is Nick Montgomery. I like this guy. He's a straight shooter, but I wouldn't cross him when it came to protecting his daughter and granddaughter. He knows that Poppy is adopted. I don't know if he knows that Joan was. I hope it's not him, but I could see him hiring someone to kill Honey if he thought she might harm his girls. On the other hand, I can't see him miscalculating the timing so badly. Also, why would he give me all these papers if he has something to hide?"

"Maybe to distract you from the truth? This fucking pile could keep you busy for weeks," Sally pointed out.

"Okay, I'll leave 'protect his girls' under his name." I pointed to the next name on the board. "Next is the Italian. I'd love it to be this guy. A completely untrustworthy asshole. We know he lied to Cassie with promises to leave his wife. We can guess he had no idea that Cassie was worth hundreds of millions. But what if he found out later?" I put a dollar sign below his name.

"Then there's the butler, Philip. And his wife Maggie. I know that Philip knows the whole story about the girls, and thus, presumably, Maggie does also."

"Mom, what possible motivation would they have?"

"This is the question," I admitted. "Killing Honey doesn't protect their girls.

"That sweet old man couldn't possibly have carried Honey's frozen body and put it on our spa," Emma stated emphatically.

"When I was your age 'that sweet old man,' as you call him, was scary as shit," I said. "He was really intimi-dating."

"That was then," Emma reminded me. "Now he's old."

"Okay. Got it." Lined up with opportunity under Philip,

I wrote 'doubtful'.

"But Philip could be protecting Joan because he thinks she had Honey killed," I said. "That brings us to the note that the police found in Philip's room. Manny read it to me and I wrote it down." I reached across the mahogany table for a small piece of notepaper.

"Here it is. 'I am very concerned about my daughter. Honey Chaffin is threatening to reveal information about her ancestry that will destroy our relationship and her future happiness. I know that you love her like a daughter. I pray that you will help me.' "

"The police took it to be Joan who wrote that, but look at it again. It could've been a lot of people," Emma said.

"What the fuck?" Sally said.

"Darling," Nikki said. "Please explain."

"Well, it could've been something that Joan's mother wrote. Joan's father, that is, Nick Montgomery, could've written it, Cameron could've, or even the Italian biological father. Philip isn't talking, beyond saying that he murdered Honey, so until he says who wrote it, and when, there's no way to know. He could've had that note for years."

"But it was found on a computer," Emma pointed out.

"So the note's fucking worthless," Sally said. "Move on."

"That leaves us with unknown bad guy or guys." I added an 's' to the word guy on the board. "We need to figure out who else could have motive and opportunity. So that's what to look for in these papers. Someone who stands to benefit and /or who knows about the babies."

I sat down with my box of papers, but instead of reading, I kept thinking about unknown bad guys. I wondered who would have thought they were to inherit because they didn't know about Joan and Poppy. I remembered that I briefly considered the possibility that my father and aunt were the heirs. Who else would have thought that? Honey had intended to tell me about Joan and Poppy so that I wouldn't make a fuss over her will. Who did she tell?

I picked up the landline and dialed Joan's number. I got an answering machine. "Hi Joan, this is Cissy. Please call me with a phone number for those men who were at your house yesterday."

Next, I tried Marty's cell. His gravelly voice answered. "Yeah."

"Hi. It's Cissy Huntington. How are you doing?"

"Alright. Doing my best to keep a lid on this thing, but rumors 're flying."

"So I hear. Listen, I was at Joan's yesterday when two lawyers for the trust came by. I want to talk to them again. Do you have their number handy?"

"I can find it, but you'll have trouble getting much outa them."

"I may have to have Joan talk to them, but I want to find out who was the beneficiary of the trust before Honey revealed the info about Joan and Poppy."

"Now that Honey's will has been opened, I can tell you that. Honey was worried about it so she talked about them a lot. You know how under the terms of old Henry's will the money has to go to biological descendants? Can't go to a museum or a charity. But the heirs are, of course, free to use the income however they want, and Honey had been giving some of the proceeds to a number of charities and research funds. She was concerned that future heirs might not be so generous, and she thought she had reason to worry based on their track record."

"So she changed her will?"

"Yep. I figure that's why she made the decision she did––to reveal Joan and Poppy's genetic history. She knew that neither of them needed money, and they have shown some philanthropic tendencies. I know she considered your branch of the family for a while. In fact before Jamie had his diff—uhm . . . er . . ."

"It's okay Marty. You don't have to be careful what you say about Jamie's frozen accounts."

"Yeah, well then, she worried that you or your father would just use the money to replenish . . . aw, you know."

"I do know." And that was exactly what I had considered doing when I thought there was a possibility we would be the beneficiaries. "Who were the previous beneficiaries?"

"It would have reverted to the Cowles clan."

"Shit, there's a lot of them."

"I don't know. Never met a one, but Honey had all of 'em checked out. I'll send you the reports."

"Can you fax them?"

"It's a lot of pages."

"Email or overnight them? I'm trying to resolve this before Joan gets into to legal trouble—like arrested or something. This couldn't have come at a worse time. Poppy's wedding is Saturday."

"I'm not too good with the computer, but I'll have my assistant send the pages to you when she comes in first thing tomorrow."

"By email please. Look, I'm sure Honey wouldn't have wanted her generosity to have ruined this week for Poppy."

"Yeah, got it. You're right. We'll get the papers to you A-sap."

"Thanks Marty."

I relayed what Marty had told me to the girls.

"You sure are right about there being a lot of Cowles. Look at this photo I found in this box. Must've been some kind of reunion up at the Lake." Nikki handed me an eight-by-ten black and white photo of a group of at least forty barefoot people dressed in bathing suits and cut off jeans and ratty looking T-shirts. Toddlers sat cross-legged in the first row, with tall men and a teen-age boy in the fourth and last row. A handwritten note in blue ink on the center of the back of the picture said "Tahoe, Summer 1988." Written in black ink on the upper right corner, in different hand-writing: "Cowles Clan."

"That must be Robby and Tommy." Emma pointed to the two towheaded toddlers. "They were cute little guys. Too bad they grew up."

Emma pointed to the teenager in the back row. "Look at Cameron. God, even as a young man he looked like he had a stick up his butt. I wonder how he ever got to be so uncomfortable in his own skin."

"The first years of his childhood were during the roughest part of the big battle between the Cowles and the Nickels. Must've been a lot of tension—and excessive drinking and drama—in those households from 1950 to 1965."

I thanked my wise great grandmother for protecting my branch of the family from the unhappiness that family feud had caused.

"Darling, there are quite a lot of them."

I thought about the number of Cowles for a moment. "Yeah, the income from that trust has gotten divided up a lot of ways. Wonder how much it's worth now."

"I'll go online and see what I can find out, Mom." Emma left the dining room and returned moments later with her laptop. She typed in 'Cowles San Francisco' to the Google search. "Shit, these Cowles are an awfully litigious group. Lot of newspaper articles about court cases here. In 1955, in 1963, in 1965, in 1971, in 1980. Nothing since 1980. I'll wade through these."

"Is this Cameron's grandmother?" Nikki handed me another photo: a black and white of a symmetrically posed wedding party with a formally gowned Beatrice Cowles Wells as the centerpiece. A note on the back identified Honey and Eleanor as the flower girls.

"Yeah, I'd forgotten she was also a Cowles. Shit, there could be Cowles relatives all over. Lot of women in that family."

I joined Nikki in digging through the box of photos. "Great clothes in this one." I handed a photo to Nikki of a group of grinning flappers and a guy in a raccoon coat, a flask in one hand, his leg jauntily resting on the running board of an impressive Duesenberg convertible.

"Oh, darling. They were having a good time." Nikki smiled.

"Hey, you two! Leave the fucking photos and help me find the papers from the fifties and the nineties. I'm fucking frustrated here." Sally said. "I don't understand why she saved some of this shit." She slammed a lid back on the box she had examined and dumped it in the pile of labeled boxes.

"Nikki, evil bitch, give me the box of photos." Sally grabbed a side of the container, Nikki held on. A minute long tug-a-war, then photos flew all over the table and floor.

"Fuck. Look what you've done."

"I don't know why I love you, darling. Behave!" Nikki gathered up photos from the floor.

Sally picked up the photo box and rifled through it. "Fucking ridiculous. Check out all the Chanel, Dior, Halston—" Sally stopped talking. Her sudden silence got our attention. She studied a photo held up to the light. "This is my Ted—er, my ex."

Nikki reached for the photo. Sally pulled it away and shoved it in my face. "Who are these other people?"

"Spreckels family."

"Why is Cameron in the picture?" Emma asked from over my shoulder. "Is Ted related to Honey?"

I thought back to my conversation with Katherine—her

response to my question as to why Honey wasn't invited to participate in the San Francisco Cotillion. "Remember, Honey's grandmother was a Spreckels," Katherine had said.

"Add the prick to your board," Sally ordered as she waved her hand at the whiteboard.

I obeyed and then returned to my box of papers. When I was certain that mine was full of papers, newspaper clippings, magazine articles, receipts, plane tickets, train tickets, journal entries, all from the sixties and not the fifties or nineties, I labeled the box "60's" with a post-it and added it to the examined pile. The next box I looked through more quickly. Thirties stuff. Then sixties. Then more sixties. More sixties.

"I'm not sure I understand what I've found. In 1969, some Cowles tried to overturn the trust and get the money paid out to the heirs. There was a lot of talk of trustees mishandling stock and the like, but they still used figures in the millions, including one settlement from the estate of one trustee of two million cash, plus land worth many millions. The court ruled that 'every Cowles who are part of the third generation were to be life beneficiaries,' but the next generation of 'those born in legal wedlock' were to receive the remainders. Does that mean what I think?"

Nikki spoke with authority. "Darlings. It means that those heirs will divide up whatever is left of the money. They won't just get the income."

"When the fuck did you get so knowledgeable?" Sally smiled at her best friend.

326

Nikki frowned. "My first husband set up a trust. He said it was to keep his children from blowing all his fortune, but it really kept me from getting the settlement I deserved. After that, I made it a point to learn all about trusts."

Sally grinned. "That's when she became the scheming bitch."

Emma continued, "Doesn't seem as though the Cowles trust fared as well as the Nickels. It's not worth more than a few million. They've managed to break into it a few times, apparently."

The pile of examined boxes out grew its corner and blocked half the archway to the living room. The room had gotten quiet. It seemed that none of us found anything interesting enough to bother to read it aloud anymore.

Sally broke the silence. "This woman was just a fucking pack rat. She was as bad as those old people who fill their houses with everything they've ever got their hands on. Except she was rich, so some poor assistant boxed it all up for her." Sally slammed her box onto the floor. "This isn't so much fun after all." But she pulled another box from the pile.

"I'm convinced she was planning to write a memoir and all of these papers were to remind her. Yesterday, I saw a few pages in a box of loose-leaf binders and a few typed pages. It looked like the start—a very rough draft of a memoir."

I didn't want to admit that I too was discouraged by the amount of papers. This tedious task could take a lot longer than I had hoped.

"Sally, you aren't being at all careful." Nikki pointed out as Sally dropped another box onto the done pile. "You couldn't've looked at everything in that box in two seconds."

"Fuck you, Nikki. There's nothing in there."

"You didn't even label it." Nikki held the post-its out to Sally, but Sally ignored the gesture.

"Fuck that." Sally walked toward the kitchen. "I'm getting more coffee." She slammed the door behind her.

Nikki looked at me and shook her head. "Darling, I thought of something scary."

She had my attention.

"Ted's a friend of Cameron's, a cousin?"

I nodded.

"Then he and BB—Bimbo Bunny—might be at the wedding."

Oh, that was a scary thought.

"How are we going to handle that?" Nikki nodded toward the kitchen. "With that one?"

I shrugged as Sally re-entered the room.

Nikki labeled her box and placed it on the examined pile. She pulled a new box onto the tabletop. Seconds later she let out a yelp. "Eureka! I found it!" Nikki madly dug through and then pulled papers from the box in front of her. "Darlings! There's hundreds of pages."

It was, per the page numbers, two hundred-and-forty typed pages, followed by maybe fifty pages handwritten on yellow lined paper.

Sally pulled her chair over to Nikki's. "Let's celebrate!

This means we're done right?"

"Let's see what's actually here," I cautioned.

"I want to see it too." Emma closed her laptop. "I'm sick of reading these cases." Emma moved a chair next to Nikki's.

I stood behind Nikki and read over her shoulder for a while. When I got tired of standing I sat across the table and Nikki handed me pages as the three of them finished reading. The typed pages started with Eleanor's description of her parent's lives and then moved on to her childhood. By page 145 we were still in the 1920's and I was concerned that we'd never see the sixties, let alone the nineties.

"Hand me the yellow sheets." I scanned the pages. The elaborate, curlicued handwriting was difficult to decipher, but it looked like these pages covered the sixties. The ring of my cell interrupted my scanning.

It was Joan. She was crying. "Cissy please come over. I have to talk to someone. I've done such a bad thing."

Chapter 44

"Keep reading," I told my crew of detectives and handed the yellow pages to Emma. "I'm going to Joan's."

I threw a jacket on over my sweats and drove to Pacific Heights. Uncharacteristically unconcerned with "what the neighbors might think", she stood in the entry door and greeted me in tears.

"Cissy, please help me! I wanted so much to do this wedding right, but it's blowing up in my face! So many mistakes."

I took her arm, guided her into the entry hall and closed the front door." What's happened?"

"C.K. is convinced I'm to be arrested. Philip, that kind-hearted old fool. He must have thought he could throw the police off my trail by confessing . . . but instead he's led them right to my door." Joan hesitated. "And the technicians found the damn note from Philip's room was also on the hard drive of my computer."

"Oh dear."

"I'm such a stupid fool—thinking I could pull this off. Oh God, I should've told Cameron years ago. But—" Joan used a soggy handkerchief to wipe away tears. "He was such a distant father. I was afraid if he knew Poppy wasn't our biological daughter—he would be even worse. Damn, damn, damn." Joan broke off, sobbing.

I put my arms around her shoulders and pulled her to me.

As I held her she spoke between sobs. "Poppy was handed to me right after she was born. I took her to my room and lay down next to her on the bed." Joan sniffled. "I wanted to soothe her—by rubbing her back. My hand was so huge compared to her tiny body. I was careful to use a light touch on her teeny little back."

"I thought about how, as she grew, my hand would be smaller and smaller in comparison," Joan choked back a sob and shuddered. "This perfect, miniature creature who had been entrusted to my care was so dependent on my love, I promised her I would love, and protect her and do everything possible to give her a happy life." Joan sank into my shoulder.

I walked her into the living room and we sat down on the sofa.

"I was absurdly overconfident in my ability to be the perfect mother. But I'm so shit." Her usual self-consciousness forgotten, this was a Joan she had never allowed me to see. Oblivious to how she looked, tears flowed over her cheeks and dripped off her jaw.

"You're not shit."

My eyes teared. I couldn't help but remember feeling the same responsibility for Emma when she was a newborn.

"You've been a wonderful mother."

Joan pulled back from my hug enough to look at my face. "I wanted to at least make her wedding as nearly perfect as possible. I've tried to keep her in the dark about any problems; I wanted her day to be blissfully ignorant of my impending divorce. Cameron's been a hopelessly neglectful father, but he can at least do a good act of it and be a proper father of the bride by walking her down the aisle, twirling her around the dance floor, and toasting their happiness."

I nodded my agreement. Damn. The divorce was news to me.

"I couldn't even provide a happy home." Tears and words gushed out. "I sent her to boarding school because I didn't want her to know that Cameron and I were fighting so much, but I think she could feel the tension between us when she was home."

"We all have the best of intentions, but—nobody's perfect." I couldn't help but think that perhaps if Joan had been honest with Cameron, their marriage wouldn't have been so rocky. But what did I know about successful marriages? I didn't even know where my husband was.

"These last few years—since she's been on her own—I begged him to keep up the pretense of a happy marriage whenever she was with us, but he mostly just stayed away . . . living up at the Lake—or supposedly traveling on business—which really meant staying with his various girlfriends." Joan pulled away from my embrace, grabbed the box of tissues off the table, took a handful and noisily blew her nose. "I've bribed him, I've borrowed money from my father to pay for this wedding so that Cameron didn't have to pay for any of it."

And here I had been thinking that Joan had no use for the Nickels's money.

"I've tried to make up for my shortcomings by giving her every material thing she could possibly desire, but of course, that doesn't make up for love. I couldn't give her a father."

"Her grandparents—Nick has been devoted to her," I said. "And your mother doted on her."

"That's another thing—I didn't protect her from the pain of my mother dying. In fact, I moved Mother into this house at the end. That was really stupid. Poppy spent that entire summer vacation in a house where death was expected any day."

"Joan, you did what you thought was best for everyone."

"I didn't know her genetic medical history. I didn't tell even her pediatrician that she wasn't mine," Joan said. "She would've been better off with Cassie."

"Cassie's dead." A little dose of reality interjected into her guilt trip.

"Maybe she wouldn't have died. If I hadn't taken Poppy, Cass would've had to be responsible, she wouldn't have been in that plane. Maybe she would've worked it out with the father."

That reminded me that I had failed to confirm the father's name. Probably was not a good time to bring it up. Joan had piled such a load of guilt on herself. She was really suffering. "Not much chance of an Italian getting a divorce back in those days." I reminded her.

"You see, I can't let Cameron find out that she isn't his daughter until after the wedding. After her honeymoon, when she's safely living in London, it won't matter. She'll be far away from all this mess with a new life. Then what we do here will have less importance. I have to give her this one thing." Joan had stopped crying.

She pulled herself upright. "I don't know how he'll react to the news about the Nickels trust. He can't know. He's liable to have a squad of lawyers getting court orders and filing suits even as we are having a wedding. Cissy, please help me figure out how to keep him from finding out. Until after the wedding."

"I'm not sure what I can do," I said but then I looked at Joan's tearstained face.

"Please, protect Poppy."

"Okay, I'll speak with Marty. He's already agreed to keep what he knows a secret until after the wedding, but I'll reinforce the importance of not breathing a word."

I thought of the rumors that were already flying around. Odds were Cameron would hear about the staggering amounts of money involved.

I thought for a moment about a strategy. "You order those trust lawyers to disappear. They work for you now."

Joan bit her lip, but nodded her agreement.

"C.K. can just handle the DA. I won't tell anyone—and neither will Emma." I thought better of mentioning Nikki and Sally, but I knew they could keep a secret. "What else can I do?"

"I guess nothing." Joan sighed. "If only you could find out who really killed Honey." She took a deep breath. "Peter and his family, his parents and siblings, arrive tomorrow. Cameron promised to get back before they show up. Maybe Emma could spend some time with Poppy until it's time for the family . . . I don't want Poppy around Cameron anymore than necessary. She'll feel that she has to tell him."

"I'll take Poppy home with me now."

"Good. I'll go tell her." Joan stood up to leave the room.

"Joan. Where do you have the name of the Italian? Could you give it to me now?"

"I'll find it as soon as I've spoken with Poppy." She walked up the wide oak stairs.

I turned to watch the misty fog roll under the bridge filling the bay with gray. Typical of a Sunday afternoon, the bay was populated with hundreds of white sails dancing merrily in the wind and waves. How happy all those people must be, enjoying the fresh air and the last few minutes of sunshine.

I heard footsteps on the stairs. Joan walked over to where I stood studying the view. She pulled a slip of paper out of her skirt pocket and read, "Giovanni Luigi Antonio Chiari."

"What?" I said. "Didn't I meet him in the clubhouse at La Rinconada yesterday? While I was with your father?"

My mind raced. What is he doing here? Living a few blocks away from his biological daughter's grandfather?

Did he come to get in on the money?

"What are you talking about?" Joan's eyes widened, her face paled.

"I met Luigi Chiari at the club yesterday morning."

"No!" she shrieked. "Can't be." Joan took a deep breath. "Probably not him. Cassie called him Vonni. How old was this man you met?"

"In his fifties."

"Oh, no." Joan sank down to the chair. "My God."

"But he doesn't get any money out of the deal." I thought about how much those houses around the La Rinconada Club go for. He can't be hurting for money.

On the other hand, he could be leveraged to the hilt. Maybe he figures that his daughter will 'loan' him money. And she might. Maybe he figures, what's a few million when you have billions. Imagine the income on an amount like that.

"Hmm, damn." Her face went whiter. "Oh, what am I going to do? Why would he turn up just now?" Joan stood and paced in front of the windows.

"He's been around for awhile. He has a house near the entrance to the club. Done up like a villa in Chianti country, complete with vineyard and olive trees."

"What—" Joan was interrupted by the sound of the front door opening. She stood perfectly still and stiff, perhaps in anticipation of Cameron entering the house. But it was C.K. and Philip.

"I'm so sorry Miss Joanie." Philip hung his white-haired head. "I didn't realize I would make things worse."

C.K. explained, "He's recanted his confession. Couldn't explain how she was killed, and the investigation turned up no evidence against him. And he was seen in Auburn several times over the three-day period surrounding Mrs. Chaffin's death."

Joan tenderly hugged Philip. "I very much appreciate what you tried to do." She stepped back from the frail, bent old man. "But I'm terribly disappointed that you felt you needed to do so. Did you really think I would murder anyone, especially Honey?"

With tears in his eyes, Philip spoke, "I didn't think. I was frightened for you . . . and for Poppy. And over the years, I've seen people do out of character things when they are desperate. I know how very much Poppy means to you . . . I . . . I'm sorry."

"So, does this mean that Joan is also cleared of any charges?" I asked C.K.

"Unfortunately, not." C.K. turned to Joan. "I agreed to bring you down to the station for further questioning. Would tomorrow morning be convenient?"

A wide-eyed, white-faced Joan struggled to speak. "Peter and his family, . . . Poppy's in-laws to be . . . they're to arrive tomorrow. How perfectly awful—that I will be at the police station when they arrive."

"You should go now," I suggested. "Get it over with."

"Can we?" Joan asked C.K.

"Yes. I just thought you . . . . Yes, let's go now."

"I'll get my coat and purse." Joan trudged up the stairs as though in a trance. She paused to hug Poppy who was coming down to go with me.

"Mother, what's wrong?" Poppy returned the hug and hung onto her mother's arm.

Joan pulled herself together. She stood upright and smiled. "Nothing, Dear. C.K. and I just have to take care of a little business."

"On Sunday afternoon?"

Joan ignored Poppy's question and continued up the stairs.

Boot-clad Poppy bounced down the remainder of the stairs. When she spotted Philip standing in the living room, she dropped her overnight bag and ran into his embrace. "Oh, my God, Philip. Thank God you're home. Whatever were you thinking?"

Philip awkwardly returned the hug. He patted Poppy's gleaming, golden blonde hair and grinned.

"I'm going with Cissy to spend the night with Emma. My last night of girlie stuff. Peter and his family arrive tomorrow."

"Everything will be ready. I'll see to their rooms." Philip said.

"Peter's sister has a thing about cut flowers. Doesn't like them. Her room should have a plant. An orchid I think."

"Good. Thank you for letting me know. Any other special requests?"

"Peter's mother is allergic. No fragrances of any kind in her rooms. Including the laundry soap for her linens." Poppy tenderly hugged the frail man. "Oh Philip, I'm so glad you're home. This place just doesn't work without you."

Philip beamed and stood more upright.

I thought it best to get Poppy out of the house before Joan and C.K. left for the police station. I hurried her out to my car.

I gave the car a quick look over before I reached for the door handle. A low cloud of water droplets sat on the ground and a layer of dew covered the car. But the door handle was wiped dry.

I looked for Joan's driver in the vicinity. He wasn't nearby, but there were shadows in the mist too far away to make out. A foghorn could be heard above the traffic noise.

I opened the car and pressed the unlock button for Poppy to get in the passenger side door. I turned on the windshield wipers to deal with the heavy mist and drove out of the circular drive.

Remembering the boxes of Poppy's grandmother's papers strewn all over the dining and living rooms at Seacliff, I stopped at the curb in the next block to call Emma. I didn't want Poppy to hear both sides of the conversation so I didn't use the Bluetooth.

"Hi. I'm on my way home. I'm bringing Poppy with me. Perhaps you could set the dining table for dinner." I hoped Emma would get the hint.

"Does that mean we should do something with the papers?"

"It would be best. What are we doing for dinner? Should we pick something up?"

"Sally sent their new driver to Chinatown, to her favorite restaurant. She ordered more than enough for all of us."

"Great. We're five minutes—" I felt a bump on the back of the car. I looked in the rearview mirror and saw the shadowy shapes of two men in dark baseball caps exit a black BMW. Something about the way they walked was not only threatening, but also familiar. One walked on each side of the car. The man on my side reached into his pocket.

I didn't wait to see if he pulled out a gun. I tossed the phone in Poppy's lap, punched the gas, and jerked the steering wheel hard to the left. Over the roar of the engine, I heard a thump and a yelp. Must have gotten a piece of the one on the left.

"Cissy, what's happening?" Poppy picked up the phone. "Emma, your mom's lost it. She's driving like a crazy woman. Two men—what's going on?"

"Poppy, look to see if they're following us."

Poppy turned around. "Yep, got back in their car and they're racing after us."

I abruptly turned right and then left at the next corner. "Tell Emma to call the Seacliff security and have them meet us at the east gate."

I couldn't see the BMW in the rearview mirror, but I wasn't taking any chances. I turned right again, left again.

Due to the dense fog, I couldn't see more than half-block behind me. I didn't see any headlights.

The adrenaline pumping had my heart racing. The necessity to keep Poppy safe had turned me into a super-woman. My perceptions were heightened. I felt competent.

I zigzagged for a few more blocks. Then I headed west on California Street for a direct route to Seacliff.

Details of signs and buildings blurred by the mist jumped out at me. Ten blocks to go to the Seacliff pillars and security.

"Poppy, look behind us. Do you see them?"

Poppy turned in her seat and studied the street behind us. "I don't."

Six blocks to go.

Four blocks.

I turned to the right on 26th Avenue. The fog thickened as we approached Seacliff.

Two blocks.

One block to go.

The mist sat just above the ground. I could barely make out the white pillars of the gate up ahead.

Out of the blanket of fog, the black BMW roared across the street and screeched to a stop, blocking the road.

Wham! We slammed into the side of the black sedan.

Air bags in both cars popped. Propellant dust shot into the air.

Poppy screamed.

I fought back the airbag that enveloped me, managing to hit the button that locked the doors.

But the airbags and the chemicals made the inside of the car uninhabitable. We had to get out.

Chapter 45

My arm stung from the burning chemicals in the exploded airbags. I held my breath and fought to find and undo the lock mechanism.

Shit! Finally—I heard it click and I opened the door.

I caught my breath. I shouted, "Poppy, are you okay?"

I shoved the bag aside, put my feet on the road.

A large, suntanned hand grabbed my arm and yanked me out of the vehicle. I struggled to my feet and looked up to see what ape owned the hand. I swung my fist and knocked the cap off his head.

I recognized the bald patch surrounded by scraggly, dirty dishwater blond hair. "Tommy! What the hell?"

"Hey! Uh. That's not Emma!" Tommy shoved me against the side of the car.

Shit! Robby had Poppy by the arm. The cretin pulled her next to me against the car and slammed his fist into the top of the car next to her head.

A scowl of frustration marred his once handsome face. Daggers of anger flashed from his eyes. He threw his clenched hand at her face. When Poppy ducked he rammed his knuckles through the window. Robby stared at his hand as the blood spurted off his fingers and ran down his arm.

"Hey! Where's Emma?" Tommy pushed my shoulder with the palm of his hand. Behind him I caught a glimpse of a familiar arm in motion. Thank God.

"Right here, asshole." Emma swung a tennis racket in a serving motion and landed a solid hit on Tommy's bare head. She followed with a backhand blow to his face.

Tommy wrapped his arms around his face and head in a futile effort to protect himself. Emma used the edge of the racket to whack his arms and bald patch.

Robby's bloody arm did not deter Nikki and Sally from raining blows onto his head with their shoes. Wham went Nikki's five-inch stiletto heel into his skull. Sally's heavy wedge heel caught the side of his jaw.

When he fell to the road in a duck and cover position, Nikki put her shoe back on her foot, thrust the pointed YSL toe into his ribs, and stomped. Sally attacked his back with her Givenchy wedge sole. Poppy repaid Robby for frightening her with several quick jabs from her Balenciaga ankle boots.

Three security guards ran between the pillars toward the cars in the middle of the intersection. When the uniformed men arrived at the scene, both Tommy and Robby were on the ground, on their backs in fetal positions trying to protect themselves from Poppy, Nikki, Emma and Sally who pummeled them with hands and feet.

"Ladies, ladies, we can take it from here."

Sally jumped at Tommy with both feet in the air and

would have landed square on his stomach had one of the guards not had quick reflexes. The guard wrapped his arms around her waist and held her back until she calmed down.

Poppy and Emma continued to work over Robby.

"Ladies, please!"

The second guard took hold of their slender arms and pulled them back from Tommy and Robby. Within seconds the girls were laughing.

The second and third guard hauled Tommy and Robby to their feet and shoved them against the BMW. They patted them down for weapons.

I leaned against the side of the car. I had recovered just enough from my shock to find my voice. "What the hell? What were you two clowns doing?"

Still shocked at being viciously attacked by four beautiful women, Tommy whimpered. "Hey, uh, we just wanted you and Emma to agree to give up your claim to cousin Honey's estate."

"What claim? We are not beneficiaries," I said.

"Like, she told us you were." Robby spit.

"She did not tell you we were. What did she actually tell you?" I asked.

Tommy wiped the snot and tears from his face with the bottom of his t-shirt. "Hey, uh, why'd you do that?" He looked at Emma.

Emma raised her racket and prepared to swing. "Answer Mom's questions!"

Tommy studied the hood of the BMW. "She said she, uh, totally wanted to be sure that we didn't like fight her will. She totally didn't want like, uh, a repeat of the, uh, fifty-year-battle that the Aunties had over great grand-father's estate."

"She gave us some cash and had us like sign a paper." Robby tried to wipe the blood from his hand and arm with his shirt. When the blood continued to gush, he wrapped his hand in his sweatshirt. "She said that the trust was going to a mother and her daughter."

"Hey, she said the mother and daughter were, uh . . . blood relatives to great grandpa Henry. But their grand-mothers . . . and their parents . . . had, uh, made decisions that had kept them from being, uh, considered heirs." Tommy sputtered.

"And you assumed that she was talking about Emma and me?"

"Uh, who else?" Tommy said. "That fits, doesn't it?"

"So, you wanted to get rid of us so that the trust would revert to the Cowles?" Emma kicked Tommy in the shin.

"Hey. Ow! Hey. Christ! We weren't going to hurt you— uh, just scare you so that you would like uh, sign away your claim."

"And if we didn't?" Emma kicked Tommy one more time. Lucky for him, she wore her soft soled boots.

"Well, uh, shit." Tommy hung his head.

"What were you going to do about the paper you signed?" I asked.

"We got that sucker back." Robby stood tall and stretch-ed his neck, but he still didn't look us in the eye.

"When you killed her?" I asked.

"You killed her?" Emma repeated and kicked Robby in the knee.

"Fuck, that hurt." Robby glared at Emma. "We didn't think it would turn out that way. We just wanted to get the paper back."

"What, you *accidentally* poisoned her?" Unbelievable how stupid these two were. "Give me a break. Who put you up to this?" I asked.

"Whadda ya mean?" Robby glowered at me.

Emma kicked Robby.

"Hey, dumb bitch! Kick me all you want: I'm not saying another word." He pulled the sweatshirt wrapped around his hand tighter. "Like, I'm gonna bleed to death here! Any of you assholes think to call the paramedics?"

"Tommy?" I looked at my pathetic cousin. His face dripped with sweat, snot and tears.

Emma threatened with her racket. "Tommy!"

Whatever Tommy said was indecipherable between his sputters and whimpers. He cowered away from Emma.

Emma tossed her racket on the lawn and threw up her arms in disgust.

"And then when the billions in the Nickels trust reverted it would be lumped in with the Cowles trust. And then it would get remaindered out—so you'd end up millionaires." I remembered the terms of the last court battle the Cowles had with their trustees. In the next generation, the trust was to be remaindered, paid out to the heirs. The court must have assumed that the way Cowles were burning through the money, there wouldn't be enough left in the trust to bother with. What a windfall the Nickels's billions would have been to the Cowles cousins.

"What the fuck 're you talkin' about? What billions?" Robby growled.

"You didn't know the trust is in the billions? Whoever put you up to this knew. Who was it that was cheating you?" I demanded.

"Hey lady, you aren't so fucking smart. Like, Tom and I figured this all out ourselves."

"Right."

The thought of what brain-damaged dopers like these two would do with millions was scary as hell.

Chapter 46

The sirens that had been in the distance minutes before now blared in our ears. While we awaited the arrival of the San Francisco Police Department, I regained enough presence of mind to call Manny and explain what had happened.

"Oh, hell, I'm sorry I left too soon." That was as close to saying I was right as I'd ever heard Manny come. "I'll catch the next flight up. Let me speak to the officers there."

Three patrol cars pulled up to the scene of the collision. Six officers got out of the vehicles. Two uniformed policemen had handcuffed the two clowns and read them their rights. Another officer took notes as he questioned the security personnel. Thankfully the security guards had all three heard Tommy and Robby confess to murder.

Policemen number three and four measured tire skids and photographed our cars as though they assumed they were there to document a traffic accident.

I approached the man who watched the other men perform their duties. "Officer, I have Homicide Detective Manny Rodriquez of the Beverly Hills Police on the phone.

He'd like to speak with you." I handed him the phone and felt my legs buckle. I sat down on the curb.

"Mom, are you okay?" I heard Emma as though she was a long distance from me.

I put my head between my knees.

"Come on, Mom. Let's go to the house." Emma put her arm around my waist and lifted me to my feet. "Officer, I need to take my mother inside. We'll be right there." Emma pointed out my father's house and helped me up the steps.

Still stunned from the car accident and my cousins' evil, I allowed myself to be led up the steps of the porch and into the dining room.

I was further surprised to see that in the few minutes I had been trying to lose the menacing car following us, the girls had managed to clear the room of not only all the papers, but also the boxes.

Poppy stood in the living room speaking into her cell. "Mom, when you get this message call me right away. We caught the real murderers and they've have been arrested."

"Wow, where did you—?" I said to Emma.

"In the garage. Fortunately—or unfortunately, we won't have much use for those papers now." Emma led me into the kitchen. I sat down in the breakfast window seat. My trembling hands gratefully accepted a glass of Gamay Beaujolais from Nikki. I allowed myself a gulp.

Poppy came into the kitchen with a wide smile.

"Are you okay sweetie? Did those guys hurt you?" I asked.

"Not really. Might have a bruise or two on my arm.

Good thing I didn't go with a sleeveless wedding dress." She giggled. "Mom's going to be okay, right?" She asked in a shaky voice.

I nodded. "Yes, I'm sure she'll be home soon."

"Fuck." Sally sat down next to me and slugged down half a glass of the wine. "What the hell? Do you know those two creeps?"

"Yeah, they're kinda distant cousins." Emma opened a white container of wonton soup, and ladled the steaming liquid into six bowls.

She looked at Poppy leaning against the counter. "You're shaking." Emma hugged Poppy. "Let's call your mother's lawyer." She ushered her to the library.

"Nice fucking family," Sally said. "It was fun beating the shit out of them."

"Darling, I have to admit I kinda enjoyed it too." Nikki unfolded the lids of two more white containers. The aroma of sweet and sour pork and fried rice wafted across the room. "I guess we aren't dieting tonight."

"Hell no! This is a celebration," Sally said. "We caught the bad guys."

"You didn't know that when you ordered all this food." Nikki waved her hand at the three remaining white bags.

"The Golden Dragon has abso-fuck-ing-lutely the best Chinese on the planet. I celebrated being in the same city and not being in fucking training/dieting mode for a change." Sally walked over to the granite island and opened the rest of the bags removing several containers from each bag. "So now that you aren't in danger, let's go shopping tomorrow."

I checked to see where Poppy was before I whispered. "This isn't over. I don't know if we're still in danger now that Tommy and Robby know Emma and I are not the beneficiaries, but those two didn't do this by themselves." In a louder voice I said, "Let's go to the design center. We can finish your screening room." I held the cool glass of wine to the sting on my wrist that had been burned by the airbag propellant.

"I wanted to buy those rugs from those cute guys in LA––Jerry and Michael." Sally stuck her chopsticks into noodles, put the sticks to her mouth, and sucked in the noodles.

"There's one of their Aga John shops at the San Francisco Design Center." My hands were settling but I poured myself more wine anyway.

"That's the name of their shop?" Sally muttered with her mouth full of egg roll.

"Yes."

"Cool. Let's go there tomorrow. Tonight let's pig out and drink." Sally held a fried wonton between her perfect white teeth and used her hands to open still another container of noodles.

Poppy carried a bowl of soup over and placed it in front of me. "I'm sorry I freaked about your driving. You didn't exactly explain—but I—well thanks. This means my mother is safe." Poppy hugged me.

"Did you speak to your mother?" I asked.

"No, I got her voicemail. She'll check it as soon as she

gets out of her meeting. C.K. didn't answer either."

"They may already know. The police should have told them."

"What a relief to get this resolved before Peter and his family arrive. Just in time. We are going to have the best week ever." Poppy danced around the room in anticipation of the parties and dancing that the week held in store.

I smiled at her excitement and hoped we could get through the week without any further complications. But Tommy and Robby weren't the only ones who might think they'd end up as millionaires. The entire Cowles clan might think they would benefit, and the main beneficiaries would be the fourth generation, the recipients of the pay out. Tommy and Robby were two of that generation. I needed to find out who else was.

"Emma, we're going to need to get out that photo of the Cowles clan again. Do you know where it ended up?"

"I can find it." Emma looked up from her plate of chow mien. "Can I do it in the morning?"

I nodded, excused myself, and headed for the study. I sat down in Dad's chair and felt the stiffness resulting from the jolt of the impact setting in already.

I dialed Skip's cell. When I got his voicemail, I explained what had just happened assuring him that we were safe. "Sweetheart, were Tommy and Robbie speaking with Ted at the club the day you and Jeff were there? Who was Ted playing with?"

Next, I called the Wells' mansion and asked for Philip.

"Speaking."

"Philip, the police have just arrested Tommy and Robby Cowles for the murder of Honey Chaffin. Have you met those two?"

"Yes."

"Well then, you'll understand when I say that I doubt that they did little more than follow directions. I need to find out who was giving them instructions, but I'm sure you'll agree it needs to be done discreetly. Especially this week, we don't want to do anything that will . . ."

"I understand."

"Philip, why did you think that Joan might have had something to do with Honey's murder?"

"There was a phone message from Tommy that had me a little worried."

"What did he say?"

"Something about Mrs. Chaffin and a new will. I didn't pay too much attention to it at the time, but later when the police came around—well, I jumped to an erroneous conclusion."

"Perhaps." I thought about how to phrase what I wanted Philip to do. "Philip, I know you love Poppy and you know how important this week is to her. That's why I think you and I should work together. We can make sure the festivities come off smoothly, but let's also do a little snooping. Hopefully, once the week is over we can have enough evidence that the person, or persons, behind Honey's murder is brought to justice."

"That sounds fine, but I don't see what I can do."

"It seems to me that the Wells household will be the

center of activities in which most of the possible suspects will be participating. Keep your eyes and ears open. If you should find anything at all that could be evidence, bag it, and save it."

"I'll do my best."

"Do you supervise the unpacking of bags?"

"Of course."

"Watch for anything unusual."

Chapter 47

Sally's driver pulled the town car into the driveway in front of the Wells's mansion. Sally and Nikki had joined Emma and me as guests for dinner.

My faithful car had been declared totaled by the insurance company, and I was now on a waiting list for a new Prius. It seemed a betrayal to put down my poor car, but the agent insisted that having sustained a powerful hit, it might never be the same.

I was somewhat surprised that Joan had included Sally in the invitation for a dinner party in honor of Peter's parents and siblings. But it was convenient that her driver could deliver all of four of us to the same location. We needed some fun after all the hours spent at police headquarters giving statements and answering questions.

We four donned our Little Black Dresses. Sally's LBD was entirely covered in sequins and accented with dangling diamond earrings. Nikki wore vintage Chanel—the original LBD—and several long strands of glowing pearls. Emma's golden skin and hair were enhanced by Fortuny pleated chiffon. I wore a simple Michael Kors black sheath.

Philip greeted us at the door and took our coats.

He whispered as he helped me remove my black cashmere coat. "I have something interesting to show you after dinner, if you'll excuse yourself after the desert is served. Can you find the laundry?"

I nodded. "Thank you."

Philip took Sally's mink and Nikki's faux ermine before he showed the four of us to the living room where cocktails were being served.

I was surprised to see Luigi Chiari deep in conversation with Cameron Wells and Nick Montgomery in the far corner of the room. Joan left that conversation to join us. I suspected she had been monitoring them, concerned as to where the talk might lead.

Poppy squealed with delight at our entrance. She ran to hug Emma and grabbed my arm as well. She dragged us both to the sofas flanking the fireplace. "Emma, Cissy, these are Peter's parents, Sophie and Malcolm. And this is his sister, Martha. His brother, George."

We exchanged handshakes and small talk. I introduced Nikki and Sally.

"How exciting this is to meet real film stars." Martha shook Sally's hand. "Now our trip to California is complete."

"Happy to have obliged you," Sally faked a smile that was closer to a grimace.

"Ms. Sally, what would you like to drink?" Philip stood at attention with a tray in hand.

"A martini. With lots of olives."

Philip took drink orders from us all. That out of the way, Joan hugged each of us. "I wanted to thank the four of you for rescuing Poppy."

"Fuck, it was nothing."

Nikki and I both shot eye daggers at Sally.

"Sorry," Sally said.

My attention went to Nick and Luigi in the corner. Nick laughed and slapped Luigi on the shoulders. I wondered when Luigi and Nick had become such good friends. They were mere acquaintances last week.

Joan must have told Nick that Luigi was Poppy's biological father. I was sure that Cameron had been too much of a tight ass for Nick to be close to him. The same did not seem to be true of his feelings for Luigi.

I took Joan's arm and walked her into the hall. "What the hell is Chiari doing here?"

"Father is completely enamored with him," she whispered. "He checked him out. Found out Luigi is quite well off. Father's convinced his intentions are honorable." Joan snuck a quick look at the three men. "I have to admit, even though it makes me a bit nervous to have him around Cameron, he is a lovely man."

Thankfully, dinner was served before Sally could ask for a second martini. Nikki and I wanted Joan to see that Sally could behave herself. Fortunately, someone had been smart enough to seat her between the young people. I was relieved to be seated at the far end of the table, far enough away that I could only hear Sally when she raised her voice. I love Sally, and usually find her entertaining, but not when I am held responsible for her unpredictable behavior.

Luigi Chiari was at Joan's right hand, her father, Nick Montgomery at her left. I sat next to Nick. Peter's mother, Sophie was across the table from me. I heard her ask Luigi how he was related to the Wells family. I wondered how he would answer.

"I'm a neighbor of Nick's."

"Aah, an old family friend?" Sophie asked.

"So to speak, yes," Luigi responded.

"You are Italian?"

"Yes, but I spend as much time as possible in Los Gatos. It reminds me of Tuscany and my family is nearby here."

"Your wife?"

"My wife died six years ago."

"I'm sorry."

Luigi turned to Joan. "I'm delighted to have been invited to your lovely home. I hope you don't mind that I convince Nick to let me accompany him on this special evening. It means a lot to me to be included."

"We are pleased to have you as our guest." Joan smiled at Luigi.

Their eyes met and Luigi held her gaze.

The two continued to look into each other's eyes long enough to make Nick squirm. "Lou harvested some of the grapes he's growing on the hill side in front of his house. We're gonna have La Rinconada wine."

Other than the occasional loud burst of laughter from Sally's section of the table, the dinner progressed normally.

As soon as the dessert plates were placed on the chargers, I excused myself and headed towards the powder room. Once I was out of sight of the dining room, I veered off to the backstairs that led to the laundry area.

Philip waited next to a countertop. On the counter sat two pair of men's boots inside clear plastic bags. And a handgun. Also wrapped in clear plastic.

"Look at the bottoms of these boots. See in here. In the cracks between the waffle pattern."

I looked at the bottom of the boot that Philip held up to the light. Small pieces of crushed granite were wedged into the cracks. I could also see reddish brown dirt.

"Where did you find these boots?"

"In the tire compartment of the Lexus SUV. Under the carpet in the rear." Philip explained. "I've done a lot of poking around this week."

"Who uses that car?"

"Mr. Wells, that is Cameron, mostly. Sometimes Mrs. Wells. But Mr. Montgomery borrowed it recently. To take up to the Tahoe house. Highway 80 was snowed over. His sedan doesn't do as well in the snow, and his Land Rover was already up there."

"Do you recognize the boots?"

"No"

"What about the size? Whose size are they?" I asked.

"This pair is Wells' size." Philip pointed to one of the high-topped après ski boots. "I don't know about the other pair. But the police will be able to get DNA from them maybe?"

"I hope so. Did you touch them?"

"Only with gloves on."

I pointed at the gun. "Where did you find that?"

"In the glove compartment."

"Of the same car?"

Philip nodded. "You better get back to the dining room. And I have to see to the coffee." Philip ushered me back to the stairs. "I'll let you know if I find anything else. If you can, there's an envelope in the library, in the desk, that I've been curious about—but she's been keeping an eye on it."

"Detective Rodriquez will contact you tomorrow. He'll need to get these boots and the gun from you."

"I'll expect his call."

I ducked into the powder room on my way back to the table. I pushed my hair back from my forehead and washed my hands, running cold water over my wrists in an effort to calm myself. The crushed rock in the soles of the boots looked exactly like the rock in the Big Bear driveway. And the soil certainly looked more like the reddish-brown dirt of the Angeles Crest than the deep brown Sierra soil of the Tahoe area. Whoever wore those boots could have been at Dad's cabin at Big Bear.

I slipped into my seat between Nick and Peter's father, Malcolm. They continued their conversation about golf. I definitely had no interest in that subject.

I toyed with the chocolate soufflé on my plate and leaned back so that my dinner partners could see each other.

"Please join me in the living room," Joan invited her

guests. She stood and the others followed her lead. Once everyone had settled into the comfortable seats around the fire, the conversation turned to wedding plans. Joan and her guests thus engaged, I slipped from the room and snuck down the hall to into the library.

I headed straight for the drawers of the antique secretaire. The center pencil drawer held only writing instruments. I rifled through the two drawers on either side of the kneehole. No envelope of any kind. I was looking for a secret compartment or hidden pigeon hole and poking at the three inset leather panels on the top when I remembered that the center panel of many of these Eastlake desks adjusted to desired heights for reading or writing. I lifted the back edge of the center panel to reveal a shallow recess. Aah, there it was. A large manila envelope.

"I've found a couple of interesting things." Joan's voice from the door startled me into losing my grip on the panel before the envelope had cleared the opening. "Careful. One of those things might break." Joan ignored my bad manners and continued to speak. "I wasn't going to do anything with them this week, but I'd like to give them to you for safe keeping." She nodded at the thick manila envelope in my hand.

"What?" I found my voice.

"Cancelled checks that came in a bank statement this week. And two interesting legal documents." Joan smiled. "I made a copy of one of them. And there's a letter. A letter my mother wrote and I found in her writing desk. But please don't open the envelope now. At least wait until you get home to call Detective Rodriquez."

I patted the envelope. I felt something other than paper. "What's the plastic thing?"

"A tape out of an answer machine. I think you'll find the conversation enlightening." Joan smiled and patted my arm. "Please, just hold onto these for a few more days. I was going to give these to you and Detective Rodriquez after the wedding, but maybe it's better now and not to chance that anything might happen to them."

I nodded and held the envelope behind my back until I reached my bag in the entry closet. I slipped the evidence into a side pouch and returned to the living room.

I called Manny from the car on the way home. He met us at the house the next morning.

Chapter 48

I buried my nose in my champagne flute to avoid the cloyingly sweet fragrance of several hundred white Casablanca Lilies and watched tuxedo-clad Cameron twirl Poppy around the dance floor to the tune of *What a Wonderful World* for the traditional father daughter number. The chiffon skirt of her ball-gown swirled gracefully over the marble floor of the Palace Hotel's Palm Court.

Poppy had changed out of the Swavorski crystal-studded, empire wedding dress she had worn for the ceremony in the cathedral into a silk and chiffon reception gown the pale blue of which matched her eyes, complemented her honey gold hair and suited the *"skies of blue and clouds of white"* lyrics.

As I watched Poppy and Cameron glide across the dance floor, I reviewed with gratitude how well the week had gone. Once the statements and questioning at the police station were out of the way, we had had a grand week. Sally, Nikki, Emma and I made significant progress on Sally's interiors. Sally and Nikki spent hours at the shops around Union Square. I avoided going with them, but I could imagine the excitement they caused there.

Per all reports, Poppy's Peter and his family's Monday arrival was welcomed by a happy, united Wells family. After we four women had dinner with all of them on Wednesday at the Wells mansion, we left the newly forming family to all of the wedding related parties.

After Philip had shown me two pair of boots, and Joan had agreed to let me have an envelope for safekeeping, I hadn't heard anything further from Philip or Joan, but I had called Manny regularly regarding the new evidence— begging him for lab results that he claimed not to have.

Poppy and Emma, along with the rest of the bridesmaids and their school chums, had a blowout time at Chippendales. Cameron hosted a Bachelor party for Peter. Peter's brother and his best man, as well as several local friends, attended. I wasn't able to learn much about that party in spite of the fact that Skip came across the bay for it.

As the wedding attendees watched Cameron lead Poppy around the dance floor of the court that had once been the carriage entrance of the Beaux Arts Palace Hotel to the music of Peter Duchin's Orchestra, I noticed that one guest was more intent on their movements than the others. Luigi Chiari had arrived at the reception with Nick Montgomery. As we stood beneath the lofty, domed, iridescent glass ceiling, light filtered down in an amber flood over the dancers and glistened on the silk of Poppy's gown. I wondered how he must feel watching another man perform this traditional ritual with his biological daughter.

I walked over to where Luigi stood next to one of the palm trees. "How are you?"

He turned and smiled. "Just fine." He nodded toward Poppy. "A bellissima girl."

"Do you have many daughters?" I asked.

His smile became wistful. "Just the one."

Luigi's eyes were riveted on Poppy and Cameron as Cameron led Poppy to where Peter danced with his mother, and for the second time that day, gave Poppy's hand to Peter.

The orchestra began a new song. *"Then suddenly appeared before me, the only one my arms could ever hold"* The bridegroom leaned his head to his new wife's ear and murmured, bringing dreamy eyed smiles to both faces as they danced in each other's arms. One could guess he sang the next lines, *"won't you please adore me, Blue moon, Now I'm no longer alone."*

Cameron escorted Peter's mother to his father. Cameron and Joan joined the other two couples on the shining dance floor below the shimmering crystal chandeliers.

"After the bride and groom dance, it is customary for the bride to dance with other guests," I reminded Luigi.

"And so I shall." He smiled at me.

I returned his smile "Where do you spend most of your time—Los Gatos or Florence?"

"I spend most of the year in Firenze."

"Do you come here for business?"

"No, for family. I'm in Firenze for business."

"You and Nick seemed to have become better acquaint ed in the last week," I ventured.

Luigi smiled in response. "Nick has been very kind to me."

"Did Nick tell you that Poppy and Peter have bought a house in London?"

"Yes."

"Luigi, or do you prefer Vonni?"

He looked at me with sad eyes. "Only Cassandra ever called me by that name. I like that Nick calls me Lou."

"Lou, years ago, I flew from Gatwick to Pisa, and then caught the train to Florence. Pretty quick trip. Just a few hours," I said. "I think you can fly direct from Florence to London now. It'll be good that you'll be nearby. Poppy may need you."

Luigi frowned at me. "I don't understand."

"You will. Please excuse me, I'm going to ask my father for a dance." I smiled as I walked across the purple carpet, away from the solitary figure.

I danced with my father and then with my son, all the while keeping an eye on the column framed entrance to the court. I sat down in one of the purple velvet chairs at a table at the edge of the dance floor with a view of the dancers and new arrivals. I sipped champagne, thanked God for letting us get through most of the festivities without in-cident, and worried because Manny hadn't showed up yet.

Joan and Luigi glided by on the dance floor. How interesting that would be if Joan were to, as my children say, hook up with Luigi. From the looks on both their faces and the way they smiled into each other's eyes, it seemed possible.

"What's with those two? They look ready to get a room." Sally threw down a concoction in a martini glass and waved down a waiter. "Fucking Joan snagged the only non-boring asshole in the place." She fell into the chair next to me. Her sequined miniskirt was riding up her slender thighs.

"Sally, let's go to the Top of the Mark for drinks after this. The sky is clear tonight, the view will be spectacular."

"Okay, I get it. You want me to lay off the booze."

I knew better than to ever tell Sally how to behave. To do so would only guarantee her going completely out of control. I smiled. "Do you know where they are handing out the bird seed or bubbles or flower petals or whatever we are to throw at the bride and groom?"

"I'll find out." Sally grinned at me before she walked over to the wedding coordinator. She returned moments later with two small lavender silk bags of rose petals and two gold mesh boxes, each containing two monarch butterflies. She placed a bag and a box on the table in front of me.

"Thank you." I nodded in gratitude not only for the bag and box, but also for her decision to cooperate.

Where the hell was Manny? Had he changed his mind about coming? Did one of the lab results turn out differently than expected?

"Why do you keep looking at the fucking lobby? Who are you expecting?"

"I thought Manny might come."

Shit, he needs to come soon. After all week worrying about timing working out so that the wedding wouldn't be upstaged, now I was concerned that we would miss our chance.

Soon it was time for the bride and groom to slip away. Emma sent Jeff to join the stags in the bar while she went with Poppy to help her into her travel clothes. The couple was going as far as the St. Francis hotel that night. The next morning they would leave for New Zealand.

With relief, I saw Manny walk between the towering marble columns that framed the entrance. "Would you like a glass of champagne?" I asked as he sat down next to me.

"I think not tonight. But thank you." Manny ran his hand over the table and smoothed the white linen cloth. He studied the surface while he spoke. "Okay, I'm here. And I brought back up." He nodded toward three plainclothes detectives standing in the lobby just outside the court. "But I'm not convinced this isn't a waste of time. Tell me—how are we sure this is the guy?"

"Oh, come on." I knew Manny wanted to see if I knew anything pertinent I had failed to mention earlier.

"One, I was deleting photos from my laptop that had to do with Honey's death. I finally remembered to look at the photo of the audience, the one I had gotten from the photographer in order to crop Honey's picture to show around the PDC. He was in the audience, three rows behind Honey. That was the email I sent you."

"Okay. He was there that day. Can't arrest him for that."

"Then he showed up at Honey's funeral."

Still staring at the tablecloth, Manny said, "Again, can't arrest him for being there."

"Then he was on the list of Cowles heirs—one of the generation who get possession of the money, the capital. I know—you can't arrest him for being on a list."

Manny smiled at me.

"But Honey had everyone on that list checked out. He was the most broke, with the most expensive lifestyle of anyone on the list. I know—you can't arrest him for living above his means."

Another smile.

"But how about this—he was seen with Tommy and Robby at the LA Athletic club the same week Honey was killed."

Manny shook his head.

"I know—you can't arrest him for hanging out with his cousins—but how about the cancelled checks and documents Joan found? He paid Tommy and Robby to sign over their share of the estate to him. And I'm sure that same bribe was to pay for their silence."

"Doesn't prove he was involved in the murder."

"The recording I gave you Thursday. You heard him say to them that he couldn't inherit if convicted of the murder that benefited him, so Tommy and Robby should keep their mouths shut. He promised he'd hire the best dream team of lawyers to represent them, but if they implicated him, he wouldn't have the money to do that."

"There's a chain of custody problem with that tape as

evidence." Manny said as he looked at me. Perhaps he knew I hadn't brought him here on a fool's errand. "What else do you have?"

"That conversation was over a jailhouse phone line. Records are kept of phone calls placed by prisoners, right?"

Manny nodded.

"How much more to you need to tie him to Tommy and Robby?"

"Okay, he knows them."

"When Philip cleaned out the SUV, the vehicle that supposedly was in Tahoe, he noticed that the soil on the boots was a different color than Tahoe dirt. Philip showed me a pair of boots he had bagged to protect a reddish shade of soil he'd noticed in the waffle pattern on the soles. I'm sure you found that dirt is from Big Bear area."

"Yes."

"And the boots are his size. Everyone else who uses that car wears different sizes."

"The chain of custody on the boots hasn't exactly been kept intact."

"Then there's the gun found in his glove compartment. A .38 registered to him. Isn't that the caliber that shot up the Big Bear cabin?"

"But Tommy and Robby admitted to shooting at the Big Bear cabin."

"Who gave them the gun?"

Manny asked, "What about the threatening phone call Emma got?"

"Setting us up so that when Tommy and Robby demanded that we sign away our claim on Honey's estate we would think we had to protect Jamie as well as ourselves."

"What if you went to the police?"

"Tommy and Robby were expendable, and we wouldn't be able to prove he was involved."

"How did he know that you don't know where Jamie is?"

"Honey could've told him. She and I used the same PI. The investigator told me stuff about her. Could've been a two-way street."

Now I had him. Although I suspect he was half teasing.

He looked at the glass ceiling for a quick second and then said, "I guess that note could've been from him."

"The note was a feeble attempt to frame Joan and Philip. He copied it into the computer from a piece of paper he'd discovered stuck in a drawer of the library desk, a page of a letter Joan's mother Eleanor wrote. That was in the package of papers from Joan. I recognized Eleanor's handwriting. That secretaire . . . the one with the hidden niche . . . was an antique Eleanor gave to Joan."

"What did he think it meant?"

"Who knows . . . or cares. But he, not Tommy or Robby, was the one with access to Joan's computer in the Wells' mansion library. His fingerprints will be all over it. And the police took custody of the computer and the printer. So you're not going to have any 'chain of custody' problems with that."

Manny's eyes gave away his suppressed grin. His lips pressed together for a moment before he spoke. "Where is he?" He glanced around the room.

"Ooh, please. Just a few more minutes."

"Are you kidding? What if he gets away?"

I frowned, raised an eyebrow and looked at the plainclothes detectives.

"Ok, ok. How soon do the bride and groom leave?" Manny asked.

"Maybe half an hour."

Now Manny frowned and raised his eyebrow.

I pulled my cell out of my evening bag and called Emma. "How long?"

"Come out to the lobby," she said. Manny and I arrived in the lobby just as Joan and Emma followed a creamy, Chloe coat-clad Poppy down to the bottom of the stairs where Peter waited with a huge smile on his handsome face. The happy couple linked arms.

The guests had migrated to the hotel entrance leading to the valet park where the couple was saluted with floating flower petals, and monarch butterflies were released to see them off. A beaming Poppy waved to the guests, Peter's family and her parents as the limo slid out from the marquee.

"Damn, these fucking petals aren't much fun. I'd much rather pelt the couple with rice."

"Now Sally darling, you know the rice is bad for the birds," Nikki said.

"Well, how about fucking birdseed then?"

Nikki ignored Sally's whining, winked at me and we exchanged smiles. We'd survived the festivities without

Sally traumatizing guests or parents.

The wedding party straggled back into the courtyard. Now that the official festivities were complete, Cameron ignored Joan.

Joan walked over to the table and I introduced her to Manny. Joan was so tired she failed to ask why Manny was there.

She even failed to comment on the fact that Sally had pretty much behaved herself. Only that one suggestive dance with Nick Montgomery.

Emma, Sally and Nikki sat down at the table. Sally flung off her high heels and put her feet on the chair next to her.

"Where is he?" Manny asked.

"I saw him head into the bar," I said. Most of the male guests had congregated in the bar.

Peter's family, Sophie and Malcolm and their children Martha and George, walked over to the table where Joan sat with us and thanked Joan for a beautiful wedding, a brilliant week, and said their goodbyes.

Joan remained standing and smiling while several more of her guests said good-bye. She held the handsome Governor's hand and kissed his cheek. "Goodbye Gavin."

Handshakes, hugs, and kisses.

"Rita, Tom, thank you for coming."

More hugs.

"Give my love to your lovely mother, Billy."

"Sandy, thank you for everything."

A handful of young people remained on the dance floor, and the bar was still fully loaded with stags, but nearly every guest over thirty had departed. Joan collapsed into a chair and let out a muffled groan. "We made it through the week."

Cameron sauntered over to the table with a tumbler of whiskey in one hand and an unlit cigar in the other.

"Thank you for this week," Joan said.

"I hired a divorce lawyer," Cameron said to Joan without acknowledging her thank you. "I want to get this over with as soon as possible."

"Have you had papers drawn up?" I asked. Of course, I knew that Joan had found the papers and had given me copies of them along with the agreement signed by Tommy and Robby.

"Yes." Cameron looked at me, annoyance sparking in his eyes.

"Where are they?" I turned to Joan. "Joan, don't you want to be done with the proceedings too?"

"Yes, let's get this over with." Joan sighed. "Where are your damn papers?"

"Don't you want to know the terms?" Cameron raised an eyebrow.

"What are they?" As if she hadn't already had a copy read by her attorneys.

"I'll give you a lump sum settlement, but then you have no claim on any future income I may have."

"Does that go both ways?" Joan sipped the champagne.

"What do you mean?" Cameron stared at Joan.

"Do you then have no claim on my future income, or assets?" Joan asked.

"Of course." Annoyed, disdainful Cameron pulled papers out of his breast pocket.

"You've had divorce papers on you this whole day!" Joan shook her head.

"I also thought it a good idea to get it over with."

"Let's sign them." Joan reached across the table for the papers and slid them to her.

Cameron looked at Manny, and then at me. He looked around the table at Sally, Nikki, and Emma as though he was suddenly aware that he had an audience. "Don't you want to consult a lawyer?"

Joan ignored Cameron's question and signed the papers. She handed them back to Cameron. "Here."

Cameron folded up the papers and stuck them back in his breast pocket.

"Don't you want Joan's signature witnessed?" I asked. "You sign the papers too and then we'll witness both signatures."

Sally, Nikki, Emma and I held our breath while we waited to see what he would do.

Cameron pulled the papers back out of his pocket, flipped to the last page, and signed his name. He handed the papers to me. I signed on the witness line. There was a second witness line. I handed the papers to Manny.

"Cameron, this is Manuel Rodriquez. Detective Manuel Rodriquez. He's a perfect witness."

Manny added his signature to the papers.

"Detective Rodriquez is with the Beverly Hills Police Department." I said to Cameron. I was rewarded with a visible crack in Cameron's stiff composure.

I continued. "By the way, Cameron, surely you've figured out by now that Emma and I are not the beneficiaries of the Nickels estate. Right?"

Cameron stared at me and then glanced at Manny.

While Cameron was distracted, I slid the divorce papers across the table and onto my lap. "Don't you want to know who is?"

Cameron raised one eyebrow, but did not answer. He looked away. I was no longer of interest, nor apparently was anything I might have to say. I continued anyway. "You might be interested to know, Joan and Poppy are Honey's heirs."

Cameron's face first flamed red, then paled to white. He slammed his fist onto the table- top and stood up. "What? How the hell—?" he sputtered.

"You are under arrest for conspiracy to commit murder, for assault of law enforcement officers, unsafe discharge of a weapon, and attempted murder. You have the right, to remain silent . . ." Manny closed the handcuffs on Cameron's wrists.

"What the hell?" Cameron shouted. He glared at me. "You stupid, stupid bitch." He swung around and swept his gaze over all the women at the table. "You stupid bitches. You stupid, stupid interfering—dumb—fucking—idiot—whores—" Cameron continued to rant as a uniformed officer led him out to the awaiting police car.

Manny nodded at us ladies with a smile. "Thank you once again," he said before he followed the officer.

Joan looked at me stunned. "Cameron?"

"What did you think when you found the papers?"

"I guess it was hard to imagine that he was a murderer."

"So, he was the third man on the snowmobiles?" Emma asked.

I nodded. "He was the mastermind. Tommy and Robby couldn't have thought this up by themselves."

"That's obvious." Emma chuckled. "Those two bums don't have enough brain cells left between them to plan a meal, let alone a murder. So Cameron must've told them that you and I were the beneficiaries of the trust."

"He probably thought he was clever to figure that out."

I had to chuckle too.

I placed my hand on Joan's and looked to see that she was doing okay. "Love that he wanted to get you out of his life so he didn't have to share the money with you. If he'd only waited until Honey died of natural causes, he would've gotten half of your share of the income as community property. A larger portion than if he'd had to share with all of his cousins. Three billion dollars creates a decent income I imagine." I passed the divorce papers to Joan.

"Patience was never one of his strong points. Too bad for him." Joan shook her head and folded the papers. "In this case, a little patience would have paid off."

"Big time! Sure proves crime doesn't pay." Emma raised her glass. "Mom, you did it again."

Sally waved down a waiter. This time I made no effort to distract her. When all five of our glasses were full, Sally raised her glass. "Here's to Cissy"

"Oh God yes, thank you so much Cissy," seconded Joan. "We got through the week without a hitch." Joan smiled and sighed. "Imagine, I thought that Cameron neglecting Poppy was all we had to worry about. No wonder you so readily went along with not telling Cameron about the trust." Joan sipped her champagne. "Did you already know then that he had planned Honey's murder?"

"I suspected him as soon as I remembered that his grandmother was a Cowles. But I needed proof to satisfy Manny."

"Here's to Cissy." Sally drained her glass and held it aloft for a refill.

"Here's to the two new contracts made today. A new happily married life for Poppy. A new happily unmarried life for Joan," I said. "Cheers."

Acknowledgements

Thank you to retired University English and Creative Writing professor, Candy Somoza for encouragement, super editing and attempting to teach me the important points of punctuation. Your support means a lot—plus I particularly enjoy our meetings.

Thank you to my writer's group, Mark Hosack, Shari Shattuck, and Sharon Doyle for making writing so much fun. I miss you guys!

Thank you to my family for encouragement, critiques of and contributions to cover designs, providing material for characters, opinions regarding titles and most of all for media management.

Thank you David Oh for patiently providing beautiful book covers.

A few years ago, I joined the Clueless Mystery Book Club. In mystery writing classes, we seldom discussed what drew mystery readers to mystery novels. I planned to go to a few meetings to see what mystery readers liked and disliked. To my surprise, despite the lack of wine at this book club's meetings, I have been attending for years now and hate to miss a meeting. I have become quite fond of this impressive group of ladies (and occasional attendee Tommy). My thanks to the members for welcoming me and teaching me more than I had hoped.

Thank you to Michael for preparing my manuscripts and lots of backup. Most of all, thank you for encouraging and supporting my love of writing.

Turn the page for an exciting early look at:

BURNT ORANGE

Sherri Leigh James

A Cissy Huntington Mystery

Coming 2020

Prologue

Splat.

Bam.

Smack.

What was hitting the building? Something soft and wet hit the window above his head. Too big, too heavy to be rain. He sat up and shook off the sleep. Shit, he'd fallen asleep while he was supposed to be chaperoning the pledges and now something was being thrown at the bar.

He checked his phone—2:20 a.m. Shit! Time to take them home.

"What the hell is that?" the young man shouted.

He slid off the sofa, faced the window in time to see another missile pelt the glass. Chunks of goo ran down the pane. Not water balloons; something round and sticky. He stumbled, knocked over a half full cup of beer and ran for the stairs.

Traffic was heavy on the stairs as students scrambled to the front of Kip's Bar and Grill. He pushed past his pledges to take his place at the front of the group. He would face whomever—whatever was outside.

Three white males and one female stood on the front sidewalk picking up gooey balls from a box that lay at their feet, then hurling them at the façade of the building. Clothed in black baggies like gangstas, but without the attitude, the four wannabes doubled over with laughter as each of their missiles succeeded in hitting its mark. The large yellow Kip's sign that hung above the second floor balcony dripped with sticky dark orange liquid.

He spread his arms to hold back the herd of young males and shouted at the troublemakers "That's enough!"

The black clad group continued to hurl.

"Get out of here! Go home!"

The foursome continued to laugh and pick up project-tiles. A round glop sailed past his face

"That's enough. Go! Now!"

The pack behind him surged forward. He took two steps and held.

"You need to leave."

The four stopped mid-throw staring at the threatening pack he held at bay. He saw in their faces the realization that they had awoken trouble. The female pulled her black hood over her purple head and slunk behind the frozen male wannabes.

What seemed a long silence broke with the sound of a half dozen students spilling from the bar's karaoke room. Drunk, loud, laughing, yelling teasing insults at each other, the young people staggered and lurched toward the gathering on the sidewalk. "Hey, wassup?" said his best friend as he walked down Durant avenue to join him.

Caught between the two groups, one angry, the other drunk, one of the wannabes shouted, "I have a gun," and swept a weapon in the air demonstrating the truth of his statement. A second wannabe picked up a whiskey bottle and twirled it above his head.

Testosterone broke loose. The karaoke revelers joined the herd of pledges.

The young man managed to stay at the front of the melee, shoved the girl out of danger, but control was impossible. A bottle flashed before his face, then smacked the side of his head. A blow to his back knocked him to his knees. When a sharp pain hit his chest; his hand came away from his shirt covered in blood.

"I've been shot," he tried to shout. "Shot."

He crawled out of the midst of the brawl to collapse in the gutter before blackness waved in and out, the skirmish faded away as his vision closed to a small circle.

His best friend's face appeared above him. He felt pressure on his chest and heard the words, "Stay with me Dude. You're gonna make it. Paramedics are on their way. Come on! Stay with me! Look at me!"

He felt his friend's tears splash on his face.

Chapter One

I smiled across the round table at my father while I hissed out of the side of my mouth at my daughter, "Where the hell is your brother?

Emma shrugged.

"We agreed to Chez Panisse for his convenience," I said under my breath as I continued to smile and nod at the small talk of the table. "He's a half-hour late."

I excused myself and hit speed dial as I walked to the ladies room. As I entered the bathroom, I reached my son Skip's voicemail. "What could be so damn important that you're missing your grandfather's birthday lunch? Everyone's here. We've had our cocktails, and we're ready to order. At least call me with your order," I told the recording.

I hung around the washbasin, looked in the mirror, rearranged my blonde hair, and fluffed the yarn trim on my tweed Chanel jacket, killing time waiting for Skip to notice the call. I tried his phone again. Direct to voicemail. Must have been some party last night if he was still asleep at 1:30 on a Sunday afternoon.

This lack of consideration was unlike my son. Where was he? What was he doing? My stomach sank and then flip flopped. Oh God, please let him be okay, I prayed as I walked between the open farmhouse style kitchen and the dark wood Arts & Crafts booths back to our sunlit, white-clothed table in the glass enclosed patio.

My two movie star friends Sally and Nikki, my father and his wife, and my daughter all smiled at me as I resumed my place.

"Let's order," I said.

The waiter asked if he should remove the seventh place setting.

"Just leave it for now." With my usual optimism, I waved him off not wishing to mar my father's celebration by underscoring his grandson's absence.

"It's fu—freaking hard to decide. So many things on the menu look awesome."

I smiled at my friend Sally, appreciating her self-censoring. She is unusually fond of the F-word, typically working it into every sentence, but she refrained in consideration of my father's eighty-something sensibilities.

Nikki brushed her champagne-blonde hair back, shot her friend an appreciative nod, and in her soft breathless voice asked my father, "Which birthday is this?"

"Eighty-two."

"No."

"No way."

Emma stated the obvious, "Grandpa, you really look damn good."

With his full head of white hair and blue eyes set in contrasting golden tan skin, it was hard to believe anyone could look that good at any age. He got more admiring looks from our fellow diners than the two gorgeous movie stars.

"What *is* your secret?" Sally asked, her jade eyes intent on his handsome face.

"I still work out every day."

"Fuck, should've known. I hate that." Sally caught her reaction. "Shit, I'm sorry." She brushed her mahogany hair off her shoulders and bestowed her famous smile on us.

My father laughed and returned Sally's smile. He took his pretty blonde wife's hand and said, "She takes good care of me."

Emma studied her lap. I glanced over and saw she was reading a text message. Her thumbs flew over the keys of her phone.

I hoped it was from her brother, although I was miffed that he contacted her instead of me. It better be Skip and not a friend or one of our interior design clients. My children failed to see how rude this constant texting was.

"Grandpa, ladies, please excuse me." Emma pushed her chair back from the table and walked out of the beams of sunlight, past the dark booths and through the maitre de's station to the top of the stairs. From where I sat in the bright light under the glass ceiling, looking into the dim, I saw her silhouette put the phone to her ear. Within seconds she grabbed the counter with her free hand, leaned into it, and listened without speaking for several minutes.

My heart fell; something was very wrong.

My father raised an eyebrow at me.

My turn to shrug. I pushed down the fear that had popped up, tried to listen to the small talk.

Sally was holding forth about the Queen Anne Victorian mansion she had just bought in Pacific Heights. It seemed she had actually read the notes I'd sent her explaining the different phases and styles of Victorian architecture.

"You see, it wasn't literally Queen Anne style, since her reign ended two centuries before the Victorian Age, "Sally explained. "The label American Queen Anne refers to the fanciest houses built on the West Coast in the late Victorian era—the ones with turrets, and towers, and covered verandas, and dormers, and everything detailed with the most elaborate, exuberant woodwork."

Emma closed the phone and stood staring into space for half a minute. By the time she walked back to the table, she'd plastered on a forced smile.

"Uhm, Grandpa, Skip's got hung up, an unexpected, but important problem he has to deal with." Emma pulled out her chair. "He sends his apologies and says have a good lunch."

"Emma, what?" I demanded.

"Later Mom." She slid her eyes from my face towards her grandfather and back to me, signaling she did not want to talk about it in front of her grandfather. "Skip's okay."

Chapter Two
Sunday, late afternoon

"This better be good." I said to my daughter as I slammed the car door. Emma waved to her grandfather and closed her door. Sally and Nikki slid into the back seat.

"What the fuck is the matter with you two?" Sally asked.

"Mom, guys, something really bad happened at the frat's outing to Kips last night, . . . in the middle of the night."

My heart stopped. I turned to my daughter. "What?" I demanded. "Your brother? Is he okay?"

"He's okay Mom. Skip's physically fine. But very upset. One of the guys was killed."

"Killed?" Had I heard her wrong? "What?"

"There was a brawl. Or something. He didn't really explain."

"Who?"

Emma shook her head.

"Emma?"

"I don't know much else. It was a fight or something."

I drove the dozen blocks toward the campus, fighting panic.

We turned the corner onto Durant Avenue. The stacked stone façade of the bar was measled with dried dark orange goo. Yellow crime scene tape encircled the sidewalk and the entrance. The street in front of us was filled with media vans.

I drove around the vans and continued to Piedmont Avenue, then made a right and a left around Channing Circle. We passed two fraternity houses also covered with dark orange pockmarks. I was shocked to see more media vans in front of Skip's frat house. Men shouldering TV cameras and heavily made up young women holding microphones filled the sidewalk.

"Oh shit." Nikki ducked and stayed down.

"Fucking vultures." Sally defiantly stayed upright. "Hate'em . . . . I don't think Nikki and I should go in there with you. In fact, we better get the fuck outa here or we'll make things much worse."

"Stay down damnit, Sally!" Nikki pulled her down behind the seats.

"I need to go in there now."

Sometimes my friends' movie star status could be such a pain in the ass. My concern for my son trumped their fear of bad publicity. I pulled the car past the vans and TV reporters holding microphones, and into the parking area.

"Cissy, you do-fucking-not want us going in there."

"I need to know my son is okay."

My voice sounded gruff even to me, but I was too distracted to be patient with this media phobia shit.

Nikki placed her hand on my shoulder. "Darling, think

about this for a minute. If this is local, or even national news now, if Sally and I go in there, it'll be international."

"And this place will be crawling with papa-fucking-razzi for weeks."

"And it'll never go away. Photos taken here will be archived."

"And every time rabbit here," Sally tapped Nikki on the arm, "gets preggers . . ."

". . . and every time Sally gains a pound, it'll play all over again."

"And here's the punch line—Skip will no longer be James Huntington the fucking fourth, he'll be that frat boy who was involved in a FATAL drunken brawl."

"Forever."

"They're right, Mom."

"Shit." I slapped the steering wheel, but moved the car so that it was partially hidden behind a tree. "Okay, which one of you is going to drive?"

"What?"

"Emma and I are going in there. One of you can drive the car away."

"NO! Don't you fucking get it? We're gonna hide behind the seats while you drive us the fuck outa here."

I pulled my purse toward me, dug out the Prius keys, and tossed them to Emma. "Go drop them off some place where they can call their driver and then get back here A-sap. I'm going to find your brother."

Nikki reached over the seat and put her hand on my shoulder. "I'm sorry darling."

I pulled away and unfastened my seat belt. "I know."

Her hand massaged my shoulder. "No, really. We do know it's not always easy being friends with us."

"Cissy, we're really fucking sorry. We would like to help however we can with this thing. If you need help, maybe lawyers—"

"or maybe PR people . . ."

"call us."

I frowned as I realized I was being a bitch, and said, "I'm sorry, I'm scared and worried. I want to see Skip, see that he's okay." I looked at Skip's frat house. "What do you think that orange goo is that's all over the outside of the house?"

I closed the car door before they could answer and waved them away as I walked to the side entrance. I pushed past a couple of microphones and punched the code on the door lock, hoping it hadn't changed since Skip last gave it to me. I pushed the door and it opened onto the enclosed side porch.

Beer pong tables sat unused but still smelled of hops and fermented malt and populated with large plastic-coated cups. The interior of the house was eerily quiet.

A boy I didn't know said hello in a hushed tone.

"Do you know where Skip is?" My voice sounded loud in the unusual stillness.

"Yeah, he's here." He waved his arm through the Tudor arch to the adjoining room.

I brushed past him, past the billiards table, the fireplace, across the sticky hardwood floor and headed for Skip's room.

"Mom."

Despite his sad expression, blood shot eyes, and dejected stance, my tall, blonde, handsome son never looked so good to me. I stood on my toes and reached around his chest. He wrapped his arms around my shoulders and held tight for the longest hug of our life together.

* * *

A week filled with quiet conversations, trips to escort boys to the police station for questioning, seeing to it that they ate and slept, and chasing reporters out of the house passed.

Memorial services were held on campus, in a sorority house, and at the frat.

Within two days, a cell phone video of the incident surfaced. Berkeley Police showed it to each of the young men, but the quality was so poor it was hard to identify the participants.

Early Saturday morning the boys loaded into vans to travel to the funeral and Emma and I finally left for home in Los Feliz.

Nikki and Sally greeted us with hugs, kisses and somber expressions as we entered the house on Saturday afternoon.

"We're okay," Emma said. "Skip's doing okay."

Nikki shot a look at Sally who was strangely silent. Nikki spoke softly, "You haven't heard?"

"Heard what?" Horrible thoughts flashed through my

mind. "What?"

"There's been another shooting in Berkeley, on Greek Row. Another student, at a party."

"What?" I sank onto the cold stone step of the stairs. "Is he—or she—okay?"

Sally wrapped her arms around my shoulders. "He died.

About the Author

Sherri Leigh James began her interior design career with a prominent Los Angeles interior design firm whose clients included well-known figures in the entertainment industry, billionaire families, and even mob bosses.

As a partner in her own company, she went on to work for equally interesting personalities. Her work has been featured on the cover of *Architecture Digest* and in the books *Private Washington* and *Hollywood at Home*.

Her intimate view of the private world of the rich and famous inspires her exciting stories of interior designer, Cissy Huntington.

She lives in Los Angeles with her husband.

You can visit her on line
www.SherriLeighJames.com
www.Facebook.com/SherriLeighJames/